missing

Kelley
Armstrong

ATOM

First published in the US in 2017 by Crown Books for Young Readers
First published in Great Britain in 2017 by Atom

1 3 5 7 9 10 8 6 4 2

A CIP catalogue record for this book
is available from the British Library.

ISBN 978-0-349-00264-4

Printed and bound in Great Britain by
Clays Ltd, St Ives plc

Papers used by Atom are from well-managed forests
and other responsible sources.

MIX
Paper from
responsible sources
FSC® C104740

Atom
An imprint of
Little, Brown Book Group
Carmelite House
50 Victoria Embankment
London EC4Y 0DZ

An Hachette UK Company
www.hachette.co.uk

www.atombooks.co.uk

missing

also by kelley armstrong

The Darkest Powers Trilogy

The Summoning
The Awakening
The Reckoning

The Darkness Rising Trilogy

The Gathering
The Calling
The Rising

The Age of Legends Trilogy

Sea of Shadows
Empire of Night
Forest of Ruin

The Masked Truth

For Julia

one

REEVE'S END IS THE KIND OF TOWN EVERY KID CAN'T WAIT TO ESCAPE. Each summer, a dozen kids leave and at least a quarter never come back. I don't blame them—I'll do the same in another year. We thought it was just something that happened in towns like ours.

We were wrong.

"Twenty dollars an hour," I say to the guy who's stopped me as I head for Doc Southcott's. I know his name. When your high school has only two hundred kids, you can't even pretend you don't. But from his expression, you'd think I've clearly forgotten him. Forgotten who he is, at least.

I lean against the crumbling brickwork. "You asked if I can help boost your math grade. The answer is yes. For twenty dollars an hour."

"But . . ."

"I know, Garrett. You expected I'd do it for the pleasure of your company. That's what you're used to—girls jumping at the chance to spend time with you. You're a decent guy, though, so I'll warn that it's not so much *you* they're after as a one-way ticket out of Reeve's End. Preferably with a cute boy who'll earn a football scholarship . . . as long as he can get the grades for college. Which is why you're here."

"Uh . . ."

I sigh and look down the road. There's nothing to see. Pothole-ridden streets. Rust-plagued pickups. Even the mutt tied outside the Dollar Barn gazes at the fog-shrouded Appalachians as if dreaming of better.

I turn back to Garrett. "I'm happy to help. But you're not the only one who wants out, and college is expensive."

"Not for you. With your grades, you're guaranteed a full ride."

"Nothing is guaranteed. And I doubt I'll get a full ride for my post-grad."

"Med school?" He glances at Doc Southcott's office. "You're not serious about that."

"Are you serious about a football scholarship?"

"Hell, yeah. It's just . . . med school?"

Kids from Reeve's End don't go to med school. Especially those like me, who even here would be from the wrong side of the tracks . . . if Reeve's End had tracks. Sometimes I figure the train purposely diverted around us for the same reason we don't have buses or taxis—so it's harder to escape.

Tutoring won't get me through med school. Neither will

working for Doc Southcott. But I've got a plan, and every penny counts. It's always counted.

"You have your dreams, Garrett, and I have mine. Yours will cost twenty bucks an hour. If you put in the effort, I can bring you up to a B. And the bonus to paying me? You won't need to flirt to win my help."

He shakes his head. "You're a strange girl, Winter Crane."

"No, I'm just strange for Reeve's End. So, do we have a deal? I've got one tutor slot open, which will fill in another week, when kids finally admit midterms are coming."

He agrees, still looking confused.

"Tomorrow, after school at the library," I say. "Payment in advance."

.

I have a short shift at the doc's that day. Mrs. Southcott has managed to convince her husband to take an extended long-weekend vacation, leaving this afternoon. I tried to argue that I could do office work while they're gone, but apparently she figures Doc Southcott isn't the only one overdue for time off.

I head to the trailer park. My official address, even if I spend as little time there as possible. Mom died when I was seven. My sister left last year. It's just me and Bert now. He prefers Rob, but Bert better suits a guy who traded an engineering career in the city for a string of crap jobs that pay just enough to keep him in bourbon. He lost the right to be called Dad when he decided I was a burden to be borne and not gladly.

I pass our trailer and duck into the forest. My real home is out there—an abandoned shack that's far more habitable than our trailer.

Thick forest leads from the town to the foothills, and what used to be a good source of income back when the local coal mine operated. Shitty work—old-timers still cough black phlegm decades later. But that doesn't stop them from reminiscing as if they'd had cushy office jobs. There was money then. Good and steady money. Then the mine closed and the town emptied. Those who stayed did so because they had no place else to go . . . or no place else would have them.

My shack is nearly a mile in. That's a serious hike through dense forest, but it means I don't need to worry about local kids using my cabin for parties. Hunters do stumble over it in season—and out of season, Reeve's End not being a place where people pay attention to laws if they interfere with putting food on the table.

I check my boundary thread. One section is slack, as if something pushed against it and then withdrew. Humans barrel through without noticing, so I'm guessing this was a deer. Or so I hope, because the alternative is a black bear or coyote or, worse, one of the feral dogs that have been giving me trouble.

I tighten the thread and duck under. My shack is exactly that—a dilapidated wooden structure maybe eight feet square. It's empty inside except for a rickety chair near the wall. I pry up a loose floorboard and remove my gear. Spread my carpet. Pour a cup of water. Set aside my sleeping bag and lantern. Home sweet home.

I write up a lab experiment while the light is good. Then I go check my snares, the bow over my shoulder doubling my chance to add meat to my ramen noodles. I forage, too, but it's the hunting that marks me as a girl who lives in a place like Reeve's End, as I discovered when a scholarship sent me to science camp in Lexington. Some city girls must hunt, but you wouldn't think so from my fellow students' expressions when I told them how I got my ace dissection skills.

"Aren't there supermarkets where you live?" one girl asked.

Well, no. Reeve's End only has a grocery and a small one at that. But food costs money, and as much as possible, money is for my savings account. At least I know where my meat comes from, which is more than I can say for those kids.

I'm drawing near the second snare when I notice something white lying beside it. I inhale, hoping it's not a skunk—polecat in these parts. But it's just white. Shit. I hope I haven't trapped someone's cat.

I jog over to see . . . a sneaker?

I peer at the surrounding forest, expecting a prank. My snares are far from the trails, and even if someone stumbled on one, the trap is hardly life-threatening. Yet from the looks of the flattened ground cover, this person fought hard to get free.

I examine the shoe. If the mate were here, I'd take it. At size eleven, it wouldn't fit me, but it's a nearly new Air Jordan, which I could sell for at least fifty bucks. I turn the shoe over.

That's when I see the blood. Then I spot a red handprint on a sapling, where he must have righted himself after the trap. I figure "he" given the size of the shoe. That shoe also means he's not from Reeve's End, where wearing three-hundred-dollar sneakers would be the equivalent of riding to school in a chauffeured Escalade.

I follow his trail for a bit. Mostly I'm just curious. But as I track him, I start to worry. He's like an injured black bear, staggering and stumbling and mowing down everything in his path. Wounded and lost in what must have seemed endless wilderness.

I should try to find him. It's inconvenient, but it'll be a hell of a lot more inconvenient when some hunter finds his body and I suffer the guilt of knowing I might have been able to help.

I continue tracking him for close to a mile. That's when I hear the distant growls of feral dogs.

two

Old-timers talk about back when we had wolves and mountain lions in these woods, and roll their eyes at hunters these days whining about a few stray dogs. The old-timers are full of shit. At least a wolf or a catamount would slink off if they heard me coming. These dogs know humans, and we don't scare them.

I'm moving at a jog now, praying those aren't the snarls and snaps of a feasting pack. I found a body out here once. I don't want to ever do it again.

The light is fading fast. That's one problem with being on the east side of the mountains. Once the sun drops behind them, it's like snuffing a candle. I've learned to hunt in twilight because it's the best time for game, but this is too dark for safety, so I clip on my headlamp. It's modified from old mining equipment, which we have plenty of. For a weapon, I'm more comfortable with my bow, but when I'm moving at this rate, the hunting knife is more reliable.

There's no doubt now that I'm hearing the dog pack. I slow and make sure I'm downwind so they won't smell me. Then I exchange the knife for my bow and turn off my headlamp. Each step lands in silence as my eyes adjust to the twilight. I can smell the dogs now. They reek like an old cat that's lost any interest in keeping itself clean.

I round a bush and spot Reject, the pack omega. She keeps to the edges, eating whatever the others leave. Last spring, she was pregnant, the dogs having apparently found a use for her. I never saw the pups. I suspect the alpha bitch killed them. These aren't wolves or foxes or even coyotes—they're half-mad beasts.

I pity Reject, but trying to tame her would be foolhardy—she's as crazy as the rest of them. I keep an eye on her as I move closer, in case she notices me and sounds the alarm.

Reject stands at the edge of a clearing, watching the others. When I pass more bushes, I see them: Flea, Scar, Mange, One-Eye, and Alanna. I named Alanna after a girl at school. She's the alpha bitch. The dog, that is. The girl is just a bitch.

The dogs are barking at something in a tree. When I see that, I exhale. I ease around the bushes for a better look, but even an unobstructed sight line doesn't help much in the darkness. Whatever they're barking at is just a shape in a shadow-enshrouded oak. Then I lean to the side and spot a white Air Jordan, dangling from a leg, at just the right height to convince the beasts that if they keep jumping they'll eventually snag it.

Assuming the guy isn't stupid enough to intentionally tease feral dogs, I'm guessing he's unconscious. Or so I tell myself. He climbed up there and passed out. That's all.

I could leave him and go for help. But there's no guarantee those dogs *can't* get his leg in a freakishly high jump. Nor any guarantee he won't bolt awake and fall.

I survey my options, find a suitable oak, and shimmy up. Hunkering down on a wide branch, I notch an arrow and let it fly into the tree trunk, over the pack's heads. That's not a misfire. There's no way in hell I can take down five dogs with a bow and a half dozen arrows.

The first arrow gets their attention. My second flies into the underbrush with a crackle and thump . . . and the dogs take off after this new threat. I jump down and race to the tree holding the one-sneakered stranger. I take a few precious seconds to fire another even more precious arrow. Three gone, and they're good ones—carbon hybrids—a luxury I allow myself because they're more effective. I'll have to mentally map this spot and come back for them.

I climb past the stranger, well out of reach of the dogs. Then I look down. It's a guy, not much older than me. Dark hair hangs as his head lolls. His eyes are closed, and he's sprawled on the branch, as if he collapsed there. His shirt is bloodied and torn, as is one leg of his jeans.

I can't tell if he's alive. That's the main thing right now—not his age or his hair color or the condition of his clothing.

Is he alive?

The dogs are back, yipping and yelping as they scent their old enemy. I barely hear them, too focused on answering that critical question.

Please be alive. Please.

I keep seeing flashes of that other body—the one I found two years ago—and I'm shaking as I lower myself onto the branch beside his. My boot touches down, and I catch a better view of his face, battered and bloodied, and I'm trying to see if he's breathing and I lift my other boot, confident the first is securely planted. It isn't.

My foot slips.

As I drop, I wildly grapple for a hold. Alanna lets out a crow of victory. She jumps and her fangs graze my leg. Then my arm snags a branch, awkwardly catching it in the crook of my elbow, my arm scissoring shut, pain ripping through my shoulder as my full weight slams down.

My free hand finds and grabs the branch as Alanna's fangs sink into my leg. My yowl only whips the dogs into a frenzy. I pull my leg up as far as I can, but Alanna is hanging off it, her teeth digging in.

I gather all my strength and kick. She might be fierce and wiry, but she's small, and I send her flying. There's pit bull in that bitch, though, and her teeth rake down my calf, furrows splitting open as I howl in pain.

The damn dogs join in, howling along, and rage fills me— frustration and fury—and there's a split second where I almost drop from the tree. Drop to face them, armed with my hunting knife, like some crazed action hero pushed one step too far. Finally facing off against my canine nemeses, blade flashing, blood spraying, taking down one, maybe two . . . before they rip me apart.

Here lies Winter Crane. So brave. So daring. Such a freaking idiot.

I resist the urge to go Lara Croft on their heads, and instead swing up my legs until I'm hanging off the branch like a sloth. I stay that way, catching my breath and ignoring the pain in my leg and the blood trickling down it. Then I clamber up and climb opposite the one-sneakered boy.

He's dead. I'm sure of that now. With everything going on, he hasn't even stirred.

As I lay my fingers on his neck, I get a better look at his face—inky black eyelashes against a pale cheek, dark stubble, arched brows, one split lip bitten under impossibly white teeth—and I have this bizarre urge to kiss those lips and see him wake, like Sleeping Beauty. Which proves I'm in a lot of pain and possibly hallucinating.

When I first feel his pulse under my fingertips, I don't trust myself. I want it too much. I want this boy to be alive. I want to be the one who saved him, as if that justifies living in a shack and hunting rabbits and squirrels, because it means that I could be here for this stranger, to save him from the wild beasts.

Yep, pretty sure I'm hallucinating. I just hope that damn bitch isn't rabid.

I check twice more before I am convinced the boy is, indeed, alive. Which only means that his heart beats. Not that he isn't comatose or brain dead. Or that he'll survive until I get him help.

Well, that's more like it. Welcome back, sunshine.

I honestly can't do much more than confirm he's alive, as frustrating as that is. The dogs are still circling below. I'm stuck on this branch, unable to get close enough to examine him, and even if I could, I wouldn't, for fear of startling him into waking and tumbling to the jaws of the hellhounds below.

I can only wait until the dogs lose interest, however long that might take.

three

It takes a while, but the dogs eventually tire of their fruitless leaping. They still linger after that, not quite ready to abandon their prey, but when Alanna catches a scent in the breeze and takes off, the others follow. I wait until I hear the thunder of them chasing fresh quarry. Then I climb down.

Getting the guy out of the tree isn't easy. He must be close to six feet tall, with an athletic build. I'm in good shape but barely five six. It takes serious effort and even then it's more breaking his fall than lifting him down.

Still he doesn't wake.

I conduct a brief examination with my headlamp. His pupils are normal. The blood on his shirt seems to be mostly from his nose and split lip, the facial injuries that tell me he's been beaten. He's breathing fine, but when I pull up his T-shirt, I see bruising there too. Someone worked him over good.

I'm accustomed to treating the fallout from Saturday night fireworks. The fact we're in a dry county only means you shouldn't walk the back roads on a weekend night or you're liable to get hit by some asshole who picked up his booze next county over and couldn't wait to open it.

But this beating isn't frustration—it's rage.

There's a sheen of sweat on his forehead, and when I touch it, his skin is feverishly hot. That suggests infection, but I don't see anything worse than cuts and scrapes, none of them oozing pus.

I use both our jackets and some branches to fashion a makeshift stretcher, a little leftover know-how from the summer Edie and I worked at a Civil War reenactment site.

Edie Greene befriended me the summer after we moved here. She'd found me in the forest, sick from eating toxic berries, and got me to Doc Southcott. She's the one who taught me to forage, hunt, and fish. Edie's been gone two months. There's nothing in Reeve's End for a girl from the hills who dreamed of a career in fashion design. Also no place for a girl who found her gaze as likely to stray to the cheerleaders as the football players.

Edie would have done a better job with the makeshift stretcher, but it'll have to do. I get the guy on it. Then, with my headlamp affixed and my knife within reach, I start out.

Any hope of hauling him all the way to Reeve's End evaporates fast. My injured leg is soon screaming for mercy, and I veer to the shack instead, where he'll be safe while I go for help.

I pull him inside. Then I spread my ground sheet between

him and the sleeping bag to keep the blood off it. It's an expensive bag, even if I did buy it secondhand, and I'm sure this guy won't begrudge me protecting my investment. I've already potentially lost three arrows helping him. Slashed up my leg, too, but it's my stuff I'm worried about.

Once he's situated, I clean his face to make sure I haven't underestimated the severity of his injuries. I haven't.

I squeeze a few drops of water between his parched lips. Then I stretch the cloth over his forehead and run my hands over his scalp, searching for bumps. When I touch a goose egg, he bolts awake, hands flying out, knocking me back.

"Don't move," I say. "You're—"

He grabs my wrist, and he holds me there, his blue eyes wide and unfocused.

"No," he says. "No, no, *no.*"

He flings me away. "Go! Run! You need to get out of here!"

"I'm trying to help—"

"No! Just go. Now! Before . . ." He trails off, as if his brain sputters off midsentence. He blinks. Then he runs his hands over his face and winces as he brushes his split lip.

"You've been—" I say.

"You need to go. Now. He'll come back."

"No one's coming back. I brought you here."

He's shaking his head, and I know he's delirious from the fever and can't process my words. I clasp his shoulders to calm him, but he grabs me again and, *shit,* he's strong. Fueled by that delirium, he's one good twist from breaking my wrists, and I struggle to get free, but he doesn't seem to notice, just grips me tighter.

"You need to go. Run! As fast as you can. I'll—I'll take care of this."

"I'm fine," I say, trying not to panic as he squeezes my wrists. "You're in my cabin. I brought you here. I need you to calm down so I can go for help."

"*Yes.* Go. I'll fix this." He throws me off then, pushing me toward the door. "I'll fix everything."

"Okay, you lie down . . ."

Another vehement shake of his head. "No time. Just *go.*"

He staggers to his feet and pushes me toward the door. He wants me to escape his nightmare, and I realize the best way to calm him down is to pretend I'm doing exactly that.

I open the door. A startled grouse takes flight, the undergrowth crackling. The guy lunges and grabs me, saying, "No! He's out there!" and I'm twisting to tell him it's okay, but he's put everything he has into that leap, and his injured leg gives way.

He smacks into me. My hands shoot out to break my fall, and I hear a crack, his head hitting the wall as he goes down. He collapses on top of me. I know he's fallen, and it's not his fault, but I panic under his dead weight, and I scrabble out from under him, clawing and kicking and—

Holy shit, Winter! Get a grip!

I stop short and crouch there, heart pounding. Then I see him in a heap on the floor. I crawl over. He's out cold again.

No, *cold* isn't the word—he's burning up. Shit!

I make some effort to drag him back to the sleeping bag, but I'm afraid of hurting him, so I lay him on his back with my pillow under his head. I'm not worrying about bloodstains now. I'm freaking, knowing how dangerous a fever can be, but if I leave and he wakes up, delirious again . . .

Cell phone.

I don't have one, obviously, but he might. I check his pockets. There are people I can call, people who will come if I ask. I don't like to ask, but for this, I will.

His pockets are empty except for a wallet. I open that with some reluctance, feeling like I'm prying. No ID. Just money. A lot of money. A corner of my mind can't help seeing a wad of cash like that and whispering that a twenty or two wouldn't be missed. I close the wallet quickly.

Someone took this guy's ID and left a few hundred in cash? Was he dumped, left for dead, his ID removed?

I look down at him.

What happened to you?

Forget that. I need to lower his fever so I can go for help.

I pull my backup water jug from under the baseboards. I take out ibuprofen, too, and bandages. The dressings can wait. First, I grind the painkillers into a glass of water. I tilt the boy's head back so he won't choke and then drip the water through his lips. I'm patient. Drop by drop until it's gone.

Cold compresses follow while the ibuprofen has time to kick in. I strip him down to his boxers, lay water-soaked towels across him, and open the door to let the night air in.

When I return with the bandages, he's already cooling. As soon as I'm sure the danger has passed, I shut the door before another kind of danger wanders in. Once he starts to shiver, I tuck my sleeping bag up to his armpits.

He needs a doctor. Which is a problem. Reeve's End has

exactly one—Doc Southcott, who's gone out of state. I'll have to get him to the next town, twelve miles over, beg a lift, as uncomfortable as that will be. He needs help. I will get it for him. That isn't a question. I took on that responsibility when I followed his path, and maybe I didn't mean to commit myself to this, but there's no going back now.

four

I CLEAN AND BIND MY LEG WHILE HE SLEEPS. THEN I'M WAITING for him to wake again, and I have my eyes closed, resting. When he gasps, I bolt upright.

"Hold on," I say. "You're safe. Just let me get some light."

I fumble to ignite my lantern. It hisses and casts a wavering glow over the shack. The injured guy is sitting. He sees me and gives a start.

"It's okay," I say. "You're safe."

"Where . . . ?" He looks around and then squints at me. "Do I know . . . ?"

"I brought you here. I found you, in a tree. Looks like you climbed up there to avoid the feral dogs."

"Feral dogs?"

"Like feral pigs, but even more dangerous." I smile, but he

frowns, as if I'm talking nonsense. No feral dogs and pigs in *his* backyard, I'm betting.

He starts to push up, and I say, "Whoa, hold on. You're—"

"Naked," he says, looking down.

"I left your boxers on. I was going to say you hurt your leg. Best not to jump up."

"Also . . . naked."

"You had a fever." I retrieve his clothing and hand it to him. He looks at me, and it takes me a moment to realize why.

"You want me to turn around?" I say. "Pretty sure I've seen whatever's on display, being the one who undressed you."

He says, "No, that's fine," but his expression is somewhere between bemusement and bafflement, as if he expects me to turn aside, blushing and stammering at the sight of a naked cute guy. And, yes, the word *cute* suggests I'm not oblivious. But it's a cursory assessment, as neutral as noting he has a scar on his shoulder.

He pulls on his jeans. "So I was in a tree, escaping the, uh, feral dogs."

"You don't remember?"

"Nope. But it happens so often, they just blur together, you know? Another day, another feral-dog-escape." A hint of a smile as he buttons his fly. "How'd you get me out of the tree?"

"Very carefully."

"I bet. And then . . . ATV transport?"

"Stretcher." When his brows rise, I say, "I fashioned a makeshift stretcher with our jackets and some branches."

"Of course you did." He chuckles, and I feel that familiar sensation, the one I get when I venture beyond Reeve's End. The feeling I'm being mocked. Mocked and judged.

20

"You don't believe me?" I say.

"Well, you said I had a fever, and I'm thinking maybe I still do. Treed by feral dogs? Rescued by a pretty girl who handily fashions a stretcher, drags me here, and nurses me back to health? Clearly I'm still delirious. Or dreaming."

"If you were dreaming, I'd be wearing a string bikini and holding a pitcher of beer."

He chokes on a sudden laugh. "With the way my head is pounding, I think I'd better stick to water. And this isn't really string-bikini weather."

I move toward him. "I noticed you wincing when you laughed. Does your chest hurt?"

"Everything hurts."

He stops putting on his shirt and lets me examine his ribs. As I do, he says, "So what is this place?"

"My hunting cabin."

"Hunting?"

"Not many girls do that where you're from?" I say.

"Some, sure. You just don't look like a girl with a hunting cabin."

I'm wearing worn blue jeans with a butt patch. Thick socks because my boots are two sizes too big—another bargain. Secondhand sweatshirt. Oversized denim jacket. No makeup. Chestnut hair ruthlessly braided back. If there's a type of girl who hunts, I'm pretty sure I fit the bill.

He continues, "Of course, you don't look like a girl who can haul my ass out of a tree, either."

I shake my head and continue my examination, concluding he has some bruised ribs but none seem broken.

"It's Lennon," he says when I pass back his shirt.

"Hmmm?"

"I just realized I completely skipped proper introductions. My mother would be appalled. I'm Lennon."

"I'm Winter," I say. "Winter Crane."

"Cool." He makes a face. "Sorry. Unintentional joke. It is a cool name, though."

"Thank you. I usually get 'That's kinda weird.'"

"Join the club. With me, it's teachers who misread the roster and call me Lemon. Which is awesome."

I chuckle and hand him the water cup, telling him to drink more.

He does and then says, "I also skipped the extreme gratitude part. Thank you, Winter Crane, for saving my life."

"It isn't saved yet. I'm going to run into Reeve's End and—"

"Reeve's End?"

"It's the nearest town."

"Yeah, I . . ." He sits straighter, wincing again. "I'm familiar with the area. We used to have a summer place near here."

"Unfortunately, the local doctor is away. So is his wife, who's the nurse. The only other person who works there is, well, me."

"Which explains the excellent care I've received so far."

"I'm just a high school student. Which means I need to get you to an actual doctor. It'll just take some figuring out."

"*Do* I really need a doctor? It's just bumps and bruises."

"You had a fever, but there's no sign of infection, which suggests you were already sick."

"Actually, the fever was from me trying not to *get* sick. I had a flu shot, and it made me a little feverish. I'm guessing the tree ordeal made it worse. I'm fine now." He taps his forehead. "Feel."

"The fever is gone because I gave you something for it. You need a proper examination."

"If I get worse, sure, but right now, I'm just suffering the lingering effects of stupidity."

I sit on my haunches. "What happened to you out there?"

"I'm still sorting that through. Brain's a little fuzzy right now."

"Then how do you know you did something stupid?"

A wry smile. "I could call it a gut feeling, but it's more a matter of probability based on past experience."

"You were assaulted. You need to speak to the police."

"And tell them what? For all I know, I got the shit kicked out of me because I was a smart-ass to the wrong person. Wouldn't be the first time."

"When you were delirious, you thought we were being held captive. You kept telling me to escape before *he* came back."

A strained chuckle. "Well, my brother always said I watch too many cop shows."

He's full of shit. But there's a steel thread of determination in his eyes. If I try to force his hand, he can just leave, and he'll get into worse trouble, lumbering around in the wilderness.

"Can I call your parents?"

"No need to notify them. I'm eighteen."

"I'm not talking about legal obligations. Someone should know where you are, even if you're living on your own."

That's an opening for him to supply more. He only says, "My parents are out east on business this week. They aren't

23

expecting to hear from me. My mother will suspect something's up if I call, and I'd rather skip the drama. Let me get back on my feet, and then I'll check in."

"But you should notify someone. What about your brother?"

"Hell, no. Mom might suspect something was up. My brother would know it the moment I said hello, and track me down."

"He's overprotective?"

He shrugs. "We're tight. But he won't freak if I don't call for a few days."

"So no police, no family, *and* no doctor."

"Because I don't need any of that until I remember what happened. If you can help take care of me, that's enough. I'll pay." He takes out his wallet and then quickly adds, "Paying for your nursing services. That's only fair."

"So I take your money and keep my mouth shut. And if you die from some internal injury I missed, I can probably pawn your shoes and jacket, too, if I can clean the blood off them."

He shoves his wallet back in his pocket, looking abashed. "Sorry. I'm just . . ."

"Used to buying your way out of trouble?"

Another of those crooked smiles. "Yeah. It's a family tradition. I'd have offered to pay even if you weren't . . . you know."

"From Reeve's End?"

His cheeks color. "I'm digging this hole as fast as I can, aren't I?"

"I come from a town where thirty percent live below the poverty line. I know my county's rep, and it's well deserved. If Doc Southcott was in town, I'd insist you get care, but as it stands, I'll agree to drop it. With conditions. I'm going to check you over again. If I find a broken bone, I'll get you to a doctor. If that leg needs stitching, I'll get you to a doctor. If that leg shows signs of infection or your fever returns . . . ?"

"You'll get me to a doctor. I agree to your terms, Winter Crane."

He extends his hand. I don't take it. I'm annoyed by the position he's put me in. "Shirt and jeans off again," I say.

He opens his mouth, his eyes glinting as if he's going to crack a joke. Then he catches my expression and begins to undress.

five

I HEAD TO TOWN FOR MEDICAL SUPPLIES. I EMERGE BEHIND THE trailer, as always. There are good people in Reeve's End. The kind who keep too close an eye on a girl living with her drunk father. The kind who notice every bruise and don't accept "I fell" as an excuse. Also the kind who, if they knew I was living in the forest, would find a bed for me. I appreciate that. I just don't want it. This is another thing Reeve's End has taught me: pride and self-reliance. I'll survive and I'll escape and I'll do it on my own.

To my relief, Bert's pickup is gone. I slip into the trailer and shower off the blood and dirt and any other sign that I haven't spent my evening studying. Then I re-dress my leg and head to Robson's Pharma.

I'm there in less than ten minutes. I cut through the food aisle on my way to the medical supplies. It's Wednesday, which

26

is when the sales start. Protein bars are half price. Past the sell-by date, but they're a cheap and easy meal. I'm dumping a handful into my basket when Mr. Robson comes by.

"Hey, Winter. You're out late."

"I lost track of time studying."

He smiles. "Course you did." He moves closer, voice lowering. "Can you tell your daddy I ain't gonna be able to pay the usual for his dope?"

Despite this being the pharmacy, *dope* doesn't mean drugs. It's the local term for soda pop. As for why Mr. Robson would be buying that from my father, it's food-stamp fencing. Bert buys Coke with his stamps and resells it to Mr. Robson for cash.

"Tell him I'm real sorry," Mr. Robson says. "But maybe this month he ought to use his stamps for food."

I resist the urge to snort. Mr. Robson means well. That doesn't stop me from taking advantage—just a little—of his discomfort, picking up one of the protein bars from my basket and saying, "Huh. I didn't see these were past the sell-by date."

"Are they? Well, now, you're right. Good eye. How about I give you another half off? Take a few more if you want 'em."

"I will. They ought to be good for a while yet. Thanks." I grab another handful. "Oh, and if you hear of folks needing the doc's help, he's having trouble with a polecat coming round his chickens. He'd 'preciate someone getting rid of it."

"I know a few families with little'uns who'd like to hear that. I'll tell 'em directly, Winter."

I take my bars with another thank-you and head toward the medical supplies section, where I can hear an old-timer at the pharmacy counter.

"—just about ate up with the cancer, poor thing," she's saying.

"Uh-huh," comes the reply, in a voice I know well. Tanner Robson, the owner's son. I try to duck around the corner before he spots me, but he calls, "Hey, Winter," hoping to free himself from the ear-bending.

I rescue him with some school chatter as I gather my supplies for Lennon. We lose most of the local dialect as we talk. We're taught "proper" English, but if we use it with older folks here, it makes us seem stuck up. We speak school English with each other and outside Reeve's End. Well, mostly. When Edie and I worked at the reenactment site, she'd ramp up dialect for the tourists—"Where y'all from?" and "An iPad? We ain't got nuthin' like that in the holler." I'd rolled my eyes until I realized she was getting double the tips, and I decided I was fine with reinforcing cultural stereotypes if it fattened my bank account.

Tanner and I talk for about twenty minutes. I like him. As a classmate, that is. A kinda-friend. Nothing more, even if he's hinted—hard—that he'd like to change that. In another life, I'd be happy to go along with it. He's shorter than me but cute, with a shock of blond hair, freckles, and a really sweet smile. He's smart, too—he'll go to college for pharmacology next year. But then he'll come back and take over the store, and that's the problem. I'm afraid I'd fall for him and tell myself Reeve's End isn't such a bad place and decide to come back.

Tanner said that to me once. *Have you ever thought of coming back? After you're a doctor? Reeve's End could really use someone like you.*

I'd made some excuse and hurried home. I'd wanted to

curse Tanner for being insensitive. Instead, I'd buried my face in my pillow and cried. I know Reeve's End will need a doctor. I know kids here need role models. But let that be someone else, like Tanner. Not me. Never me.

When I return to the shack, Lennon is awake but groggy. That alarms me, but the thermometer assures me he's only a degree above normal. I find no reason to insist he get help, not when that means a twelve-mile trip to a doctor who'll get pissy at a midnight call for a non-emergency.

I've brought my old sleeping bag, which smells faintly of mildew, and when Lennon insists on taking it, I let him. I still don't sleep well. I'm a mile from town, lying beside a stranger. Yet I can't leave him when he's injured. So I doze on and off until dawn seeps through the window boards.

Once I'm ready to leave for school, I wake Lennon to check him over. His temperature is back to normal. The cut on his leg is cool and dry. His chest still hurts when he inhales deeply, but that's to be expected—while bruised ribs hurt like hell, even Doc Southcott would only tell him to rest. I'm still not thrilled with the situation, but it's the best I can do for now.

SIX

I HAVE GARRETT'S FIRST TUTORING SESSION THAT AFTERNOON.
He shows up, pays me, and pays attention, which is all I ask for.

At the shack, Lennon is napping, and I wake him to check
his temperature, but he seems fine. The grogginess still bothers me enough that I suggest that doctor visit again. At this
hour, we could easily get a taxi from the next town over. It'd
be a hefty fare, but the wad of bills in his wallet says that's not
a problem.

"Do you *see* anything wrong with me?" he asks.

"Just because I don't see anything—"

"You want me to get undressed again? Just say the word. I
don't mind."

I shake my head and touch his ribs, feeling for sore spots
and asking if he's having any trouble breathing.

"I wasn't until you started running your hands over my

chest. You sure you don't want me taking off my shirt for this? Not every day a guy gets to strip for a pretty girl who actually *knows* how to play doctor."

"I'm sure you know plenty willing to try. You don't need to do that."

"Do what?"

"Pretend to flatter me, flirt with me . . ."

"It's not fake flirting or false flattery," he says. "But I get the feeling you don't appreciate either, real or otherwise."

"Good instinct." I back up and look around. "You need fresh air."

I pull the chair to the middle of the room, stand on it, and undo a latch on the ceiling.

"Is that an escape hatch?" he says.

"A skylight. I needed to board up the windows on account of the dogs, so I made this."

"You cut a skylight into your roof." He smiles. "You are remarkable, Winter Crane."

When my eyes narrow, his hands fly up. "That is not flattery. It's honest admiration. Whole different thing. And you can't ban me from saying nice things altogether."

"I can try."

His smile grows as he shakes his head again and says, "You sound like my brother. He hates compliments. And he gives that same look when he gets them."

I reach to open the hatch. A tendril of hair falls from my braid, and I shove it back in.

"He does what you do too," Lennon says after a minute. "Dress down. You don't want anyone to notice you."

"Practicing for a degree in psych?"

"Nope, just experience. With him, there's more to it. Same as you, I bet."

"Possibly so I'll be left alone, and not have to worry about guys pestering me because I'm not paying them the attention they think they deserve."

"Mmm, no. Partly, maybe. Not entirely. And, yes, you're taking a jab at me there, but I am ignoring it. You're an interesting girl—an interesting *person.* I'm trying to figure you out, and I don't believe in hiding that."

"Are you sure you don't want me contacting your brother? It sounds like you guys have a good relationship. Maybe he could help."

The animation falls from his face as he glances away. He's brought his brother up a couple of times now, and there's obvious affection, but I sense discomfort, too, and I wonder if they had a falling-out.

Now who's practicing for a psych degree?

I can't help it. When he talks about his brother, I think of my sister, Cadence. I grew up dogging her footsteps. Then . . . things changed. Changed so much that she's been gone over a year now and didn't even send a Christmas card. I understand how desperate she was to leave and why she doesn't want to talk to me, but it still hurts. Hurts so much.

I hop off the chair. "I need to check my snares." I glance at him. "Yes, I have snares."

"At this point, I don't doubt anything you tell me. You're like something off a reality show. Med-school-bound student by day, Appalachian survivalist by night."

"The second part isn't really a life choice," I say, and my tone is soft, but his smile falters, and he says, "I know. Can I come check traps with you? I can clean anything you've caught. This city boy is still a Kentucky boy."

"All right. But we aren't going far, on account of the dogs. If the traps haven't caught anything, it's protein bars and soda pop for dinner."

"Suits me fine," he says, and waits outside while I get my knife and bow.

seven

LENNON IS QUIET AS WE CHECK THE SNARES. HE'S LISTENING FOR the dogs, his gaze swiveling with every noise. It's only after I find a rabbit that he clears his throat. "I want to talk to you about why I was here. In the forest."

"I thought you didn't remember."

"I don't know exactly what happened, but I remembered why I was here. There was a girl. Actually, a lot of stories about me getting into trouble start with a girl. But this one I met last year at a concert in Lexington. She's from Reeve's End."

I cut the dead rabbit from the snare. "What's her name?"

"Edie Greene."

"What?"

"You know her?"

I nod.

A look flickers over his face, and I tense, but I stop myself before asking if Edie's okay. Of course she is—she's in New York at design school. We talked just a few weeks ago.

"So you met Edie . . . ," I prompt when he doesn't go on.

"We hung out after the concert," he says. "And kept in touch after. I'm guessing she never mentioned me?"

"I know she met a guy at a concert and stayed in touch. That's it."

"We went out a couple times, but it didn't work. I liked her, though, as a friend, and we talked maybe once a month. Then on Tuesday she called, middle of the night, in trouble. I was heading to Reeve's End to help."

"But Edie's in New York."

"Not on Tuesday. She'd hitched a ride from Lexington, and then she was walking to Reeve's End when . . . I don't even know what happened, exactly. I could barely make out what she was saying. It sounded like someone was following her. Someone in the forest, and she was freaking, and I asked where she was, and I was going to tell her to call the police when the line went dead. I took off to find her. I found the spot. There were signs of a struggle in the dirt. I was crouched, checking them, when I thought I heard someone behind me. That's the last thing I remember."

We're sitting on the roof edge, having moved up there when the light got low. While my roof hatch is technically a sky-light, I do use it for an "escape hatch"—escaping the dingy confines of my shack. It reminds me of when Cadence and I were young, after our mother died and Bert started the wandering that eventually landed us in Reeve's End. Wherever we were—a townhouse, an apartment building, a hotel, a motel . . . the endless series of deteriorating residences—Cadence and I would find a place where we could sit on a roof, each time telling ourselves the next one would be better. Maybe our father would find a decent job. Maybe he'd meet a nice woman. Maybe he'd stop drinking and start smiling again. Maybe, maybe, maybe . . .

We'd sit on those roofs and dream of life after one of those "maybes" fixed the life we had. Then we got to Reeve's End and the trailer park and, after that, Cadence never wanted to hear another "maybe," never wanted to climb another roof, never wanted to talk about the futures we could have, never wanted to talk to me about much at all.

"Winter?" Lennon says. There's genuine concern in his voice.

"Sorry. You were saying . . . ?"

"I know you'll want to go to the police, and I'm not going to stop you. But my gut says we should check a few things first. If I took this to the city cops, they'd tell me Edie's eighteen and unless I have proof she's in trouble . . ."

It's worse here. Our sheriff keeps his position only because no one dares run against him. The mayor is eighty-seven, in poor health, and does whatever the sheriff wants. And what the sheriff wants is an easy job with a good paycheck for him and his family—one deputy is his son, the other his son-in-law, and his wife and daughter do the clerical work. The last time we had a murder in Reeve's End, by the time the state police showed up, Sheriff Slate had already arrested the poor guy who reported the crime, trampled over the scene, and forgotten to notify Doc Southcott.

I do need more. I need to confirm Lennon's story. Maybe that sounds unreasonable—why would he make up something like that when I've said I know Edie, meaning I can just call her and straighten this out? Why make something like this up at *all*? The truth is that I don't know Lennon. I must confirm his story, as best I can.

When I last spoke to Edie, she never mentioned coming home. Still, she *is* impulsive, and if she made the decision last minute, it's not as if I have a cell phone she can text.

I've made my mental list of ways to confirm his story—call Edie, talk to her family, take him to check the spot where he says she was taken. And until all of that is done, I'm certainly not going to the police.

eight

As Lennon roasts the rabbit, I add a pot of water to the
fire for ramen noodles. We talk as we cook and as we eat, and
as night falls, I'm faced with the same predicament as last
night. I don't like sleeping beside a stranger, but I'm terrified
that I'll return to find him dead, the feral dogs having come
across him wandering deliriously through the woods.

"I'll be fine," he says as he sips his water.

"Hmm?"

"You're trying to figure out whether it's safe to leave me
tonight."

I arch my brows. "Mind reading?"

"Nah, just following the clues. It's dark, you've stopped
talking, you're looking between the sleeping bags and the
door. You don't want to leave me on my own, but I'm not your

responsibility, Winter. You rescued a total stranger from a tree, braving feral dogs to do it. That's quite enough."

"Anyone would have done that."

He laughs so loud he startles me. "Uh, no. The only other person I know who would have done that is my brother. *I'd* have gone for help."

I'm ready to change the subject, but he says, "I don't need a nursemaid tonight, and you shouldn't sleep next to a guy you barely know—though, arguably, one who's very cute and charming and witty, which I know makes it much tougher to leave. But since you forced me to promise not to flirt with you, I'm afraid you don't stand a chance of a good-night kiss."

"Well, damn. There goes my reason for staying."

He grins at that. "I'm sure it was. But I'll be fine, and you'll sleep better at home."

Not true, but I only say, "I'll go soon."

"I'll walk you." He lifts his hands. "No argument. It's the right thing to do."

"Says the guy who got treed by feral dogs. You're not walking me back." When he opens his mouth to argue, I say, "I'm not leaving yet anyway. I need to get my homework done first."

I pull books from my backpack. He takes my copy of *Heart of Darkness* and flips through it.

"Read that one?" I ask.

"Nope. If they don't assign it, I don't read it. Drives my brother nuts, because apparently I am totally missing the opportunity to expand my understanding of the world through

39

classic literature. He's a little weird. But I remember him try-ing to get me to read this one. Do you need it right now?"

I shake my head. He takes the novel and lies on his sleeping bag to read. I open my biology text and get to work. Less than ten minutes later, I hear the sound of soft snoring, and look over to see him with the book fallen on his chest.

"That good, huh?" I murmur, and take the book away.

I'm having the nightmare, the one rooted in that most ter-rifying of places: memory. I'm returning to the trailer after working at Doc Southcott's, and I catch Cadence burning something in the fire pit. When she sees me, she tries to shove the pages in quickly, but I see the Western Kentucky Univer-sity logo on one and I snatch it. I back away, reading the paper as I pinch the flame devouring one corner.

"You got in," I say, and I turn to her, grinning. Then I look from the fire pit to her. "Cady . . . ?"

"I'm not going," she says.

"Is this about Colton? Seriously, Cady? You'd give up col-lege for a guy whose big dream is expanding his parents' pot farm?"

"You don't understand."

"No, I don't." When she tries to retreat to the trailer, I plant myself in front of her. "You say you love him and he loves you. Well, let him prove it. Either he goes with you to Bowling Green and gets a job there or he waits here until you're done with school. That's what *girls* do if they love a guy who goes off to college."

"It's not the same."

"It damned well should be."

"Stop swearing, Winter. You only do that—"

"No, I don't only do it to piss you off. Shockingly, I don't do *anything* to piss you off. I just do. By existing, apparently."

"Let's not—"

"Fight? Yes, let's fight. You're my big sister. I know we aren't close anymore, and I'm not really sure why, but I still want the best for you. And throwing away college for a boy is nothing but trouble. You'll resent him for it. You won't mean to, but you will. If you love him, then you can't start like that."

She stares at me. Then she hugs me, and I'm so shocked I stumble back, but she pulls me into a tight embrace. She says, "I'll think about it." A week later, she tells Colton she's going to college.

And then . . .

And then . . .

I jolt awake, hearing something outside the cabin, and I'm trapped in that nightmare, in the aftermath, and I think it's my sister beside me. A figure rises, and I grab it and blurt, "Don't go out, Cady."

Lennon falls back, his eyes wide.

"S-sorry." I drop his arm. "I was . . ." I swallow. "I didn't mean to startle you."

"Who's Cady?"

I shake my head, and I'm trembling. He ignites the lantern and reaches for the bottle of water and hands it to me. Then he stops, his head tilting as if he's heard something.

A creak sounds outside the door. The hair on my neck rises. The wind whistles and something hits the door, making us both jump.

Lennon's on his feet, darting toward the door, and I'm opening my mouth to stop him, but he's just checking the latch. He puts his shoulder to the door, as if to stop anyone coming through. I turn down the lantern until it's only a dim glow, one that casts his face into half shadow. He shuts his eyes and his Adam's apple bobs as he swallows. He glances over, sees me watching, and leans against the door, his ear to it, listening—

Thwack.

nine

THE DOOR QUIVERS AS LENNON JUMPS WITH A LOUD "SHIT!" AND then slaps a hand over his mouth. His back shudders as he inhales. When he turns to me, his face is set.

"It's okay," he whispers. "I'll take care of this."

The hairs on my neck prickle again as his words echo the ones he said last night, in his delirium.

He reaches for the latch, and I realize he's about to open the door. I jump up and hold the latch shut.

"Are you nuts?" I hiss.

I swear I can smell the fear wafting off him. His gaze goes to my sleeping bag.

"Right," he says. "You need your knife. Stay in here until it's quiet and then go through the hatch. Get to town. I'll be fine. I'll fix everything."

"What is going on, Lennon?" I whisper.

"I have no idea, but it must be whoever attacked me. If I go out there, he'll see me and leave you alone."

"And I repeat, *are you nuts?* I swear if you open that door, I'll run out ahead of you."

When he stops, I back up to the floorboard compartment, gaze fixed on him as I retrieve my hunting knife and bow.

Another *thwack* against the door makes us both jump.

"What the hell is he doing?" I whisper. "Throwing rocks?"

No, it sounds like …

The noise is familiar. But as calm as I'm acting, I'm too freaked to analyze it.

Lennon looks at the ceiling hatch. I say, "We'll take that. Let me get a look—"

"No, I will." When I start to protest, he says, "I brought this danger. You know I did, Winter. I'll take the risks."

It's not an absolute certainty he *did* bring this here. It could be local kids goofing around. But Lennon's already pulling over the chair to climb up, and as much as I want to argue, it'll only slow us down. Someone is outside that door. We need to find out who and get the hell out before—

That creak outside the door comes again, and all I can think of is bonfires with Cadence and her friends, the older kids telling ghost stories. The urban legend of the girl in the car after her boyfriend has gone to see what's outside and she hears something scraping the top of the car.

I hurry over to Lennon and put my hand on his leg. He jumps.

"Sorry, just … be careful. Please."

He smiles. It's strained and anxious, but he manages it. "I will."

He lifts the hatch an inch, and I snuff the lantern so no light will betray our escape route. He looks left to right. Then he pushes the hatch another inch. He peeks out again and then flips the hatch completely up and grips the edge to hoist himself through. Then he bends and whispers, "Stay in here. Whatever happens. Whatever you hear. Lock this and stay inside."

That urban legend creeps back into my head, and I want to grab him and say this is silly; it's nothing but the wind in the trees and bugs hitting the door. But I know it isn't, and that's all the more reason to grab him and drag him back down before—

He's gone. Heaved himself out and closed the hatch behind him.

I scramble up onto that chair and reach for the hatch. I hold it as I strain to listen, ready to throw it open at the first sound of trouble.

"You trying to get my attention?" Lennon's voice booms through the still night. "Come where I can see you, and I'm all yours."

I shove at the hatch. His foot stomps it down.

"You want me, just show yourself. I know you're there."

I keep shoving on the hatch, but the angle is awkward, over my head, and Lennon's standing on it.

"I'm not playing games," Lennon calls. "You found me. You win."

I jump down and run for the front door. I'm not thinking— I only know that Lennon is summoning the demon who beat him half to death. Summoning him to finish the job, and I'm sure as hell not letting him do that.

My recklessness has limits, though, and I ease open the door. Lennon realizes what I'm doing and breathes a curse as his footsteps pound across the roof. I have the door half open and—

I recoil, letting out a gasp and a cry and a whimper all rolled into one. There's a shape hanging in the tree, swiveling in the wind, and that's the noise, that creaking noise, and all I can see is that shape and I flash back to—

Lennon jumps off the roof and accidentally strikes my shoulder, and I stagger, and the image flies from my head, and when I look back, I realize it's One-Eye, the alpha male, strung up outside my shack. He's hanging by his neck, dead, his stomach slit open and . . .

I turn away quickly. Lennon doesn't. He's staring at the dog. Just staring. When I touch his arm, he jumps and his face reddens.

Just because he can field dress a rabbit doesn't mean he's seen anything like this. He's in shock, and embarrassed by it, and I take his arm and turn him away. That's when I see what hit the door. Three arrows are embedded in the wood.

My arrows.

They're the ones I used with the dogs. I see those and somehow it's even worse than the eviscerated dog. It's so much more personal.

I peer into the forest. It's silent and still, but I know whoever did this is here, and if he had those arrows, does that mean he was *there,* too? Watching me rescue Lennon? Following us here and then biding his time?

"We need to go," I whisper. "Now."

Lennon prods me into the shack, but I shake him off.

"We're sitting ducks there."

Sitting ducks anywhere, really, given how far we are from town. But it's worse in the shack because it's not as if anyone will come looking for me in the morning.

We go back inside. I get my penlight and give Lennon my hunting knife, keeping my switchblade. Then we set off into the woods.

ten

AT FIRST LENNON TRIES WALKING BACKWARD BEHIND ME. AFTER a couple of his stumbles, I'm about to comment, but he moves up beside me and settles for frequent glances over his shoulder.

I don't run. Our best weapons right now are our senses and our brains, and if we run, we'll be moving too fast to hear or see trouble, panic and adrenaline dulling our thoughts.

The human predator I know best is Bert, but his attacks end as quickly as they begin, smacks and shoves that are worse than full-blown attacks because I don't feel as if he's venting misdirected frustration and rage on me. It *is* about me—I've pissed him off or gotten in his way—and those blows are as casual as kicking a dog.

Sometimes I want to be the kicked dog that leaps up and bites back. But I'm afraid that will unleash something truly ugly in him and earn me the kind of beating that leaves more than bruises. I still feel like a coward for not doing it.

And I feel like a coward running from whoever killed One-Eye. As if I should stay and fight and say I won't put up with this shit. Yet that's as stupid as leaping into a seething pack of enraged canines.

With Bert, I've learned that the best way to avoid trouble is to remain alert. That's what we do as we move quickly through the dark forest. I leave my penlight in my pocket and steer us onto a clear path, even if it's not the most direct route. It's a riding trail—horses, ATVs, dirt bikes—and it gives us breathing room and sight lines so our pursuer can't sneak up on us.

We catch no sign of him, though, and that's more terrifying, giving us no clues. When my breathing quickens, Lennon takes my hand. He squeezes my fingers, his grip light, reassuring. We hold hands like fairy-tale children walking through the dark forest, the wolf slinking through the shadows beyond our moonlit path.

A dog howls. Others join in, and I recognize the sounds of the feral pack.

Lennon stops short, and I'm wrenched back. He's looking to the side, and I whisper, "What is it?"

"I thought I saw something move."

We survey the woods, knives in our free hands. The howls die, and eerie silence descends, and we're both looking and listening so hard that when an owl hoots, we jump and fall into one another.

Then someone laughs.

It's a low laugh, barely audible, and when we both spin, it

49

tapers off, but slowly, and there's challenge and mockery in that tapering off.

Here I am, children. Right over here. Step off that safe, moonlit path and come meet me.

Children holding hands against the darkness.

You aren't afraid, are you?

Silence falls again, but I swear I still hear the echo of that laugh, and then Lennon shouts, "Damn you!" and I jump, but he only tightens his grip on my hand and his fingers are trembling and when I look over, there's such rage in his face that I suck in my breath, the sound sharp in the quiet. He's quaking with fury, but his eyes glisten, and he blinks back tears, and snarls and shouts, "Damn you to hell!" and I know what he's saying, because I've said it so often, in the safety of my shack.

Damn you for making me cry. Damn you for making me afraid. Damn you for making me less than I want to be.

I squeeze Lennon's hand to tell him he's not alone, and he glances away and I wonder if I've embarrassed him. He entwines his fingers with mine and gives me a crooked little smile. It's only one moment and then we're surveying the woods again, our weapons raised.

The forest has gone still.

I know he's still there. I know it. But he's enjoying our fear too much to strike. This isn't a feral dog chasing down its prey. It's a cat toying with mice.

"Let's go," I say, and we resume walking. Shoulders straight. Chins high. *See, you don't frighten us.*

Except that's a lie, and the man doesn't laugh, but I know he's out there, and he's smiling.

eleven

WE DON'T EXIT AT THE TRAILER PARK. I WANT TO GET OUT OF
these woods, but if people spot me at night with a guy they
don't recognize, someone will follow, maybe out of curiosity, or maybe to ensure I haven't made some gravely naive
mistake . . . like finding a cute guy in the forest and bringing
him home.

Maybe we should have made a beeline for the sheriff's department. But I never even consider it. I'd just be "Rob Crane's
stuck-up brat" bringing along some city fella and playing a
prank. Being chased through the forest by a psycho dog-killer?
Yeah, because outside of teen slasher movies, that happens *all*
the time.

I could probably take the sheriff back and show him One-
Eye's corpse, and he'd think it was part of a really sick joke.

I select a safe path that will take us behind the main street.

Our stalker won't follow us here—I'm sure of that. Ninety percent anyway.

Once we're away from the forest, I whisper, "About my place . . ."

"Hmm?"

"I live . . . Well, it's my father and me. . . . He's probably not home, but . . ." I inhale, and blurt, "It's a trailer."

"Mobile home, you mean."

"Technically, yes, but . . . it's a trailer. In a trailer park."

"Okay." He glances over at me, through the moonlit dark. "I don't care where you live, Winter."

"I'm just warning you. The place is clean. Or it was. Well, it's as clean as I can make it, which isn't really—"

"Winter? I don't care."

I do. I know what I'll see when we get there. Judgment. He'll try to hide it. He'll still be surprised, though, because he'll have thought I was exaggerating. And he isn't the kind of guy who's been in a trailer where you need to move stuff off the chairs to sit down, where you won't find a matching set of cutlery and you're just happy that a spoon is clean and, really, it probably isn't—Bert likes to just rinse stuff off and stick it in the drawer.

"You guys don't have much money, Winter. I get that. You want to know my secret?" He leans in and mock-whispers, "I'm rich."

I roll my eyes, and he says, "No, seriously. I come from old Kentucky money. The kind that means I've been going to the Derby since I was old enough to sit still."

"The eye roll wasn't doubting you."

"It's mocking me, I know. It's saying, 'you poor baby.' And that's totally legit, because I know exactly how good I have it.

But I don't go around advertising my background. People have certain preconceptions if your family's rich. Preconceptions and expectations. Still, I know life's a whole lot easier for us because we have money, and if I ever forget that, Jude's quick to remind me."

"Is Jude your brother?"

"Yep."

"Jude and Lennon? Is there a Beatles fan in the family?"

He chuckles. "Good catch. Most kids don't get the connection."

"My mom was into the old stuff. The Beatles, Rolling Stones . . ."

He's quiet for a moment. Then he says, "You use the past tense, and you said you live with your dad. Your mom's . . . gone?"

"Died when I was seven. Cancer."

"I'm sorry. Jude and me . . . Our parents died when I was six months. Car crash. We're adopted." He shoves his hands into his pockets. "I shouldn't have jumped in with that. No one likes people comparing their situation to theirs. Jude says—" He makes a face. "I keep doing that, don't I?"

I resist the urge to say something lame, like *You look up to him.* No one over the age of ten wants to hear that. I can't help a pang of envy, either. People used to say that about Cadence and me. *You look up to your big sister, don't you, Winter?* Because I did. And then it changed, and I'd give anything to have that back.

Instead I just say, "He's your brother," as if this explains everything, and he nods as if, yes, it does.

"He's older, right?"

"A little."

"Off at college?"

"He should be, damn him." He says the last two words as if in affectionate exasperation, but there's real exasperation there too. "He had the grades to get into any school he wanted. Hell, he could have gotten a music scholarship if he didn't want to take our parents' money."

I want to ask why he *wouldn't* take it. If his family is wealthy, he has a right to a good education, adopted or not. But instead I say, "Music?"

"Piano. He's a freaking prodigy. No exaggeration. Or he was—he gave it up last year, the idiot."

I'd have to agree. If I had a talent, I'd treasure it. But I can also imagine that "concert pianist" isn't the dream of the average teenage boy.

"How long ago did he finish school?" I ask.

"Just this year. We're—we *were*—in the same grade."

"You're twins?"

He laughs softly. " 'Irish twins' is the not-quite-politically-correct term one of our nannies used. Jude's ten months older than me."

"That's . . ."

"About as fast a turnaround as a mom can manage." Another chuckle. Then, "Enough of this shit. I should call him. Do you guys have a landline?"

I shake my head. "There's a pay phone just over on Main."

"Can I get change somewhere? Any I had fell out in my tree-climbing escapade, apparently."

"I have some. I'm not sure if it's enough."

"I'll keep it short."

He keeps the call *very* short because his brother doesn't pick up. Lennon leaves a message. "I'm in a bit of trouble. Big surprise, right? I, uh, wouldn't call, but . . . yeah, it's . . . more than a bit of trouble. I've . . . I've done something really stupid, Jude, and—" He inhales. "I'll confess later. For now, I'm calling from a pay phone, which apparently still exist. So no point calling me back. I'll try again in the morning. Please keep your damn phone on for once, okay?"

He shakes his head and hangs up.

twelve

WE DO RETURN TO THE FOREST, BRIEFLY, SKIRTING THE TRAILER
park. I suspect if we hadn't lost our pursuer, he'd have been
unable to resist letting us know.

I'm still here. Did you think you'd escaped that easily?

But we haven't escaped. No more than we've "lost" him.
He's left.

We reach the trailer. Thankfully Bert's pickup is gone.
When I usher Lennon through the door, I fuss with relocking
it to avoid watching his reaction.

"Light?" he whispers.

"To your left."

He flicks the switch. Then he walks in without a pause.
That nonchalance lasts only a moment, though. Then he stops
in the middle of the kitchen and gives a slow look around.

"Shit," he says.

"It's—"

"Turn off the light, Winter."

I do, too nervous to ask why, but he only moves through the kitchen and living area, pulling the shades.

"There, okay. Turn it on."

When light fills the trailer, I try not to look around with fresh eyes. Try not to see the thrift store sofa, one arm bleeding stuffing where Bert stabbed it with a knife after losing a gig mowing the cemetery lawn. Try not to see the pyramid of empty bourbon bottles near the door, an altar to the god that rules his life. Try not to see the Chinese food containers left on the counter. I don't know if he's just too lazy to put them in the fridge or if he leaves them to taunt me with food I don't dare eat unless I want to risk salmonella poisoning.

I grab the takeout containers and open the trash. "Sorry about the smell. Let me open a window."

"It's fine, Winter."

I reach for the window over the sink. "No, I'll—"

He catches my hand. "Opening a window isn't safe. And it really is fine."

"It wasn't like this when I left."

"I know. If you insist on being hospitable, I see a case of Coke over there. I'd love one."

"That's, uh, not mine." I hurry on before he can question. "I have some in my room. Just give me a sec."

I come back with a can and hand it to him. It's even cold. I have a bar fridge. Edie and I found it put out for the trash.

"We can sit . . ." I look around. There's crap everywhere. The trailer has zero storage space, so our belongings just get moved from surface to surface.

"Let's just sit over here." He moves into the living area.

I dart ahead to clear the sofa.

"I can do that," he says.

"I just— It's— I'm sorry."

"Yes," he says. "You should apologize for making me move stuff to sit down. And apologize for not having a bigger home. Because clearly this doesn't meet my standards."

There's a chill in his voice, and I know I've insulted him.

"I don't mean—" I begin.

"You're embarrassed by your place. I get it. But I don't give a shit. You saved my life and took care of me. And what did I do in return? Brought some psycho to your doorstep. Do you honestly believe I'm looking around and thinking—"

"—maybe next time you can attract a better class of rescuer?"

I smile when I say it, but the look he gives me makes me murmur an apology.

He sets the can down and steps toward me, his face softening. "I don't mean to give you shit, Winter. I'm just trying to say that I think you're pretty damned amazing, and this"—he waves at the room—"doesn't change that."

His hands go to my hips, and he leans in, and his lips barely brush mine before I back from his grip.

"You don't have to . . . do that," I say.

His face tightens in annoyance. "Do what? Kiss you to say I think you're *worthy* of my attention. That's not what I meant, Winter."

"I know. Just—"

He moves away. "Oh, right, no, I must be kissing you as a *reward* for saving my ass. Or maybe to ensure you don't kick me out the door. Give you a little incentive to keep risking your life for me."

"That isn't—"

"I kissed you because I want to kiss you. I think my little speech should have made that clear."

"Okay. But . . . no. I don't want—" I inhale. "Let's not go there, okay."

He blinks, and there's genuine surprise in his face. Then a flash of hurt, and he pulls back, picking up the Coke and turning away.

There's silence. Long, awkward silence, and I'm about to go tidy the kitchen when he turns to me, his gaze slightly downcast, his lips crooked in a rueful smile.

"And that was a really shitty thing to do," he says. *"You don't want me to kiss you? Well, screw you."* He shakes his head. "Have I mentioned I can be a jerk?"

"Not many girls tell you no, I'm guessing."

"I'd say it's never happened before, if that wouldn't add 'arrogant' to 'jerk.' But, hey, new experiences are good. They build character. Let me apologize. Deeply and profusely. Not for trying to kiss you, which I think is acceptable, but for being an ass when you said 'no thanks.' "

"Apology accepted."

He smiles. "Most girls would cushion the blow by telling me I *wasn't* being an ass. I like that you don't. One of many things I like about— And let's stop there. Sorry. Couldn't resist."

59

"Under the circumstances, I think it's best to . . . avoid anything."

"The practical and wise course of action. I'm the strange guy you met in the forest. You've already taken risks for me. You have no idea what I've brought to your doorstep. Being nice to me is one thing; kissing me is quite another."

"I didn't mean—"

"No, you're right." He waves at his face. "See this expression? It's my serious one. I'm not angling for a compliment."

He takes a basket of laundry from the couch and clears us a spot. We both sit, and he continues, "You are absolutely right to be wary. I *want* you to be. That's what'll keep you safe from . . ." He looks at the window, and I know he's thinking of the man out there.

"I stumbled onto something," he says, "and I'm an idiot for bringing it to your door."

"You didn't exactly have a say in being rescued."

"Yes, but . . ." He shakes it off as he straightens. "I just want you to be careful, Winter. You didn't sign up for this."

"Neither did you. But I take your point. Trust no one."

"I used to think everyone was a good person, deep down. I remember Jude—" He makes a face. "Sorry."

"No, go on."

He pauses and then says, "Even in private school, kids can be bastards. Jude wouldn't put up with that shit, but he'd also say that the bullies probably had crap going on in their lives too. Divorce, abuse—stress of some kind. He'd say that doesn't excuse it, but you need to remember that everyone else is dealing with crap, and bear that in mind before you write them off."

His brother has a point, but as someone who's been bullied, I don't particularly want to grant it. It's easier to imagine that when I'm a surgeon at a big city hospital, my father will be stuck in Reeve's End, drinking himself to liver failure and realizing if he'd just been a better father, I could have saved him. Enjoying that fantasy makes me petty and vindictive. Jude's way is better. Probably healthier. But I can't bring myself that far.

"Jude might be right about seventy-five percent of assholes," Lennon continues. "But the other twenty-five percent? They have no excuse. They're just bad. Born bad." He fidgets with his Coke can. "They might seem good on the outside, but it's a disguise. Sometimes I feel that way. Like everyone thinks I'm this great guy—student council president, captain of the volleyball team, Mr. Popularity—but I've done shitty things. I've *thought* shitty things. And when other kids looked up to me in school, I wanted to run and—"

He thumps the can down so loudly I jump. "And very clearly I haven't had nearly enough sleep in the last couple of nights. Sorry."

"No," I say quietly. "It's okay. I know . . . People think . . ." I swallow. "They tell me I'm a good person for helping Doc Southcott. For tutoring other kids. For setting a good example. But I get *paid* for the work and the tutoring. And how am I setting a good example? By being smart? By working hard so I can get out of this town and never come back? If I *were* a good person—"

"You risked your life to save me, Winter."

I push to my feet. "We both haven't had nearly enough sleep. There are only a few hours left until morning. I'm going to insist you take my room because if Bert comes home and finds you on this couch, he's liable to mistake you for an intruder and grab his shotgun."

"Which would be bad."

"Yep. He has crappy aim, but that doesn't matter with a shotgun."

thirteen

I WAKE IN FLIGHT. I'M FALLING, AND I SCRABBLE, ALL FOUR LIMBS flinging out before I hit the floor. I leap up, my hand going to my pillow for my knife, before I realize my pillow is on the sofa and I'm on the floor and staring at a man's boots.

Familiar boots.

I lift my head and look up to see my father. He's stocky and fair-haired and blue-eyed; nearly the polar opposite of my slight build, brown hair, and dark eyes. There was a time, in eighth grade, when a boy at school found out his dad wasn't really his father, and I wondered if that was why Bert hated me so much, if he thought I wasn't really his. I am, though. We have the same nose—too strong on me— and the same chin—too sharp on him. But I've seen the photos of my mother that Cadence squirreled away, and I know who I take after more, and I've wondered if *that's* why he hates me.

Bert's standing there, holding the blanket, having yanked it off me and toppled me to the floor in the process, and now he's glowering, like I've fallen to spite him.

"Get up," he says.

I do, as I try to see past him to my bedroom door, which is thankfully shut.

"You're back?" I say, raising my voice in hopes Lennon will hear.

"I live here. Right now I'd like to know why the hell my daughter is on the couch and who the hell she brought home last night."

"Br-brought home?" I straighten and look around in panic that I don't need to fake.

"Miz Reid stopped me at the gate. Said she saw a boy sneak in with you."

I open my mouth to protest and then shut it fast. I'm still half asleep, and I need to get my panic under control or he'll know I'm lying. I also need to get Lennon out of my bedroom. I'm not sure if he'll fit through the window, but he sure as hell needs to try, because if Bert finds him here . . .

"Boy?" I manage a snort. "Mrs. Reid is overdue for her cataract operation. Long overdue. She probably saw Susie sneaking a man back while Pete's on the road. You know what she's like."

Bert's eyes narrow, as if I'm pointing out that he knows that from personal experience, being one of the men Susie invited over when her husband was on a long haul.

I continue, "I slept on the sofa because my room got hot and I had to shut my window before I got a contact high from all the pot smoke blowing in. Someone was definitely celebrating the long weekend early."

"You didn't have a boy over?"

"I didn't *bring* a boy over. If one was sneaking around, he sure wasn't invited."

Bert surveys the trailer. His gaze lights on Lennon's Coke can.

"That better not be mine," he says.

"I don't touch your stuff, Bert."

His eyes narrow more. "Don't call me that."

"What do you want me to call you? Dad?"

"Show a little respect."

"I will . . . when you earn it."

He raises his hand, but I dodge and he doesn't come after me. My flinch is satisfying enough when he's sober. The exchange has the desired effect, though—he's forgotten about "the boy."

"Get ready for school and go," he says. "And keep it down. I need sleep."

I wait until Bert stalks toward the bathroom. Then I say, "If you want me gone, I'm going to need to use that first." He slams the door behind him. I hurry to my room and ease open the door.

There's no sign of Lennon. I exhale in relief . . . until I see that the books piled by the window are still there. He couldn't have slipped off without moving them. There's nowhere else in my room to hide—it's a twin-sized berth with every spare inch converted into makeshift storage containers.

That's when I see the note on the bed.

WINTER,

I'M GOING TO FIX THIS.

—LENNON

Shit! No, no, no. You idiot.

I race out the door. Bert's still in the bathroom, shower running. I fly outside, bow over my shoulder, knife in my pocket.

I run straight for the forest. I get ten steps in before I freeze.

I'm running into the forest. Where we escaped a dog-killing psycho. And I called *Lennon* an idiot?

I bounce on my toes and look around. Lennon isn't in there. I know he isn't. But I need to do something. I need to talk to someone. Who can I confide in?

No one.

For the first time in my life, I'm utterly alone. As estranged as Cadence and I became, she'd still been my sister. I could count on her when it mattered. Edie had been there too, for anything I needed, even after she left, telling me to call anytime, night or day. And I do have friends. I'm not a complete loner.

No, let's be honest. I have school friends. Kids I see in class and in the halls and maybe chat with if I bump into them around town and stop—like Tanner—but that's it. There is absolutely no one I can go to with a problem like this. No one I can run to and say, "I'm in trouble and I need help."

Except it's not me in trouble. It's a guy I met two days ago.

That doesn't matter. I'm not even sure it's about him as much as it's about me. Like why I helped him in the first place. Why I didn't want to leave him alone at night. Because if anything happens, I'll suffer the guilt of it.

I head back into my room, on the off chance Lennon left something else there. He did, tucked under the pillow. Three hundred dollars. I curse him for that—I don't want his damn money; I want him to take better care of himself.

Don't go running off to save a girl you met at a concert, Lennon. Don't go running off to protect a girl you met in the forest.

His heart might be in the right place, but his brain really isn't. He's not stupid—just impulsive. I could add *brave,* but honestly, there's a line between brave and foolhardy, and he's crossed it.

Damn him.

I take the money, namely because I don't want Bert finding it. I check the note again for clues, but it's written on paper from my stash.

I'M GOING TO FIX THIS.

What exactly are you going to fix, Lennon? How are you going to fix it? Have a reasonable chat with the guy who beat the shit out of you?

I can't even fathom what was going through Lennon's

67

head. His words make no sense, and I don't think they're meant to. They are a talisman to ward off the boogeyman in the night.

I can handle this. I can fix this.

Except he couldn't.

fourteen

I SPEND SOME TIME TRYING TO TRACK LENNON. BUT IF HE WENT
into the forest, I can't find a trail, and I have no idea where else
he'd go.

School started an hour ago, but that's the last of my concerns today. For once, I have something more important to do.
It's the Friday before a long weekend, when I swear half the
kids skip out. For once, I'm joining them.

The first thing I do is call Edie. I thought of sneaking from
the trailer to do that last night, but if she didn't answer at two
a.m., that might only mean she didn't hear her phone.

I call at nine. It rings through to voice mail. I leave a message. Then I wait ten minutes and call again, in case she was
screening. I don't expect her to answer. Lennon wouldn't have
told me a story I could explode with a single call. But I needed
to be sure.

When I try to leave another message, I'm told her inbox is full, which means I'm not the only person who's been trying to get in touch. Edie doesn't ignore messages. A full inbox means she hasn't been answering her phone in days.

As for Lennon, I can't report him as a missing person. He's not actually missing—the note means he left of his own accord. I do need to tell someone what's happened to him, though. Someone who will care.

I make another call, dialing 0 for the operator.

"Hello," I say in my professional answering-the-doctor's-office-phone voice. "I'm calling from a pay phone in Reeve's End. This telephone was used last night by a young man who placed a call to a family member. I need to contact his next-of-kin—it's an emergency—and this is the only information I have."

I sound very grown-up. Pleasant and yet confident, as if I have no doubt this is a perfectly valid request, one she can and will fulfill.

The operator isn't fooled for a second.

"Who is this?" she asks.

I take a deep breath and send up a silent apology to Doc Southcott. "I work at Dr. Edgar Southcott's office in Reeve's End, Kentucky. As I said, it's an emergency. The only way we have of reaching this young man's next-of-kin is using the number he dialed last night."

"Then have the doctor speak to the local sheriff's department. Only they can request that information."

"But—"

She hangs up.

fifteen

THE GREENES ARE PROPER HILL FOLK. THAT'S THE LOCAL TERM. They're also known as mountain folk and sometimes hill-billies, the latter being one of those words we don't let anyone else apply to us.

Those of us down in the holler are supposedly more civilized than hill folks, with none of that "moonshine and coal mine" nonsense. Which is bullshit. Moonshine is a cultural tradition, and the good stuff is considered an art form. As for coal mines, well, that's historically a major form of industry, along with trapping and hunting and other things that fit right into the stereotype. But like any stereotype, it's only a small part of who we are. More people here drink beer than moonshine. They're far more likely to work in an office than a mine, and they get more meat with cash and credit than bullets and arrows. For the record, I don't even know anyone who plays the banjo.

In the hills, people are more likely to conform to the stereotype, and that's more a matter of necessity than choice. They can't afford store-bought liquor and meat. They don't have the education for office jobs. Up here, folks survive and thrive under conditions that make me look like a suburbanite.

This is where Edie comes from. And this is where I'm headed: making my way through endless Christmas ferns, under towering tulip poplars, pushing aside the massive leaves of the umbrella magnolias.

When I get close to the Greene homestead, I start hunting. I scare up a couple of rabbits and a grouse, and I'm starting to think that's what I'll have to settle for, when I see the buck. It's young, antlers suggesting it's in its second or third year. It's been a good summer, and the buck has grown fat, ready for winter.

I slide behind a stand of trees and assess my prey. I haven't taken a deer since Edie left. It's a waste for me—too much meat and no way to store it. But this isn't for me, and this buck is better than I dared hope for.

There's a second stand of trees closer to the deer. I'm about to step out, when it lifts its head. It's looking the other way, though, and it's a casual glance, the buck still chewing, grass hanging from its mouth. When it resumes grazing, I creep to the second stand of trees. Then I ready my bow as I mentally run through my checks. The wind is heading my way, which means the buck can't smell me, but that wind also adds resistance to my shot. It's a light breeze, though, and a little more force behind my draw will compensate.

When the kids at summer camp discovered I hunt, the first thing they said was "How can you?" Not literally "how," asking how I came by the skills. They meant how could I stand here, looking at a young and healthy buck, eating peacefully, and end its life.

How can I? Easy. Because this is not a sport for me. I can't add items to a grocery list and know the food will miraculously appear after my parents go shopping. I hunt to eat. In this case, I won't be the one dining on my kill, but someone will, someone who can use the meat even more.

While the buck grazes, I line up my arrow. The kill spot is behind the shoulder, aiming at the heart. It's a shot best made while standing broadside, and that's exactly the view I have. The buck pauses again, this time glancing in my direction, and I freeze. When it resumes grazing, I recheck my aim and then let the arrow fly. It hits the right spot. It goes in—and the buck rears with a bleat.

I didn't have enough force behind my draw. Shit, shit, shit!

I have a second arrow nocked when the buck collapses on the ground in a skid. It's lying there, snorting, nostrils flaring, eyes rolling. And this is the worst. The absolute worst. I want to apologize, want to undo what I've done, wish I could walk away and know the buck will be fine. But that too is a luxury I do not have. The deer is suffering, and I must fix that.

I walk behind the buck. It doesn't hear me—it's too panicked. I lower myself to the ground, position my knife at its throat, and finish what I've begun.

I wait until it's dead. Then I check, touching an arrow shaft to its eye. The first time I hunted alone, I started field dressing a rabbit before it was dead. I was in a hurry, dark falling, elated

73

at my first solo kill. I still have nightmares about that horrible mistake. So I check even when a beast has stopped breathing and its chest has stopped rising.

I grab the antlers, drag it to a slope, and use the incline to drain some blood. If it was my kill, I'd field dress it here. But it's not and I don't have far to go, so I start dragging, which is not unlike hauling Lennon, and by the time I near my destination, I'm huffing and puffing, my injured leg blazing.

I can see Edie's grandmother as I approach the house. I call it a house out of respect. It's a shack, maybe twice the size of mine. Edie does what she can to keep it in good repair, but it's not easy getting supplies up here. The roof lists and it's a patchwork of shingles—wood, asphalt, even asbestos—but it keeps the rain off. The front porch sags and the railings are rotted, but Edie propped it up well enough that she didn't have to worry about her granny or pappy falling through when they sat on their rockers. That's a stereotype—about as hillbilly as you can get—but it's what they do. They sit on the porch and look down the mountain as they sew or peel or whittle.

Edie never knew her parents. Her mother got pregnant in her teens. Her grandparents said they'd raise Edie while her momma went off to the city and settled into a life. She never came back for her daughter. She sent birthday gifts, roughly at the right time, presents that grew increasingly lavish as her fortunes must have improved. Edie hocked them. That wasn't anger and resentment. She just needed the money more than an MP3 player or new cell phone.

When I see Granny Greene hanging the laundry, I lift my hand and call a "hullo!" quickly adding, "It's Winter," knowing her sight is poor and her shotgun is always close by.

"Winter?" she calls. "You sure? I thought it was still fall." It's an old joke, and she cackles as I smile obligingly.

She squints at me, her face screwing up. That face is as brown and wrinkled as a walnut, despite the fact she's not even sixty. Sunscreen is a luxury folks up here can't afford.

"That a buck you got there, Winter-girl?"

"It is," I say, dragging it closer.

"That's a fine one. You're getting to be a better shot than my Edie."

I shrug. "I got lucky. It was busy stuffing itself, not a care in the world. Course, problem now is that I can't drag it back down the mountain. You mind if I dress it here? Leave it for you and Pappy Greene?"

"Not gonna argue with that. You need a knife? Edie's got a good one."

"I'm fine, thanks. I came prepared."

"Let me getcha something to drink."

As she goes into the house, I position the buck and start cutting. It's the same procedure as cutting up a rabbit or squirrel—just tougher getting through the hide. I've sliced straight up the abdomen when Granny Greene comes out with my beverage. It's apple pie—the local name for apple-pie moonshine. As the name implies, it tastes like pie, made with apples and cinnamon, so it's drinkable, though I'll let most of it spill when she isn't looking.

I continue cutting while she settles in on the porch to watch.

"You heard from Edie?" I ask.

"Got a letter last month. And fifty dollars. She'd done some work, casual-like, said she made a little extra. I sent a return letter, telling her not to do that no more. We don't need the money and she shouldn't be working when she's going to school. You talk to her, you tell her the same thing. She's there for an education."

"I'll do that." I sever the deer's windpipe, preparing to remove the internal organs. "I heard someone saying she was coming back to Reeve's End for a visit. That's why I came up. Last I heard, she wasn't coming until Thanksgiving. I tried calling, but she's not answering. Busy, I guess. You know anything about her coming home?"

Granny Greene shakes her head. "If she does, she might stay down in the holler, knowing she'll catch hell if we find out she wasted money on a bus ticket. She'd come to see you, though, Winter. First person she'd come see, I wager. And if she does, you tell her to get her ass up here, so I can kick it, and then make her a proper dinner with that buck you're carving so nicely. She'd like that. Be real proud to see your work. Better yet, she comes home, you bring her up here yourself. I'll put some of that buck in the icebox, just in case, do it up the way you girls like it. Okay?"

I nod and fervently pray Edie will come home to eat it.

sixteen

I STAY FOR LUNCH. THAT'S EXPECTED. THEN I HELP A BIT AROUND the house, and when I leave, Granny sends me off with an apple pie. An actual apple pie, which I will appreciate much more than the liquid version, even if it means I need to detour to the shack to drop it off.

I'm about a half mile away when a twig cracks. I spin, like I used to in my early days exploring these woods, and I imagine Edie's laugh.

You're like a cat in a roomful of rocking chairs, Winter, she said.

That doesn't make any sense, I replied.

She explained the analogy—the cat dashing through the room, just waiting for one of those rockers to crunch down on her tail. That's how I felt *everywhere* in Reeve's End. Tense, waiting for trouble. Forest or town, it was unfamiliar territory, filled with dangerous rocking chairs.

These days, in the woods, I usually process the noises as simple data, potentially a threat but more likely to be dinner. Now I'm jumping.

I catch a flicker of movement in the trees. Dead leaves crackle behind me. I wheel as a rabbit zooms across the path, and I hear Edie's laugh again.

I take a deep breath and continue on. I'm nearly to the shack when I hear buzzing.

A cell phone?

It's a testament to my nerves that I even jumped to that conclusion when the answer is one I'm far more familiar with. The buzzing of flies. Lots of flies, from the sound of it. I take another few steps, and there—jutting onto my makeshift path ahead—is something white.

Something white.

I race forward to see—

It's a rabbit. A dead rabbit with its white rump and tail extending from under a bush. That's all there is—the rear half. The rest is gone.

I stare at the mutilated rabbit. Its hind leg moves. I jump and hit a tree behind me and something falls, striking my shoulder. When I leap away, I see the other half of the rabbit lying near my feet.

I drop the pie and let out a yelp. I jam my fist in my mouth, but those notes echo through the forest.

I look back at the rabbit's hindquarters. The leg twitches again. It's the flies, crawling underneath, making it move. The other half is just the head and part of the upper torso. The middle is gone.

I yank off my jacket and look for blood on it. There's nothing. I scour the tree branches, but I see no sign that the other half of the rabbit was up there and fell on me.

It looks like an animal kill. A brutal one, but no worse than I've seen from those damned dogs, tearing something in two, gulping down the choice middle pieces, and leaving the rest.

It's a disgusting mess, but nothing unnatural, nothing I haven't seen before.

I take a deep breath and resume walking. I've gone only a few yards when a footstep sounds behind me. That soft thump can be nothing else, but when I spin, I see only trees.

I turn slowly and begin walking, ears pricked for that careless twig-crack or leaf-crumple behind me. I even wheel suddenly, hoping to catch my pursuer off guard.

Nothing.

I take three deep breaths. I'm freaking myself out. I know that. There's no one else here.

I continue on to the shack. I approach from the rear and climb onto the roof. I left the hatch undone last night, and I crawl to it on my stomach and peek in.

The shack looks empty and untouched. I creep farther to peek over the roofline. No sign of anyone. My gaze swings to where One-Eye . . .

I don't see the dog's corpse.

I jump to the ground and hurry over to the tree.

The dog is gone.

Every sign that the dog's corpse ever was here is gone. There's no rope in the tree. No blood on the undergrowth.

I search and find what looks like a few droplets in the dirt, but when I rub one between my fingers, it's only tree sap.

I climb the tree and crawl onto the limb the dog had hung from, but there are no rope marks on the bark.

One-Eye's killer returned and took the body and erased the evidence.

Yet it's more than that. One-Eye had to weigh a hundred pounds. The rope *would* have left marks. The dog had been split open. There'd be blood or viscera left in the undergrowth.

One-Eye's killer *prepared* for this. He cushioned the rope so it wouldn't cut into the tree bark. He laid something on the ground to catch any falling evidence.

No, that's crazy—I've seen too many of those damn CSI shows. Cadence used to watch them with me, and she'd threaten to gag me when I'd point out that no one can analyze DNA while you wait, like ordering a burger at the drive-through. But it's that very television show that compels me to look closer here as I search for exactly the sort of evidence I rolled my eyes at on-screen. And I find it. Fibers caught in a knot on the limb, proving he cushioned the rope. More fibers in the dirt, proving he laid a cloth below the dog.

This isn't a psycho haphazardly cleaning up after himself. He planned this meticulously. String up the dog. Scare us with it. Then clear away the evidence, so if we tried to bring the police back, we'd have nothing to show.

Wait. The arrows.

I turn. My arrows are gone, but he can't hide the marks

in a wooden door. I jog over . . . and I can't tell where the arrows went in because he's added scratches and knife gouges, all rubbed into the wood so they look like old damage.

I carefully open the door . . . to see my arrows, neatly laid out on the floor.

seventeen

He's returned my arrows to me.

Mocking me with them.

I slam my fist into the wall. I hit it again and again, and I've never done anything like that, never vented my anger like that, and once I start, I can't stop until I have to, my hand throbbing, my lungs burning. I double over, catching my breath and struggling to rein in my temper, and I realize I'm crying.

It's not just this. It's everything, piled up, and this seems like the culmination of the rest, proof that no matter how carefully I organize my life, no matter how much control I try to exercise over it, I'm like an ant meticulously constructing my hill, only to have a boot stomp out all my work and continue on, oblivious.

Edie is missing, and I don't know how to prove it. Then Lennon goes missing too, and I pray he's just out there looking for Edie, but he tried that before and look where it got him. Now I've attracted the attention of almost certainly the same person who took Edie, who mocks me, lining up those arrows, so helpfully returning my prizes.

This is all you get, Winter Crane. I'll take Edie and Lennon; you can have the arrows. It's a fair exchange, don't you think? Oh, you can certainly run to the police if you want. Maybe Mrs. Reid can testify that she saw you with a boy—the trailer park busybody whose cataracts are so bad she can't see five feet in front of her nose.

I want to curl up in the corner and sob. Call my big sister and tell her what happened and get her sympathy and her help. Except I have no idea how to contact her. I'm not sure she'd even take my call.

The only person who promised she'd be there for me is Edie. Who is missing. Almost certainly more than missing.

Poor Winter. Poor little Winter. Just have a good cry, then. Maybe that'll help.

I shake it off, and I'm rising when I hear a noise at the door. I turn sharply, see a dark-haired young man, and let out a sigh of relief so deep it shudders through me.

"Lennon," I say.

He's standing in the shadow of the doorway. Then he steps through, and I realize my mistake.

He looks like Lennon; he is not Lennon.

He's about the same age. A little taller. Bigger build. Longer hair, worn in a black mop of curls. Brighter blue eyes. Features that were classically handsome on Lennon are skewed on him, not quite right, like seeing Lennon through a warped mirror.

The biggest difference, though, is his expression. I've seen

Lennon angry, frightened, charming, even goofy, but always animated, always expressive. This guy's face is a stone mask.

"Where's my brother?" he says as he advances on me.

"J-Jude?"

Of course that's the obvious explanation for a guy who looks like Lennon yet isn't. But I'm thrown. I don't know how Jude could be here. It's as if I somehow summoned him, and now, seeing the look in his eyes, I really wish I hadn't.

"Lennon isn't here," I say.

"I see that."

He keeps coming at me. I back away. I can't help it. That look sends ice through my veins, and I know it's foolish, but I hear myself saying, "Let's step outside and talk," as if the shack is suddenly too small.

"No," he says.

I square my shoulders and go to step around him.

He blocks me, saying, "You're not leaving until we talk. So get comfortable."

"You can't—"

"Yeah, I can."

My hand taps my pocket, reassuring me the switchblade is still there.

"No, actually, you can't," I say as calmly as I can. "It's called unlawful confinement. Obviously you're upset—"

"Upset? My brother calls me last night from a pay phone, saying he's in trouble. I get the message at four in the morning. I find out where it came from and haul ass here. I'm checking the town and this old lady walks over and chews me out for sneaking around with some girl in a trailer park last night. Girl named Winter. I ask some kid and he tells me you've got

84

a shack this way. I find you in here and see my brother's jacket over there . . . with blood on it."

"I can explain."

"Good. Sit down—"

"Don't tell me what to do."

"You're obviously mixed up in my brother's disappearance, so I'm sure as hell not letting you outside, where you can run."

I walk to him and look up. "Move."

"No."

I try to sidestep. He blocks. When I dodge past, he backs up fast and slams the door shut with his hip and then plants himself in front of it.

I glance up at the skylight hatch.

"Yeah," he says. "Try that. See how far you get."

I slide the knife from my pocket and hit the switch. His hand chops my wrist so fast I don't even see it coming. There's a flash of blinding pain and my switchblade clatters to the floor. I dive for it. He's faster again and steps on it. I grab him by the pant leg to wrench his foot off the knife. When he doesn't budge, I leap up. His hands fly up to block and he gives me a shove that sends me to the floor. When I rise, he's just standing there, with that same impassive expression.

"Don't," he says.

I see that cold emptiness on his face, and somehow it's worse than Bert's rage.

I charge, and Jude steps aside and grabs me by my shirt. He lifts me at arm's length, onto my tiptoes, and just holds me there, saying in that same calm tone, "You done?" and fresh rage whips through me as tears fill my eyes. They're angry tears, but the shame of crying only makes things worse, and my blows rain down on the arm holding me. The only change to his expression is a flicker of annoyance, as if I'm a three-year-old throwing a tantrum.

"Done *now*?" he asks finally. "Or am I going to have to tie you up to have this conversation? I'm sure I can find rope in here somewhere."

"That's—"

"Unlawful confinement. Yeah, you mentioned that. Feel free to report me later. All I care about right now is finding my brother. If you insist on hitting me, I'll have to make sure you can't."

He says it so calmly, like he's explaining a very simple concept. I look down at my knife on the floor.

"Whoever gave you that should have told you not to pull it unless you plan to use it," he says, "and should have taught you how to hold on to it."

He tosses me aside. Literally tosses me, no rancor in it but no care either. As I hit the floor, pain jolts through my shoulder. He walks over and bends to scoop up the knife. He has his back to me and I tense, ready to—

"Don't bother," he says, rising as he pockets my knife. "Now sit down and tell me where my brother is."

eighteen

IF IT WASN'T FOR THE PHYSICAL RESEMBLANCE, I'D FIND IT HARD to believe the guy standing before me is the one Lennon talked about, the brother who doesn't like to call attention to himself, the classic-literature-loving, piano-playing virtuoso who counsels Lennon not to judge others too harshly.

I look at Jude again. Yeah, really not seeing it.

But what I do see is a guy who is insanely worried about his brother, and that *does* fit the picture Lennon painted. He said his brother would come tracking him down the moment he heard his voice, knowing he was in trouble. Which is exactly what he's done. While I'm not cutting Jude any slack, he's proven he's not making idle threats. I need to get this over with.

I start my story with finding Lennon's shoe and end at this

morning, when I discovered he'd left. After I finish, Jude just stands there, like I'm still talking. Or like I haven't even started.

Finally he says, "Feral dogs."

"Yes, there's a roving pack—"

"Seriously? You can't do better than 'feral dogs'?"

My face heats, temper surging again. "I—"

"Oh, right. Sorry. I'm just some dumb city boy who thinks your forests are filled with grizzlies and moonshiners and crazy hillbillies with sawed-off shotguns. Of course I'm going to believe feral dogs."

"There are a lot of dogs around here," I say as calmly as I can. "People don't get them spayed or neutered because—"

"—they can't afford to. And if those dogs go feral, you've got hundreds of miles of forest for them to live in. I know feral dogs *exist*. The part I'm questioning is where you single-handedly fought off a pack to save my brother."

"Because I'm a girl, right?"

"No, because you can't hold on to a switchblade. Can't fight properly, either. If you took on one of those mutts, you'd be feral dog *chow*."

"No, I can't fend off a pack of dogs. I can escape them, though, and I can wait them out. I might suck with a knife but pass me that"—I motion to my bow—"and I'll show you how well I can use a weapon."

"So you escape the dogs and then get my brother to this shack, despite the fact he has a good fifty pounds on you."

"I fashioned a makeshift stretcher."

"Of course you did. You know how to do that, and yet you couldn't get him to a doctor."

"Lennon didn't want one. The local physician is out of

town, but I work for him and plan to go to med school, so I know how to treat—"

He laughs. It's not just a snort, it's an actual burst of laughter, and my temper flares. I say, "Your brother is *missing*. He left a note—"

"Show me."

"It's back at my trailer."

"Lennon called to tell me he was in trouble. His blood-stained jacket is here. And you, apparently, are the only person who saw him."

"Mrs. Reid—the lady you met—"

"Sorry, let me rephrase. You're the only person who can confirm this story about my brother being badly beaten and set on by wild dogs after escaping a psycho who butchered one of those dogs—and then conveniently hid *all* the evidence. Which all began because Lennon came to help a girl who seems to have been taken captive by this same guy. Yet you've told none of this to the local police, despite my brother disappearing while going after the madman, which, by the way, is *mad,* so please come up with a better story. Or we're going to be here a very long time."

For an hour I tell my story, and for an hour Jude eviscerates it. I fight back, but eventually even I realize how preposterous it sounds. I have no evidence besides a note penned in block letters, which could have come from anyone. I can't even say where Lennon pulled off the road to look for Edie—I didn't ask for the exact location because he planned to show me.

I finally say, "But the question remains: What exactly do you think I've done?"

"I have no idea. All I know is that my brother was seen with you last night, his bloodied jacket is here—with you—and he's not. Also, your story stinks like horseshit."

"But what *exactly*—"

"Do you know who we are?"

"What?"

"Lennon and me. Do you know who our father is?"

"I know your family is wealthy. Old money, Lennon said. Beyond that—"

His snort cuts me off. "Yeah, *beyond that*. If you don't know who we are, then whoever set this up isn't telling you shit. And apparently, neither was Lennon, which means you didn't get to know him nearly as well as you claim."

"Okay, who is your father?"

"If you don't know, I'm sure as hell not telling you. Let's just say that there are people who'd kidnap my brother to get at our father. That's not paranoia. Sometimes, growing up, we'd need to take a different car to school—one with bullet-proof windows. Occasionally that car came with a bodyguard, who'd walk us to class. Once, we weren't even allowed to *go* to school—we were on lockdown for a week."

I stare at him. This isn't LA or New York. I can't imagine whose kids here would warrant that kind of protection. I can't imagine Lennon being one of those kids. And I can't imagine it of this guy, who honestly wouldn't look out of place at my school, in worn sneakers and a faded sweatshirt and frayed jeans.

"I didn't help kidnap your brother," I say, "since that seems to be what you're implying. I don't know how I can prove that to you. . . ."

"Tell me the truth."

"I already did."

"Then I guess we're going to spend a very long night together."

"You can't—"

"I can and I will, as I've already proven."

"Someone's out there. Someone who killed a dog—"

"Show me one shred of proof."

"He cleaned up the evidence."

"Of course he did."

"I can show you fibers in the tree, where he cushioned the rope so it wouldn't cut in. I can show you more in the dirt, where he used a ground sheet."

"Fibers? Seriously? You're going to show me fibers?"

"That's all I—"

"Then get comfortable. We're going to be here awhile."

When I stop talking, he doesn't threaten me. Doesn't get angry or frustrated and demand answers. Nor does he calm down and acknowledge that holding me hostage is ridiculous. He can't "calm down" when he isn't worked up. He's just determined—determined to wait me out, presuming that I'll get cold or hungry or tired or just plain bored. Eventually I'll crack.

I don't.

Neither does he.

So I wait. About an hour passes. Then the room darkens. It's only late afternoon, but the sun has gone behind clouds, and it's as gray as twilight. That's exactly what I need. Jude's been up half the night. He's exhausted and his eyelids flicker and then they close. He's probably telling himself he can close his eyes for a second, just one second.

Ten minutes later, his head nods as he falls asleep.

I force myself to wait twenty minutes more, to be sure he won't jerk awake. His breathing deepens. I inch past, grab my bow and hunting knife, and then I'm out the door.

nineteen

I MAKE IT THROUGH THE FOREST WITHOUT INCIDENT. TWICE, I think I catch the sound of someone following, but both times I see nothing when I stop.

I head straight for the pay phone. Of course I try Edie again. By now I'm sure she's not going to miraculously pick up, but I have to give it one last shot. I get the "mailbox full" message again. Then I call directory assistance and feed in the coins for another long-distance call.

It's a good thing I stocked up on coins earlier, because I have to keep feeding them in as my call is rerouted through several departments. Finally I get where I need to be, speaking to a young-sounding guy in Edie's college main office, who tells me he's just a student covering the desk because "everyone took off early for the long weekend—figures, huh?"

I tell him I'm Edie's sister and I'm supposed to pick her up at the bus station, but I haven't been able to get hold of her in days. Does he have a backup number? Or anything? I expect a runaround about privacy laws, but he's obviously bored, not terribly experienced, and happy to help.

He confirms that the number I have—her cell phone—is the only one on file. I ask if there's any way to be sure she's been in class.

He says, "The instructors don't always mark attendance, but you're in luck. There's a message here saying she was expected to be gone after Monday, heading hella early for the long weekend. But I wouldn't worry. She probably just decided to use her extra days off to squeeze in more partying."

"But if I were concerned, is there anyone there I could talk to?"

"Four o'clock on a Friday before a long weekend? Nope. Call back Tuesday. By then, I'm sure she'll have shown up. They always do."

I thank him and hang up. Then I'm standing there, still gripping the receiver, when a voice to my left says, "Okay, your story's legit," and I spin to see Jude walking toward me, my switchblade in his hand. When I back up, he follows my gaze to the knife and says, "If this was a threat, I'd have the sense to open it first. I'm returning it, on the condition you don't pull it on me again. I should also insist you learn how to use it, but that's probably too much to ask for."

"Put it on the ground and move away."

He sighs. It's an oddly put-upon sigh, again like a grown-up dealing with a small child. "I'm not here to hurt you."

"Says the guy who knocked me around a few hours ago."

"I defended myself. I blocked you every time you came at

94

me. Not gently, either, in hopes of convincing you to stop trying. But you're a slow learner."

"You kidnapped—"

"I prevented you from leaving. Which is still involuntary confinement. Like I said, feel free to turn me in."

"Because your parents will make any charges go away."

"If they do, you can take it to the press."

"You're telling me how to get you in trouble?"

"No, I'm proving I don't give a shit, so you can threaten me all you want. Except with the knife. I don't like being threatened with a knife."

He tosses the switchblade to me. I catch it and pocket it, and I'm trying to figure out what to say, when he continues, "Back to where we started. From that conversation I just heard, checking up on your friend, your story seems legit. So you don't need to worry about me holding you hostage again."

"That's such a relief."

He nods, completely missing the sarcasm. "We'll go over it again so I can construct a timeline. That's a start."

"A start for what?"

"Finding him and your friend. We'll gather what we can and then decide how to go about reporting them missing."

"You're serious."

"About what?"

"You want to team up after you held me *hostage*?"

He gives a dismissive wave, as if I'm holding a grudge because he accidentally stepped on my toes. "I said I won't do it again."

"You're right you won't. Because I don't want anything to do with you. If I hadn't escaped—"

"Escaped? I faked falling asleep hoping you'd lead me to my brother. I honestly didn't think you'd fall for the ruse. You did." His tone says, on second thought he's not that surprised. After all, I *am* the one who lost his brother.

"Are you hungry?" he asks.

"What?" I'm sure I've heard wrong.

"Are you hungry?" he says, slower. "We can grab a bite and talk this through."

He looks at me expectantly. *See? At least one of us is being reasonable.* When I don't respond, he starts walking away and says, "Come on."

A moment later, his sneakers squeak as he stops and turns.

"Winter?" he says.

I'm already around the corner, running as fast as I can. He doesn't curse or shout. There's a sigh, rippling through the night air. Then the slow thump of his shoes . . . continuing in the direction he'd been headed.

Bert hasn't left for the night, and for once I'm glad of it. That means Lennon's crazy brother won't follow me to the trailer. Or, if he tries, he'll be met with the business end of a shotgun. I wonder if he'd actually react to that. Or just sigh and give a slightly pained look, as if a chest full of pellets would be a minor inconvenience.

Bert's watching TV. He acknowledges me with "Pizza in the fridge," his gaze fixed on the screen, where something is blowing up loudly enough that I have to read his lips to know what he said and then check the fridge to be sure of it.

I'm wolfing down a slice as I walk toward the couch. It's a commercial break, and he hits the mute button and says, "What?"

I don't thank him for the pizza. He gets pissy about that, like I'm either being sarcastic or making him feel guilty for the times he doesn't share.

"Do you have a minute?" I ask.

He waves at the TV. "Make it fast."

"Have you heard from Cady?"

It's the question that's been poking at me since Lennon first told me about Edie. The reminder that Edie isn't the only person I care about who has disappeared. I'm sure there's no connection, but it's still raised the question.

When Bert turns to me, there's an odd look in his eyes, one I can't quite decipher.

"I . . . ," I begin. "You know we . . . When she left, we weren't talking and she . . ."

"I know why she left." He doesn't say *I'm* why she left, but I hear the accusation nonetheless.

"So, she, uh, hasn't been in touch with me," I say.

"You surprised?"

"I'm just . . . I'm worried about her, and I was wondering if you'd heard—"

"Nope."

"Or if she left contact information, some way of getting in touch."

"Nope."

"I'm not going to bug her. I just want to know she's okay."

He turns to me, and his eyes are as empty as Jude's were earlier. "I have no damn idea if she's okay, Winter. When she

97

left, she made it pretty clear she couldn't wait to get away from both of us. Can't blame her, all things considered."

My face heats. "I never meant—"

"What you *meant* doesn't matter. What *happened* matters, and that's all Cadence could see. I figure she needed time to get over it, and when she does, she'll contact you. She's sure as hell not contacting me."

I drop my gaze. "Okay." I start to turn away, and then say, "Do you think she's all right?"

He's quiet, his finger over the remote, and the show's back on, and I think he's just going to hit that button and ignore the question. But after a moment he says, "I think the fact that we haven't heard from her doesn't mean she's *not* all right, and I think that's really all we can say. That it's understandable she hasn't called."

"Okay."

When I do turn, he says, "About that boy, Winter . . ."

"I wasn't with a boy."

"I know what it's like here, not much to do. But you go getting pregnant—"

"I'm not even dating."

"One thing doesn't always have much to do with the other. If you *weren't* with a boy, that means one could have followed you here. You gotta be careful."

"I am."

"Good. Keep your eyes on the horizon, Winter. It's the only way you're escaping this shit hole." He reaches for his glass of bourbon and gulps it down. "I've got a job tomorrow, but I'll leave a twenty on the fridge. Pick up some groceries."

I say, "Okay," and head for my room as the TV blares again.

twenty

THE LIBRARY IS THE NEWEST BUILDING IN REEVE'S END, AS NICE as any small town could want. We appreciate the government funding that built it. We'd just appreciate it a lot more if they'd included money for decent computers or books people might actually read.

I walk past the Kids Eat Free sign out front. It's a double-duty campaign—feeding their minds and their bodies with something healthy, which, sadly, they may get little of at home, on either count. I head straight for the computer terminals, two old Dells, both in use by kids playing online games.

Before I can even turn around, the librarian—Ms. Dermody—is there, saying, "Just hold on, Winter." She walks to one gamer and says, "Mikey? I think that's enough. Winter needs to do her schoolwork. You can come back this afternoon."

I thank Mikey and Ms. Dermody, take a seat, and open a browser window.

I know Jude and Lennon are from Kentucky. I know they went to a private school, come from old money, and their father is a VIP—someone whose children could be targets for kidnapping. That last part isn't terribly helpful. He could be anything from a famous opera singer to a drug lord. But it's additional information that I can use to winnow down a search. And winnowing down that search is critical, given the excruciatingly slow speed of our local Internet.

The most useful information here is also the most basic: their names. There can't be a lot of brothers in Kentucky named Lennon and Jude, not ones who are important enough to warrant a mention in the media.

After a couple of minutes of waiting, I get a page of results. I presume most are mis-hits, but one catches my attention as I remember something else Lennon told me.

I click the link.

It's a newspaper article in the online archives. I recognize the town name—it's not far from here.

Crash Claims Lives of Young Local Couple

The headline says it all. A twenty-year-old married couple died in a car crash—hit-and-run on a one-lane bridge through the mountains, which sent the couple's car through the guardrails, plunging into the gorge and then the Red River. While the reporter's tone is factual—almost clinical—there's this one line where he says the coroner's office "cannot confirm" whether the couple died on impact or drowned, and that matter-of-fact tone makes it even more chilling, as if the writer sees nothing wrong with even speculating on the possibility that this poor couple survived the fall, only to be trapped up-side down in their vehicle as the water seeped in. . . .

I swallow and skim down to a line written in that same chillingly factual tone.

The couple leave behind two sons, Jude, 16 months old, and Lennon, 6 months old.

I type faster now, whipping through keywords and then tapping the desk impatiently, waiting until I get a full page of results, most dated about ten years ago. The articles center on Congressman Peter Bishop, one of Kentucky's congressional state representatives. His district is the sixth, geographically just above ours. The articles date back to his initial election, and my search caught them because they mention his family . . . including his adopted sons, Jude and Lennon.

With that I have no problem finding more. The fact that their father is a congressman doesn't make them celebrities by any means—I can't name the kids of any politician other than the president. But Jude and Lennon get their fair share of ink. A state representative is up for reelection every two years, and trotting out Peter Bishop's family for public inspection seems to be part of that process. With many teenage boys, I suspect their father would be scrambling to shove them under the carpet until they outgrew surly, acne-plagued adolescence. Not Jude and Lennon. These boys are glowing reflections of Congressman Bishop's abilities as both a parent and a human-itarian.

Every election, articles rehash the boys' tragic backstory—not only did their parents both perish young, but the boys came from extreme poverty, with chronically ill grandparents. When the Bishops heard of their plight, they adopted the boys, and from there, the brothers flourished, like rare flowers rescued from the refuse heap. Oh, of course none of the articles say that, but I catch the implication. Take two boys from backwoods Kentucky, give them every advantage, and watch them bloom, strong and hardy examples of our strong and hardy state.

You don't get much more well-rounded—or successful—than Jude and Lennon. Star athletes, top scholars, community activists. Jude, the intense musical prodigy, a future concert pianist. Lennon, the affable debate-team captain, clearly destined for politics. According to one article, the boys' achievements were so evenly matched that when their school had to pick a top student for any honor, the principal joked they'd just flip a coin to choose between the brothers. If that wasn't enough, these weren't arrogant rich kids. "Refreshingly down-to-earth," reporters said. "Just great guys," according to their peers. Lennon was charming and outgoing, Jude quiet and thoughtful. No one had a bad thing to say about either.

They were also photogenic—every article included pictures of the boys, as they went from adorable children with mops of dark curly hair and bright blue eyes to young men with the maturing good looks that had even female journalists commenting in a slightly creepy way. The brothers weren't movie-star gorgeous but—as one article said—they looked like members of a boy band, seriously cute in an approachable guy-next-door way.

As I flip through the photos, I notice that Lennon's expression never changes. It's the grin I remember, a little devilish, a little angelic, one that makes you want to smile back in spite of yourself. Once Jude reaches early teens, though, his smile dims and his gaze shifts to the side, as if he just wants the photo shoot to be done and he's already mentally moved on.

By the last election, just over a year ago, Jude looks very different, both in expression and appearance. After the boys reached high school, their hair was cut short, as if what looked cute on a preadolescent might seem too rebellious on a teen-age boy, at least in the eyes of older voters. But in the last photo, Jude has let his hair grow. There's not even a hint of a smile. And if he looked restless before, his expression now holds angry defiance—*just snap your damn picture and go away.* For the first time, I find photos of Lennon without Jude. I imagine their mother saying to the photographer, "Oh, Jude? He's very busy. Piano. Or football. Or maybe he's volunteering today. Yes, that's it—he's busy volunteering."

I look at the last photo of Jude, at his expressionless face, and deep in his eyes, I see more than defiance.

I see rage.

"Questions answered?" a voice says behind me, and when I turn, Jude's right there, as if I've conjured him from the screen. He has that same empty expression, his eyes equally flat, giv-ing nothing away.

He gestures at the monitor. "Got your answers?"

I want to flip off the monitor as if I've been caught spying. Behind him, Ms. Dermody looks concerned. I wonder why, but that's because I'm remembering the boy in those photos. What she sees is a very different young man. Jude isn't scruffy or unkempt enough that I'd cross the street to avoid him, nor is he burly enough for me to do the same, but put those things together, and I understand why the librarian seems ready to intervene.

Jude notices and glances behind him, trying to see who's making her nervous. It can't be him. The congressman's straight-A son. The piano prodigy. The quiet one. The thoughtful one. But that confusion only lasts a moment before he realizes it *is* him, and there's no flash of consternation at that. He just nods.

"Small town," I say. "We aren't good with strangers."

I don't know why I explain. I'm certainly not inclined to cushion his feelings. He gives a shrug, as if this goes without saying and he doesn't really give a shit either way.

He jerks his chin toward the window and says, "Five minutes."

He leaves without waiting for an answer. Clearly I will obey, because he is Jude Bishop.

For that very reason, I'd love to ignore him. But considering what I've just found out, I do want to speak to him.

I check a few more search terms. I don't want Ms. Dermody to think I'm following the disreputable stranger. As I go to leave, though, she says, "Winter?"

I walk over.

"Who was that?" she asks.

I shrug. "He wanted to use the computer. I didn't recognize him. Passing through, I guess." I look around, as if searching for him. "Guess he didn't want it too badly."

She nods, and I take off.

twenty-one

"Were you following me?" I say as I walk around the building to where Jude waits.

"Yeah."

I expected a denial. I should have known better. This guy doesn't see the need to lie, maybe because he's grown up in a life where he doesn't have to. The privilege of privilege.

He continues, "I saw you go into the library. I walked by the window and noticed you were on the computer. I figured I'd give you time to look up whatever you needed to look up. I had a good idea what it was. And I was right."

There's a slight smugness there, as if I should be impressed that he guessed.

"You could have just told me who you are," I said.

"What fun would that be?" There's a soft drawl to the words, as if he's teasing, but there's no sign of it in his face.

"Anyway, now you know. Make sense? Why I'm not running to the cops with this?"

"I don't care. That's where I'm going. I happen to think your brother's life is more important than avoiding embarrassing your father."

"Embarrassing my father is the absolute least of my concerns. The point is that the minute you say his name, they will involve him, and my mother will squelch the investigation because she'll figure this is just Lennon doing something stupid, which Lennon has been known to do. That's not going to help your friend. Or my brother."

"And what exactly would *you* suggest we do?"

"Look for them ourselves."

I laugh. When his expression doesn't change, I say, "You are joking, right?" I wave toward the mountains. "Do you have any idea how much land is out there? It's not like we've misplaced them in a city park."

"I mean track the clues. Figure out what happened to Edie."

"So after graduating from high school, you got a PI license."

"I didn't."

"I was being sarcastic. I know you don't have a PI license."

"I mean that I didn't graduate high school. I dropped out in my last year." He turns and starts walking. "Let's find a place to talk."

He gets about twenty feet away before he realizes I'm not following. When he turns and sees me with my arms crossed, he gives a soft sigh. I'm being difficult again, and he can't quite comprehend why, but he's being very patient with me.

"You dropped out in your *final* year?" I say. "The guy who won every freaking academic award your school offers?"

"Not math. Lennon won that. And he tied me in biology, though he should have beat me there, too."

"Yet you dropped out?"

He shrugs. "Things came up."

Earlier, I called him Lennon's crazy brother. Now I'm wondering if Jude really does have a problem, something that made a star student suddenly decide school just wasn't all that important. Either way, Edie's disappearance isn't something I can handle on my own, and while I don't trust the local police to do a significantly better job, it's time to notify them. When I say as much, Jude says, "I'm going to ask you, again, not to do that, Winter."

I take a slow step back and he pauses, frowning slightly.

"If you think you're going to stop me . . . ," I begin.

"Stop you?" He rolls the words, as if not understanding them. Then his gaze drops to my hand, which is reaching into my pocket for my knife, and his brows arch. "What do you think I'm going to do? Tackle you?"

"Hold me hostage, maybe?"

Again, I get that faintly put-upon sigh. "I already explained that. When I say I'm asking you not to go to the police, that's exactly what I mean. If I wanted to threaten you, I would. I'm asking."

"And I'm refusing."

"Can we discuss it?"

"No."

He shrugs, says, "Do what you have to do," and walks off.

I stop at the sheriff's department and ask to speak to Sheriff Slate himself. I get stuck with his son, Deputy Slate. When I finish explaining, he leans back in his chair and says, "So Edie Greene—a girl from the hills—has been hooking up with a governor's son."

"Congressman," I say.

"I know you're supposed to be smart, Winter," the deputy says, "but I always say, book learning is one thing, common sense is another. Making up stories about a governor's son—"

"—would be stupid. Same as making them up about a congressman's."

His face screws up, as if he's wondering why I'm bringing a congressman into this.

"Lennon Bishop is Congressman Bishop's son," I say. "Lennon came to help Edie after she called him in trouble. Ask Mrs. Reid. She saw Lennon with me."

"Mrs. Reid can't see her hand in front of her face."

"Lennon Bishop *was* here."

"And now he's not. Meaning I can't interview him. That's convenient."

"Because he's *missing*. Which is not convenient at all for either him or Edie."

His eyes narrow. "Don't you take a tone with me, missy. I remember what you did to Colton."

"I didn't do *anything*—"

"You think you're too good for us. Decided your poor sister was too good for Colt, and look what happened."

I pause to calm my pounding heart. "I want to talk about Edie."

"If Edie Greene is not answering her phone, it's 'cause that whole story about getting into some fashion school is such bullshit everyone can smell it a mile away. What's a girl like that gonna do in fashion? Make designer coonskin hats?"

"I called the school. She is enrolled. But she's not there. She said she was leaving early to come home for the long weekend. And now she's missing."

"Which only means she decided not to come back, and she's avoiding your calls. You're worried about her, so you think if you make up some story about a governor's son, by gosh, I'll pay attention then, 'cause I'm just a hick deputy."

"His brother—" I stop as I realize what I'm saying. Too late. I push on. "His older brother, Jude, is here in town. I can bring him in to talk to you."

"His brother's here and hasn't reported the disappearance himself?"

"He—"

"A *governor's* son is missing and the *governor* hasn't reported it himself?"

"Peter Bishop is a congressman. Which—"

"Which doesn't make a damn bit of difference. He's still a big shot politician who'd be raising Cain if his boy disappeared. You want me to even consider this story of yours? Bring that boy to me."

twenty-two

I HEAD FOR MY SHACK. I TELL MYSELF I'M LOOKING FOR JUDE, BUT that's really an excuse. I should be able to handle this better—should have been able to convince the deputy to investigate, should have been able to prove Edie was missing, should have been able to keep Lennon from disappearing. I feel helpless, which means I need to go into the forest, a place I understand, where I'm in charge.

Jude is not at the shack. As I string fresh barrier thread, I'm fixed on an image I can't shake: the walls in Doc Southcott's office. The whole clinic is decorated with photographs of the lives that pass through his doors. There's one of me shortly after I arrived, hanging on Cadence's arm, another where I awkwardly pose in my elementary school graduation dress, and a third taken last year, when I was putting away supplies and a box of cast plaster powder fell and my laughter brought Doc

Southcott running in time to snap a picture of me covered in white dust.

"That's the best one," he said. "That's the real you." Except it isn't. The other two better reflect the Winter Crane I see in my head, the awkward and somber girl. The laughing one is a stranger I never see in the mirror.

For many people, those office photos start with a first baby shot, taken shortly after Doc Southcott brought them into the world. Lives told in pictures. So many lives. Yet many sets don't progress past teenage years. People leave after that, moving away as soon as they can, and sometimes never coming back, their photo sets ending with a final shot of a sullen or smiling teen, eyes already fixed on the horizon beyond Reeve's End.

So many leave. Some plan to return, at least for visits, like Edie. Others don't. Like Cadence.

I swallow hard. That's why I'm thinking of those photos. I'm thinking of all the kids who leave and never come back. Of my sister who left and hasn't come back. Of how easy it would be for someone to grab . . .

I put aside the boundary thread, go inside, pull out my notebook, and turn to a blank page. Then I stare at that page as I fight the urge to snap the book closed. To tell myself I'm being silly. Overreacting.

But if there's a chance—any chance at all—that Edie's disappearance is part of something larger . . .

Maybe I've just watched too many of those damned crime shows. Read too many of Cady's mystery novels, the ones she rarely actually read, buying them secondhand and then telling me to take what I wanted, and now I wonder if they were really for me, a small way of continuing to be my big sister.

Miss you, Cady.

I give myself a sharp shake. None of that. I have work to do.

I steel myself and write *Cadence Crane: left last May.*

I know the date. I know the hour. I can still see her the day after graduation, walking to hitch a ride to the city, me running after her, feeling like I was five again, chasing her after I'd done something wrong and she'd had enough of her little sister for a while.

"Go home, Win."

"I just want—"

"And I just want to be alone."

"I didn't mean—"

"Go home, Win. I'll come back when I'm ready."

Are you ready yet, Cady? It's been over a year. Isn't that long enough? Whatever I did . . .

Whatever I did . . .

I force myself to keep writing, adding to my sister's entry. *Last contact: none. Last known location: none. Reason for departure . . .*

None.

I'd love to write that. Or simply *the usual.* But it isn't true. I gaze down at the paper, my pen bleeding a growing pit of black as I press the tip in harder.

Reason for departure?

Her sister.

Her stupid, foolish sister, who thinks she's so smart, thinks she has the answer for everything, knows what's best for everyone.

Her sister made a mistake.

I swallow and then I write *family tragedy.* I look at the

words, and I squirm in my seat and I want to change them. It wasn't really *family*. More *personal*. And tragedy? More of an accident, really.

An accident. Seriously?

I leave the words *family tragedy*. They do not overstate the matter. I only wish they did.

I push on to the next name.

Marty Lawson: left . . .

I continue on, dredging through my memory for the names of every kid who's left in the last few years and never returned. For the other columns—date of departure, last contact, last known address, reason for departure—many remain blank.

When I'm done, I have a list of twelve names dating to when I started high school. That's when I began paying attention to those who left, if only because they were setting out on a trail I planned to follow.

I'm eating an energy bar when I hear a soft *clink*. It's a Coke can rigged to my thread-line, letting me know I have an intruder.

I climb onto the chair and pop my makeshift periscope through the hatch. Fifth-grade science comes in handy sometimes. I scan the surrounding woods as best I can. Nothing.

I'm still looking when something pushes against the door. It's a tentative push, stopped by the latch. I jump down and snatch up my hunting knife and stand on the other side of the door.

"Who's there?"

No answer.

"Jude? If that's you, and you're trying to spook me . . ."

I know it isn't. Jude doesn't have the patience or the

personality for games. He'd pound and say, "It's me. I want to talk," and then be genuinely confused when I didn't throw open the door.

I stand poised with that knife for at least two minutes. Then I decide I'm overreacting. The wind must have set the can clinking and pushed the door. I hear the whistle of it over the roof.

I lower the knife. The door moves again.

I freeze, blood pounding in my ears, hand gripping the knife handle so hard it hurts.

There's nowhere to run. No one to call. I'm trapped here, alone, and I have nobody to blame but myself.

I back to the chair, ease up onto it, and then push open the hatch. I put my knife on the roof, making sure it's caught on a board and won't slide off. I tense, certain the maniac below will pick this moment to break down that door, and I'll grab for the knife and send it skittering down the roof and be helpless to fight back.

But that's not what happens. I slide to the roof on my stomach, staying low. Then I have a choice. Try to see him over the front or escape over the back.

The obvious choice is "flee while you still can!" Yet if I do, I lose an opportunity. So I creep on my stomach to the front. First, I scan the forest, in case he's backed away from the door. Then, face plastered to the roof, I inch forward until I can just barely see over the edge and . . .

And nothing.

*　*　*

I'm heading back to Reeve's End. Every crackle in the bushes makes me jump. I hate that. Hate feeling as if my forest has been taken from me, my place of refuge now a place of danger. I walk fast, senses on high alert. I'm a third of the way to town when a low growl ripples from the bushes. I spin as a dog leaps at me. I don't even see which one it is. I kick as hard as I can, hitting it under the muzzle. Then I run.

When I hear pounding paws, I glance back to see Flea and Alanna tearing after me. I look around wildly for a tree to climb, but I'm in the wrong part of the forest; this patch is too rocky for more than bushes and saplings. As I'm looking for shelter—any shelter—I stumble. Flea pounces. He's a small dog—some terrier mix—and I shove him away, but not before he chomps down on my arm. I manage to throw him off and resume running, but the alpha bitch has taken advantage of my stumble and accelerated, yowling as she closes in.

When Alanna snaps at my flying feet, I ignore it as best I can, but she snags my sneaker enough that I stumble again. I twist and I manage to kick Alanna's belly. Something cracks, and she goes down. Then a brown blur streaks from the bushes.

I see a flash of light blue—a filthy and tattered kerchief still tied around the dog's neck. It's Mange. He's big—part hound, part shepherd—and when he leaps, I slash with my blade. I don't see where I'm striking. I stab and I yank the knife out and blood flies and I stab again. I catch another blur in the corner of my eye as Flea lunges and grabs my arm again. I strike at him—a blind and wild strike. It makes contact, though, and he loosens his grip, and I swing the knife and slash, equally blindly. Blood sprays. Flea yelps and drops from my arm.

Mange is rising. Blood stains his coat, and I can see one ugly gash, muscles ripped, but the dog is on his feet, snarling and enraged. I kick him in the chest and run. I've kicked so hard that my sneaker—already loose from the alpha's nipping—flies off. I can't stop to grab it. I just run.

Flea comes after me. Alanna does too, having recovered. When I glance back, I see Mange lurching in my direction, staggering and stumbling.

That's when I see the tree. It's a small one, as big as they grow in this section. Sneakers hang from the top branches, where kids threw old ones up. That's not random. It marks a spot. A spot that has exactly what I need.

I race to the top of a rocky mound beside the tree. There, half hidden in the undergrowth, is a hole. I don't look down it. I don't look back at the dogs. I just jump.

twenty-three

As I jump I see the rope. The rope that I'm supposed to use to lower myself. I grab, catch it, and slide, my palms burning, until I touch down. I look around, spot a hole in the side wall, and crawl through into a mine shaft.

That's what the shoes marked: a mine shaft. The proper entrances are sealed, but this opened up after a storm maybe five years ago. Kids found it and marked it with the shoes. After a year or two, it lost the novelty factor—if you want to smoke up or make out, there are better places closer to town.

After I heard about it at school, I brought Edie, thinking she'd be keen to explore. Instead, I got a lecture on the dangers of mine tunnels and the stupidity of the kids who were exploring this one. If I wanted to go caving, she'd happily take me to one *without* deadly gases, poisonous snakes, hidden vertical shafts, rotted beams, and abandoned explosives. We did exactly that, exploring relatively safe mountain caves instead. Which explains why I didn't know about the rope, only that there was a hole kids jumped down.

I hear the dogs snarling at the top of the pit and hunt for something to block the opening into the mine shaft. I find a board and wedge it in. Then I head deeper into the tunnel, grateful for the penlight on my keychain. It doesn't do much, but it's better than stumbling around a mine in the dark.

Once I'm a little ways from the entrance, I check my wounds. Fang scrapes and punctures. I clean them with a tissue and then shine my light down the tunnel. The chance of finding a conveniently open second entrance nearby is about as good as the chance of finding someone selling ice cream bars. More likely I'll hit gas pockets and bottomless shafts and toxic mold.

I contemplate going back up. I have two knives—my hunting one and the switchblade. There seem to be only the three dogs. I probably hurt Mange pretty badly. Though Flea is small, he has a good bite, as the throbbing in my arm reminds me. Alanna's not much bigger than Flea, but she's twice as nasty.

I can't fight the three of them. Just can't.

I'm preparing to wait it out, sitting near the hole, when I hear a yelp up top. It's not a frenzied yelp of excitement. It's not even the yelp of one dog turning on another. It's a high-pitched yipping that raises the hair on my neck.

Then comes Alanna's distinctive frenzied snapping and snarling, only this time it's laced with panic. A thump sounds on the other side of the board covering that hole. Above,

Alanna keeps snapping madly, but I'm staring at the board and I can see something beyond it. Something white. Then I hear a high-pitched whine and even Alanna goes silent.

Knife ready, I creep to that board and crouch. Through a gap, I see Flea. The white fur around his ruff is stained red and he's struggling for breath, flanks heaving, nostrils flaring, eyes wide and staring.

He's dying. His throat . . .

Alanna ripped out his throat. Blood is pumping, his life-blood draining. There was a skirmish above, both of them jockeying for position, and she must have ripped into him and he fell, and now between the injury and the fall . . .

He's dying. I'm gazing into his eyes and watching him die.

I've had to put animals out of their misery before. Usually it's in traps. If I can't save it, I kill it. But after delivering the fatal cut I look away and act like I just happened upon a dying animal, like I played no role in that passing.

Now I watch. And I feel . . .

I feel like I should do something. Hasten his death. It doesn't matter that he'd have ripped out *my* throat. Doesn't matter that he'd have dined on my corpse. I'm watching him die slowly, and it is horrible, and all I can think is that this is a dog, a pet animal.

Had someone dumped him, tired of him once he was no longer a cute puppy? Or after he chewed up too many shoes? Had he been loved once? By a child who'd cuddled him? Who'd wept when he was gone?

I want to end his suffering, and I cannot because Alanna is still up there. She's back to that frenzied snarling and snapping, her claws clicking against rock. I'm afraid that if I go out there to hasten Flea's passing, she'll leap down that hole.

Flea gives one last gurgling breath, blood bubbling from his throat. He sighs then. Sighs as if he's remembering some good memory, one from a time before he was abandoned.

He goes still, and a tear slides down my cheek. I could say that tear is for him, but I'm not sure it isn't for me—for what I see of myself in that fantasy past I've created for him.

There's a yelp up top, as if the alpha has just realized her pack mate is dead. A sudden yelp of shock and then a drawn-out whine, and I wonder if I've misjudged her. I think of these feral dogs as shipwrecked killers, forced to rely on one another for survival, always ready to tear into a pack mate if he comes between them and a full belly. Perhaps they were more, perhaps as much a pack—a family—as they could be.

Then the whine turns to a scrabbling of claws and a high-pitched strangled cross between a whine and a yip mingled with a frantic growl and then . . .

Silence.

One long moment of silence.

A hollow plopping sound follows. I tug aside the board to see a growing spot of red on Flea's white flank. At first, it's just a dot. Then it's the size of a silver dollar and then another spot forms beside it, the two seeping together. It's not an injury. He wouldn't start bleeding after his heart stopped pumping. The blood is coming from . . .

I lift my gaze, and I watch a drop of blood fall onto Flea's flank from the top of the hole, where Alanna has gone quiet.

Everything has gone quiet.

That's when I hear breathing. Slow and steady breathing echoing down that hole.

Then the unmistakable squeak of a shoe. Pebbles tumble into the hole, raining on Flea. Another squeak. Then a dog collar thumps onto Flea's side.

Alanna's collar.

twenty-four

I HEAD INTO THE MINE TUNNEL, MOVING AS FAST AS I CAN WITH-out breaking into a panicked run. Every few yards, I make my-self stop so I can listen and peer back down the tunnel. There's no sign that the dogs' killer is coming after me. No sign that he's even climbed down that rope. I keep going, though. It's all I can do.

The shaft has been painstakingly blasted and carved into the mountain rock. Wooden support beams are supposed to keep stray chunks from breaking loose and bringing the whole thing down, but one look at those flimsy boards and I know they won't stop a cave-in.

The mine has a smell all its own. There's the usual odor of a cave—rock and dirt and moisture—but there's a lingering chemical odor too, from those old explosives. If I had a more creative bent, I'd say I smelled the sweat of those old miners, the stink of hard work and constant wariness, endless listening for that creak or groan that meant trouble. I'd say I smelled blood, too. The blood of those who died in cave-ins. Who fell into pits. Who weren't quite far enough away when the dynamite ignited.

I haven't gone more than fifty paces when I trip and catch a support beam. Dirt from the ceiling showers down as the beam creaks. As I scramble out of the way, my knee hits a rotted support. It creaks and dirt rains down, but that seems to be it, and I stand stock-still, listening and watching and barely daring to breathe, as if that will set off a cave-in.

Then I take a step and . . .

There's a tremendous crack as a support snaps. I dive aside just in time. Rocks pelt down and a cloud of dirt envelops me as I hit the floor. I lie there, hacking, my eyes streaming.

"Winter!"

My name echoes down the tunnel.

"Winter!"

The voice is sharp, a little annoyed, as if I'm playing a game of hide-and-seek and breaking the rules. I recognize it and go completely still as dread congeals in my gut.

Jude.

I lie there, heart pounding. I remember Lennon ducking my questions about his brother. I hear that wistful note for a boy he'd once known. A boy who'd changed.

I knew something was wrong with Jude. He looks so different from the boy in those old photos. His behavior was odd. Even his flat affect and empty expression seemed wrong. I remember what I saw behind the emptiness in that final photo. Rage.

As Jude calls my name, I understand why Lennon insisted I not go to the police. Why he kept saying he'd fix this.

Because he knew who was responsible.

"Winter?" Jude shouts. A thump, reverberating through the tunnel as if he's jumped the last few feet down the hole. "Damn it, Winter. If you're down here . . ."

If I'm down here.

Is that really how he's going to play this? Like he just happened to find me in a mining tunnel, ten minutes after two dogs were killed?

Is he crazy?

Yes. I suspect he is.

He expects me to run out and thank him for coming to my rescue because he's not thinking clearly. He can't *think* clearly.

What has he done to his brother? To Edie?

I won't go there. Not yet. I still hope . . .

When I strain to listen, I hear him cursing under his breath. Then there's a crack, as he breaks the board covering the hole into the tunnel.

"Winter?" he calls. A moment later, his dark figure appears against the pale light filtering through that hole. He lifts his cell phone, shining it my way, and ducks his head, as if trying to make out my shape in the distance.

I'm trapped. He's standing between me and the exit.

No, not *standing*. He's walking toward me. Fifty feet away and then forty and then thirty. There's something dark in his hand.

A gun? I can't fight him if . . .

"Winter? That's you, right?"

"It is." I have to speak. It might be my only chance to trick him, to escape.

"I heard what sounded like a collapse down here. And there's blood at the bottom of that hole."

"Is there." I say it deadpan, no inflection, and he stops, maybe twenty feet away, lifting his phone to shine it better on my face. I see his, then, and this time there's an expression on it. Several expressions—concern and confusion mingled.

"Are you okay?" he says. "Did you hit your head?"

"Put down the . . ." I start to say "gun," but my gaze drops to what he's holding and it's the sneaker I lost outside.

Whatever's wrong with Jude doesn't affect his intelligence. He found my shoe and now he's bringing that as his excuse. Like asking me if I hit my head.

"How'd you find me?" I ask.

"I heard the dogs, and I figured you were down here hiding from them, but you're acting—"

"What are you doing in the forest, Jude?"

He walks closer. I say, "Stop. I asked what you're doing here, Jude."

"Looking for you. We need to talk."

"About your brother."

He tilts his head, face scrunching up. "Are you okay, Winter? You're acting—"

"How'd you find me? Start from the beginning."

He peers at me, sees I'm dead serious, and says, "Fine. Let's see, step one: go to your cabin. Step two: realize it's locked." He looks over. "Can I fast-forward?"

"No."

He doesn't sigh. Doesn't even roll his eyes.

"I heard the dogs and a girl's voice. I ran to help. I found a shoe I recognized as yours. I could hear a dog yipping weirdly, like it was hurt. I followed the sound. It went quiet. Then I heard a crash underground." He pauses. "Good enough?"

"Keep going."

Now I get the sigh, his usual one, not dramatic, not even meant to be heard—just that soft sigh of exasperation for a child who is really terribly difficult.

"Hear the crash. Find a hole with a rope. Climb down. There's blood at the bottom. Rip off the board. Crawl through. Get treated to a third-degree interrogation for my trouble." He pauses. "You're welcome, by the way."

"For what? Does it look like I'm trapped down here?"

"No, but you might need medical attention. You're acting like you've hit your head—"

"My head is fine. So you climbed down that hole and found blood."

"Pretty sure that's what it was. It was soaked into the dirt, but it seemed wet." He shines his light at the walls. "Maybe it's iron in the soil?"

"You have an answer for everything, don't you?" I say.

He gives me that tilted-head frown again. "I'm just saying I shouldn't jump to the conclusion it was blood."

"And the body?"

"Body?"

"Of the dog you landed on when you climbed down."

He peers at me again. "There is no dog, Winter."

"There was a dead dog in that hole. And a collar from a second one. Two dogs that were killed—"

"Whoa. You think I—? No. There's—" He glances toward the hole. "There's no dead dog. You can check. And I certainly didn't kill—"

"Step back," I say.

He obeys, and I walk until I can bend and look through that opening.

Flea is gone. So is Alanna's collar.

"Show me your hands," I say.

He holds them palms out. I see faint red smears on one thumb and forefinger, as if he rubbed blood-soaked dirt between them, but there's no other sign of blood. I make him turn, hands over his head, as I inspect his clothing. There's mud on his knees where he crawled through the hole. Otherwise, nothing. Definitely no blood spatter.

"You're going to wait down here," I say.

"No, Winter," he says calmly. "I've been a good sport about this. I came because I thought you were in trouble. I answered all your questions. You've practically accused me of killing two dogs, and I didn't take offense. I let you check me over, presumably for evidence. You obviously didn't find any. I'm clear."

"I'll decide that. I want to see what's up top first."

He purses his lips. "Good thinking. It was only about ten minutes between me last hearing the dogs and me getting here. I could have cleared the scene or I could have changed my clothing. Not both. So if I killed those dogs, you'll find them topside, and there's no way I could have missed them, which would prove I'm guilty."

I struggle not to gape at him. It's as if I'm accusing someone else and he's just helping with the investigation.

He continues. "How about this. You go up. I'll wait at the bottom. I want your knife, though, so you can't cut the rope. As soon as you're clear of the hole, I'll come up. Reasonable?"

Frighteningly reasonable. Of course, I don't mention I have both my switchblade and hunting knife.

"Stand over there," I say, pointing.

He walks ten feet. I climb the rope. Once I'm partway up, I send my hunting knife tumbling down to him.

"Thank you," he says, without a hint of sarcasm.

I shake my head and continue climbing.

twenty-five

THERE'S NO SIGN OF THE DOGS UP TOP. THERE ARE SIGNS OF their deaths—blood droplets on ferns and a bloodied drag mark and scattered fur. Their killer didn't have time to clean up as much as he had with One-Eye.

I think about One-Eye and Flea and how they died, and I squeeze my eyes shut, push the horror of that away. Focus on something else. Something useful.

I look over to a half-fallen tree next to an outcropping of rock. I imagine the dogs' killer hauling the corpses there and hiding behind the rock, watching as Jude calls down the hole.

When I round the rocks, there's a shoe print on the ground, dug into damp earth, and blood on the tree stump. Wet drops of blood. A few white dog hairs cling to the undergrowth.

"Winter?"

Jude emerges from the hole. I imagine the dogs' killer,

hiding behind this rock, watching Jude, thinking how much he looks like another boy. . . .

"Winter?" he says again.

I rub the goose bumps on my arms and walk over to him, saying, "Lift your shoe."

"Huh?"

I wave for him to raise a sneaker, and when he does, I can see the pattern doesn't match—it's not even close. His feet are also several sizes larger.

"You found a shoe print?" he guesses.

I don't answer, just take back my knife. I've already accepted that, as coincidental as Jude's arrival was, it really *was* a coincidence, one supported by the evidence.

"About the deaths of these dogs," he says. "I noticed blood on your knife. There's more on your clothing. And I heard what sounded like a fight."

"I had to do it. They—"

"I'm not questioning that," he says. "Could the dogs have been wounded and you mistakenly thought they were dead?"

"Including the one at the bottom of the hole?"

"Yeah, that's harder to explain."

"I was heading for Reeve's End. The dogs came after me. I ran. I had to stab Mange—the big brown one. I went down the hole into the mine shaft. I could hear two of the dogs going nuts up top. Then Flea—the smallest one—fell and his . . . his throat was cut. I thought maybe the other dog did it, but then she went quiet and there was . . . blood . . . dripping. Down the hole. I heard breathing and footsteps. I think he cut her throat and let her bleed out. . . ." I swallow. "Then he threw down her bloodied collar."

130

Horror grows in his eyes, the same horror I feel when I think of it.

"That's ...," he begins. There's a pause, and when he looks at me, he says, "Are you okay?" and that startles me, the empathy in his voice. I straighten fast and say, "Sure. It was bad, but I work in a doctor's office. Blood doesn't bother me. The alpha male was ... worse. It affected Lennon more than me, though."

He tenses and asks, "What'd he do?" and that seems a weird response, as if he's afraid Lennon embarrassed himself by freaking out.

"He was just shocked. More than me. He has less experience with stuff like that."

Jude relaxes. "Right. Yeah." He looks toward the hole and then says, "Did the dogs' killer say anything?" he asks.

"No. I could hear him breathing and moving, but he didn't speak."

"You know it's a guy, though? Male?"

I shake my head. "It just saves me saying 'he or she.'"

He silently processes and then says, "Let's get back to town. We need to talk."

We've walked maybe a quarter mile. Neither of us has said a word. I'm still reeling from the death of the dogs and trying to figure out what it means, and I think he's doing the same. Finally, he clears his throat and says, "I've contacted my mother about Lennon. It changes nothing," and I realize he's changing the subject, distracting both of us.

He holds his phone. It's an older model, banged up, with

131

a crack in the screen. I read a text conversation with "Elysse Bishop." It seems odd that it's her full name—other kids set their contacts list to Mom, Dad, Asshole Brother . . .

Jude: *Have you spoken to Lennon since Tuesday?*

The message is in proper English, fully punctuated. It took nearly two hours for her to respond, and when she did, it was equally correct, as if they were exchanging formal letters.

Elysse: *Hello, Jude. Nice to hear from you. I trust you're well?*

Jude: *When did you last speak to Lennon? I know you're in DC. Did he make his weekend check-in? It's important.*

Another hour passed.

Elysse: *He texted. He said he was busy and couldn't call.*

Jude: *That's it?*

Elysse: *Yes. Why?*

Jude: *I don't think that text came from Lennon.*

The time stamp shows twenty minutes passed before his mother responded.

Elysse: *I presume this conversation means you are unable to get hold of your brother. If he is ignoring you, I'd suggest it means he's finally had enough of this—*

Jude's thumb quickly covers the rest of the message and scrolls past a few exchanges to where he tells his mother he has reason to believe Lennon is in trouble, possibly even kidnapped. It took over an hour to get a reply.

Elysse: *Your father is convinced drug use isn't the explanation for your behavior, Jude, but—*

He scrolls down again quickly, past a few exchanges. I see something about Jude not understanding how much he's hurt his father.

Jude: *I don't lie, Mother. You know that. I don't lie. Don't make up stories. Don't drink. Don't do drugs. If you knew me at all, you'd know none of those explanations hold.*

Elysse: *Your father is throwing a party tomorrow night. If you want to mend this rift—and speak to your brother—I would suggest you attend. I'd also suggest you clean yourself up and attend as the son we raised, not the sullen, ungrateful—*

Jude pockets his phone. "She thinks I'm full of shit, as you can see. Despite the fact . . ." He shakes his head and doesn't finish.

"You aren't known for lying."

He hesitates, as if realizing I read that part. Then he says, "That probably sounded like a typical guy telling his mom he doesn't lie, drink, whatever. It's not. I don't do any of that. At all. It's a personal choice."

"So I can ask you anything and get an honest answer?"

"Of course not. I have a right to privacy. If I don't want to give an honest answer, I don't give one at all."

"Okay. So . . . your mother doesn't believe you. And your father would react the same way?"

"He might worry more, but he'd turn it over to her, and the end result would be the same, only I'd be in deeper shit with her for 'bothering' him."

"This thing about a weekend check-in. I don't mean to pry, but is there a reason for that? Lennon's eighteen and living on his own, but has to check in on weekends?"

Mrs. Bishop mentioned drug use, and I'm wondering if that's the answer, if Lennon is recovering from addiction or something and has agreed to a check-in system. But Jude looks at me, his brows drawn in confusion. Then he curses under his breath and says, "Lennon told you that?"

"He said he was eighteen. As for living on his own, I think I said that and he went along with it."

"He's seventeen. Finished high school in the spring, but he's taking a gap year before college. He lives at home. The check-in is just a thing. Our parents travel a lot and they give him his space, so they just ask for a weekend call."

"He didn't want me to contact your parents. Saying he was eighteen and implying he didn't live at home made that easier."

It's Lennon's text to their mother I want to pursue next—

that's the obvious clue—but instead I hear myself saying, "This problem with your parents. It's about you dropping out, right? And don't tell me things just 'came up.'"

"I'd prefer not to—"

"Too bad. This story of yours needs to make at least a little bit of sense if I'm going to consider working together. You left high school in your senior year, and clearly not because you weren't getting the grades. You're brilliant—"

"Actually, I'm not."

"Top of your class in, what, every subject except math?"

"My IQ is 110. That's barely above average. Do you know why I got those grades? Why I got trophies and awards? Because I had the advantages other kids do not. I had wealthy parents who wanted sons who achieved those grades and those trophies and those awards. I had tutoring for hours a day. The best athletic coaches money could buy. Hours of daily work to make sure I didn't squander those lessons. I achieved those things because of training and practice. Pure and simple. I have no innate aptitude or talent—"

"Piano."

He blanches but stays casual with, "What?"

"You're a whiz at the piano. That's *talent,* not training."

"The sole exception to the rule and even there, *most* was still training and practice."

"So that's why you dropped out of school. You got tired of meeting all those expectations."

He shrugs. "That works." I know that's not a lie, not the full truth, either. Just an explanation I can accept if I need one.

He continues as we walk. "The point is that I am estranged from my family and therefore they are not going to believe me about Lennon, and short of proof, no one else will either. If I go to the police, my mother will play it down, convinced I'm causing trouble."

Which is what Lennon said too. Why he didn't want to report his own incident. I remember reading those articles and thinking how politicians probably spent their kids' adolescent years hiding the teens and their antics, but the Bishop boys had done nothing to hide. Yet even after years of model behavior, their mother was still vigilant, still ready to see the worst.

I could imagine how that maternal mistrust might build up until the quiet model son exploded from the pressure and made the biggest statement he could think of, by dropping out. The problem? Once he did it, he couldn't turn around and undo it. Not a guy like Jude. So his grand statement backfired, and the life he screwed up the most was his own. No wonder he didn't like to talk about it.

"About Lennon's text," I begin.

"Right." He takes a small notebook and pen from his pocket. "Presumably it wasn't sent by Lennon."

"*Presumably?* He didn't have his phone when I found him. Unless you can schedule a text—"

"You actually can. He's done it before. But he went to check on Edie Tuesday night, and I'm not sure he'd have had a check-in text set so far in advance."

"What if someone else sent it?"

Before he can reply, his phone sounds. He answers and listens and then says, "Yeah, I was out of range. You got something for me?"

He stops walking, tucks the phone between his ear and shoulder, and jots notes in his book.

"No, that's great," he says. "I'll take it from here. Just please don't tell my mother I was asking."

A pause as I hear a man speak, and Jude answers with a forced laugh, "Exactly. If Lennon's gotten himself in trouble, I want to clean it up before she finds out. Oh—" He glances my way. "If I give you another number, is there any chance you can get positioning for it?"

Jude covers the receiver and asks for Edie's number. I give it and he relays that, then says, "Thanks, Roscoe, I owe you."

I hear the man tell Jude to call if he needs anything. They sign off. Jude makes another notation in his book and says, "That's a guy on my dad's security team. He's the one who tracked that pay phone for me, and his contact just got the last GPS signal for Lennon. Before we go check it out, though, *you* need a cell. I figure if you were using the pay phone, you don't have one, right?"

"Not exactly in my budget."

"Okay, but you need to be safe. I'll buy one for you to use."

I could point out that I said I was *considering* joining forces. I haven't agreed. But he's thrown me off balance. The offer is considerate in a way I wouldn't have expected.

I need an ally. This is the one on offer, and I'll need help if I want the best possible chance for Edie.

"Lennon left me money," I say. "I planned to return it, but I can buy a phone from that."

"Good. Then let's go get you one."

And with that, I've teamed up with Jude Bishop to find Lennon and Edie.

twenty-six

"My ride's over here."

We've been walking along a dirt road, bordered on both sides by forest, with the occasional clearing for a house. After a mile or so, Jude cuts into the woods. There, hidden in a thicket, is an old motorcycle. And by *old* I don't mean vintage. I mean old, and that's coming from someone who lives in a town where decade-old cars are sold "like new."

He wheels the bike from the forest, and as it jostles over the rough terrain, I wonder if I should follow behind, to catch any falling parts.

"You really are taking this vow of poverty thing seriously, aren't you?" I say.

He inhales, his back to me. Then, slowly and deliberately, he knocks out the kickstand.

"Let's get this over with," he says. "Leaving home before I graduated meant getting rid of my credit cards. I live in Louisville, with three other guys, where I take the couch. I work two jobs—as a stock boy and a dishwasher. I'm not trying to be the rich kid who proves he can rough it. I do all that because I need to use an assumed name, which means everything on a cash-only basis."

He shifts his weight, leaning against the bike. "I understand that, to you, my choices seem obnoxious. You're from a place where poverty is a real thing, not something you play at when you're pissed with your parents. I'm not asking for your understanding, Winter. I'm sure as hell not asking for your approval. I'm working through some shit, but right now, all that matters is finding my brother. So if you have something to say to me, say it."

I'm quiet. Then I say, "I'm sorry."

"I'm not asking for that, either," he says as he wheels the bike to the road.

At the road, Jude tries to give me the helmet. When I refuse, he seems annoyed but doesn't argue, just gets on and waits while I do the same.

The cell phone's last known coordinates are in the forest. Jude slows the bike to creep along a mile of road alongside the coordinates, up one side and down the other, both of us scouring the dirt shoulder for signs of a struggle. We're hoping to see those signs, meaning Lennon's captor hauled him into the forest from here and we're within walking distance of wherever he took Lennon, possibly wherever he's also holding Edie. We find nothing. Knowing how meticulous this guy is, that doesn't mean this isn't the spot. He's just not leaving us any clues. Yet he left some for Lennon to find. And he was waiting for Lennon to show up. What does that mean? I'm not sure yet.

We leave the bike and walk deeper into the forest, Jude tracking the coordinates with an app, and I say, "Does Lennon's car have one of those tracker things?"

"Hmm? Oh, LoJack. Yeah. Roscoe says it's in a parking lot back in Lexington. Roscoe wants to bring it home before our parents find out, but I asked him to leave it. It's evidence. Obviously whoever took him put the car there."

"What does Roscoe think of all this?"

Jude goes quiet for a moment. Then he says, as if reluctantly, "He thinks I'm overreacting. I've . . . been known to do that when it comes to Lennon. Roscoe's been with us for years, and he's always taken . . . well, he's tried to take a role in our lives, with our father gone a lot."

"Be a father figure?"

"More like a much older brother. Baseball games when we were kids. Concerts when we hit our teens. He's always wanted to be the guy who realizes how old we are, not treating us like kids. Which means things like giving us our space. Or sending us porn links."

I smile. "Were they good porn links?"

He snorts. "I have no idea. Even if I was interested, I don't really want to know what his idea of *good* porn would be. Seriously awkward. As for Lennon's disappearance, Roscoe thinks my brother's just being a typical seventeen-year-old guy, off getting into the kind of trouble our parents wouldn't approve of. Roscoe is just helping because I'm worried."

We continue on. I don't like being in the forest. For years this has been my domain, and now I feel like that's been stolen from me, as I jump at every noise.

We're about a mile in when Jude says we've reached the right area. We start searching for a structure of some sort. That's what we're hoping to find: the place where Edie is being held and possibly Lennon, too. When we don't see so much as a hunting blind, we turn our attention to the ground, searching for the phone itself.

"Is it even likely we'll find it?" I say after about thirty minutes. "We only know that it was here the last time it had service."

"Yeah," Jude says, but he keeps searching and so do I. It's not as if I have better things to do on a Saturday night.

We've been at it an hour when Jude's arm swings out, catching me across the chest. I've got my gaze on the ground and stumble with a curse.

"Shhh," he says.

I think of pointing out that if he wants silence, he shouldn't accidentally whack me. Then I see his gaze fixed on something and realize it wasn't an accident. He's stopped, and there, in the distance, a dark shadow is bent behind a log.

A moving shadow.

Jude grips my arm and backs me up. I peel off his fingers, sidestep to a tree fall, and hunker down behind it. He crouches beside me.

I see that figure and my heart slams against my ribs. It's the man who killed the dogs. He's followed us again, and I kept telling myself I was overreacting by jumping at every noise, but I wasn't, was I? He's right there.

The head dips down. Comes up again. Dips down.

Is he peering out from behind the log? He's not nearly as well hidden as he seems to think he is.

A sound comes. A snuffling grunt that has me squinting for a better view.

The head dips again. I change position, ignoring Jude's grab to keep me close. I edge out.

I creep back to Jude and whisper, "It's a black bear."

"What's it doing?"

That's the question, and when the answer comes, I push it away. I don't want it. I really, really don't want it.

I focus on that faint snuffling sound, hoping to prove myself wrong. I hear the snuffle. The grunt. Then a wet, tearing sound I know only too well.

My stomach lurches.

"Winter?"

"It's eating," I say.

"Grubs from that log?"

I don't answer.

"Winter?"

"It—it could be grubs."

He goes quiet for a moment. "Bears are omnivores, which means they do eat meat. They hunt and they scavenge."

I nod.

"But Lennon lost his—"

He stops himself. I know what he wants to say. That Lennon lost his phone before I met him, and the last signal is days old. Yet that doesn't mean Lennon didn't return to this spot to find his phone and possibly clues about his capture.

"Tell me how to scare it off," he says.

"That's dangerous. You can't—"

"I will."

I shake my head. "If we need to, yes. But we only have to check . . ." I swallow. "To see what it has. If it charges, make yourself big and noisy."

"Then you're staying beside me. I'm the bigger one. And the noisier one."

I'm not sure about the last, but I agree. I circle us around, staying downwind as I make a wide arc to see what's on the other side of that fallen log. When I spot the bloodied brown flank of a deer, I let out a sigh deep enough that the bear raises its head . . . and looks straight at me.

Jude pulls himself up, shoulders squaring. He inhales, mouth opening to shout, but I cut him off with a whispered "Wait."

The bear rises on its hind legs. It samples the air, thick snout quivering. It's a sow, shorter than me, lighter than Jude, which doesn't make it anywhere near harmless, not with those claws and teeth, both on exhibition as it waves its forepaws and pulls back its lips in a snarl.

"It's a warning display," I whisper. "Just wait."

The bear drops to all fours. It glances down at the deer it was scavenging, and then back at us. Trying to decide whether we threaten its meal. When it rises in another display, Jude rocks, ready to shout.

"Step back," I whisper.

He eyes the bear. Tension strums from him, the part that doesn't want to back down warring with the part that knows he should. When I move away, he does the same, grudgingly.

The bear snorts. Its head bobs as if in satisfaction.

Yes, puny humans, get away while you still can.

It lowers its head to the deer again. I retreat one more step, just to be sure.

A twig cracks to our left. I spin to see a blur of motion through the trees. Jude lunges. I go to grab him, only to realize at the last second that he's lunging at *me*. He tackles me to the ground. I go down easily, caught off guard, and he drops over me, on all fours, his gaze fixed on that blur through the trees.

The bear snarls.

Jude goes to leap up, but I grab him by the shirtfront. I hold him there, over me, and we stay poised, straining to listen. The bear grunts. Then that snuffling and ripping comes again.

Both our gazes swing up over our heads, in the direction of that blur of motion.

We see and hear nothing, but we stay completely still and listening. Then I notice I've still got my hand wrapped in his shirtfront. I release it and motion for him to rise. He does, slowly, and moves into a crouch. I sit.

"Clear?" I whisper as he lifts up enough to look.

He nods.

"What did you see?" I whisper.

"A blur."

"Ditto."

He backs onto his haunches. "You okay?"

I rub my shoulder. "You played football, I'm guessing from that tackle."

"Just one season. Not my thing." He asks again, "You okay?" and I nod. I'm about to rise when a sliver of late afternoon sunlight reflects off something in the undergrowth. I motion for him to cover me and crawl over to find a cell phone almost hidden under a patch of Christmas ferns. Jude takes it and hits the power button. Waits. Hits another button.

"Dead," he whispers.

"But it's his?"

He peels the lime-green case off and shows me the back of the phone, bearing a sticker that says LENNON IS WAY MORE AWESOME THAN JUDE.

"Old joke." He puts the cover back on. "I got my first phone inscribed with 'Jude is awesome.' Lennon couldn't fit his response in an inscription, so he printed a sticker. In my defense, I was ten, and with my next phone, I skipped the engraving."

"But Lennon kept getting stickers."

"Yeah. My brother . . ." An eye roll. Then his gaze shifts toward the bear, still eating. "We should go."

I nod and we creep past the bear. We're clear when I hear a sound off to my left, something like a chuckle. When I ask Jude, though, he's heard nothing, and the forest is silent. I give one last, slow look around and then pick up my pace as we head for the bike.

twenty-seven

Jude says he charged his phone this morning at a nearby diner. I think I know the one he means but I say nothing until he pulls in. It's the one I figured, a diner lifted straight out of the fifties—a mock-futuristic building that looks like a spaceship.

As we park Jude says, "Guess I should have asked if you're okay with this place. You know it, right?"

"It's the first stop we made when we moved here. Our dad remembered it from when his family would come here in the summer."

We walk across the lot and I continue, "My sister, Cadence, and I were so tired from the drive. Then we got here and it looked like something from a movie. Dad let us order whatever we wanted. I got a cheeseburger and rings and a root beer float. It was . . ."

My gaze sweeps the diner as we walk through the door.

"It seemed like a sign, you know? That things were looking up. That we'd reached someplace special. And we *had* reached someplace special. The end of the line."

He looks over, and I rub my face.

"Sorry," I say. "I'm just tired."

"You want to go somewhere else?"

"This is fine."

I walk to one of the red vinyl booths with an outlet nearby. As I slide in, I remember how the vinyl shone that first time. How the chrome gleamed. How the Formica tabletop felt smooth as glass under our hands. Now I see the cracks in the vinyl with dingy stuffing poking through. I see the scratched chrome. I see initials carved with penknives into the tabletop. I wonder if that's just a sign of the diner's age, or if I saw it with the eyes of a nine-year-old hoping for better.

Jude already has the phone plugged in. He opens the menu, notices I haven't taken one, and says, "Cheeseburger, rings, and a float?"

I shake my head. That will be my last meal, before I leave Reeve's End forever. Not that I'm telling him that.

"Get whatever you want. It's on me. You're helping me find my brother. I'm going to buy you dinner. Don't argue. It's just awkward."

I order a burger, fries, and a shake, and Jude seconds it, changing only the flavor of the milk shake.

"You know, I always wondered about that," I say, when the server leaves and silence falls.

"About what?"

"Whether anyone actually orders vanilla when there's a choice of actual flavors."

"Vanilla's a flavor."

"I'll take your word for it."

He shakes his head, but his eyes have warmed, acknowledging that I'm trying to make lighter conversation, as lame as it may be.

When the shakes arrive, Lennon's phone is finally ready to turn on, and Jude exhales as it bleeps to life, undamaged. He goes straight to messages.

"Last text sent was . . ." He frowns. "Tuesday? That can't be right."

He taps the screen, checking a few things, and then says, "Yeah, it was definitely Tuesday. It's to a friend of ours—well, Lennon's friend now. . . ." Jude rubs his thumb across his mouth, his gaze on the screen. When he walked away from home, he'd have left behind more than credit and debit cards.

He continues, "He hasn't texted our mother in a week. Again, that's normal but . . ."

"But he—or this *phone*—apparently sent a text yesterday."

"It definitely didn't. There are unread ones from friends received up until Wednesday night. That's when it must have turned off—new messages are downloading now."

"So the number was spoofed."

"Spoof . . . Oh, right. You mean the text seemed to come from him but didn't. That must be it. But it definitely didn't come from Lennon, and it wasn't scheduled from him either—it'd show up in his sent messages."

The food arrives, and he digs in, wolfing down half the burger and fries, and I wonder if he paused for lunch today. Or breakfast. As he slows, he resumes checking the phone, flipping through screens.

"Is Edie's call on there?" I ask.

His fingers keep tapping the screen. "I don't see it."

"So he deleted the record of the call. You can do that, right?"

"Yeah."

"He must have deleted it by accident. Or maybe he was worried about it being found."

He's stopped checking the phone and is just sitting there, staring into space.

"Jude?"

He snaps to attention. "You shouldn't get involved in this. I was wrong to ask. In fact, I should have insisted you steer clear." He puts down the phone with a clack. "You were trapped in a mine by a guy who killed two dogs. The same guy presumably who took your friend. That should have been the point where I said 'enough.'"

"And you're just realizing this now?" I shake my head. "It's my choice. I know the risks. I choose—"

"I'm going to ask you to drop this, Winter. I have Lennon's phone. I can get Roscoe to check a few things, and then I'll take what I have to my parents. I'll find a way to *make* them look into it. But you need to step aside."

"You don't actually get to decide that, Jude."

"Yes, I think I do. It's my brother."

"Who went after my friend. My missing friend."

He cuts me off with a clatter of plates as he gets to his feet and slaps money on the table. "Come on, I'll give you a ride back to Reeve's End."

twenty-eight

I'D LIKE TO TELL JUDE WHERE TO STICK HIS RIDE, BUT I'M NOT
making a statement at the cost of a ten-mile walk. So I sit behind him on the bike, gripping the sides of the seat as I fume.

I have ample reason for investigating Edie's and Lennon's
disappearances. That reason? Because I choose to, and no one
is going to "order" me to stop.

Jude might have given up his congressman's son life, but
he's still the guy who thinks he can boss others around. The
birthright of money and position. What rankles even more is
that off-hand Southern "chivalry" he uses to justify it.

*I've decided this is too dangerous for you, little girl. So you'll
go home while I handle it.*

I understand where that mind-set comes from. Old-timers
really do see it as good and proper behavior toward the "fairer"

sex. *Here, let me carry that for you. Let me open that door. Let me give you my jacket.*

I'm not going to throw a hissy fit if a boy insists on opening my car door. That's how their mommas raised them, and they'd catch a whupping if they didn't. But I expect them to understand that I'm capable of opening a door myself. And if that attitude spills over into "it ain't right for a girl to go to college," then we have a problem. Same goes for "here, let me decide what's best for you," like Jude was doing.

I have Jude drop me off outside town. I walk away without a word, and I think he'll call after me, at least say he'll be in touch, let me know what happens. The motorcycle revs, and then the tires spin as he turns around. Another rev and he's gone.

I check my watch as I walk. It's barely seven, and I'm not ready to turn in for the night, not when that means staying at the trailer, since I don't dare return to my shack. The library is closed, and I'm not sure what research I'd do there anyway.

What I really need is to start tackling my list—filling in the blanks for missing kids. Maybe a parent would have more clout with the sheriff's department than I do. I'm certainly not convinced we have an epidemic of kidnapped teens in Reeve's End, but if someone starts the conversation, it will help us plead Edie's case.

After Cady's, the first name on my list is Marty Lawson. That's definitely not going to accomplish my goal. I knew Marty—he dated Cadence in her freshman year, and I was sore when she broke it off. He was a nice guy and he got hurt, and it didn't help that she dumped him for Colton, who was *not* a nice guy.

Marty left nearly three years ago. No one was surprised—he struggled in school but he was a hard worker who dreamed of taking up a trade. He left a note saying he was going to the city to do exactly that. There's no point asking his mother if he's made contact. She's a drinking buddy of Bert's, meaning it's unlikely she's around on a Saturday night, unlikely Marty wants to speak to her again, and even more unlikely she's concerned enough to talk to the sheriff.

The next name is Tanya Tate. Her family lives just outside the town proper. I stop by there and her folks tell me she just called last month to say she'd found a boy and got engaged.

Next on my list, Susie McCall, a friend of Cadence's whose father lives three doors down from the Tates. In Reeve's End, "three doors down" isn't like in the city. It's a bit of a hike, and when I reach the house, dusk is falling. That makes me nervous. Word is that Owen McCall turned to drink about three years back, which might have been one reason Susie didn't bother waiting until she graduated high school to leave. But rumor also says he's harmless, a sad drunk rather than an angry one like Bert.

McCall used to be one of the preeminent pot farmers in the county. I remember Cadence telling me how she and Susie would hang out in a storage bunker under his field before he shut down his crop. Colton used to rant about what a waste that was, how Owen McCall was a whiz with hybrids and he'd regret it when pot was legalized in Kentucky. Folks here track the spread of legalization the way others track the NBA draft.

Mr. McCall's happy to talk about Susie. We settle in on the front porch and I ask when's the last time he heard from Susie.

"Couple months back," he says. "She sent an article from the Cincy *Enquirer* with her name in it." His thin face broadens in a smile. "Can you believe that? My girl, getting her name in the paper. And you know what for? Volunteer work with the homeless." He shakes his head. "Never would have guessed."

"I'm not surprised. Susie always had a good heart."

He beams. "She does, doesn't she? Took after her momma, God rest her soul. You were friends with Susie, weren't you?" He pauses. "No, wait, that was your sister, Cadence. How's she doing?"

I can imagine the look on my face, because he says, "Haven't heard from her, huh? Don't worry too much. That's what Susie did too. Needed some space. All kids do at that age. They take off, and they don't want nothing to do with family, and then the next thing you know, they're sending an article with their name in it. Just needed that bit of space to find themselves. I've got the newspaper clipping right inside, if you'd like to see it. Might make you feel better about your sister."

I say sure, I'd love to see it. He goes inside, and I take out my notepad and draw a line through Susie's name. He returns sooner than I expect, and I set the notebook on the chair arm as I read the article. It's about a new homeless shelter where Susie volunteered, saying she used places like it when she first came to the city and now wanted to give back.

"She sounds very happy," I say. "Congratulations."

When McCall doesn't answer, I look up to see he's still standing beside my chair. His gaze is fixed on my open notebook. When he picks it up, there's a slight tremor in his hand.

"What's this?"

I take it as gently as I can. "It's just a list—"

"Of kids who've left Reeve's End. I can see that. What are you doing with it?"

"It's my senior year project, on kids who leave. I'm following up on them."

His voice chills. "I thought you came by to ask about Susie because she was your sister's friend and you were interested."

"I am. I—"

"Your sister took off and now you're poking your nose where it doesn't belong, asking questions, upsetting folks who lost their kids and won't appreciate the reminder. *You* want a reminder, missy? Remember why your sister left."

My mouth opens. Shuts.

He continues. "You think I don't know? Everyone knows. But you seem like a nice girl, and I figured you made a mistake and you've paid for it. We all make mistakes. We all pay. But you don't go rooting through other folks' miseries so you can feel better about yours."

He's hit full-steam boil, and I'm just staring. I can see how he might be a little put off that my interest has turned out to be a school project, but that doesn't explain this Jekyll/Hyde transformation. I try getting to my feet, which requires bending almost backward to slide past him as he looms over me.

"I—I'm sorry," I say. "I really was interested in how Susie's doing. It's reassuring to know that kids find success when they leave Reeve's End."

"They do," he says, spitting the words on a snarl. "They get away from this hellhole and they make good lives for themselves, and that's all you need to know. You go digging like that, and you're just stirring up trouble for the folks who *don't* get a newspaper article with their baby's name in it. No one here needs that. We've got enough problems as it is."

"Yes, sir. I'm sorry, sir."

"Why don't you give me that notebook, then?"

"Wh-what?"

"You're done with this nonsense, aren't you, missy?"

"I . . . I'm going to reconsider the focus of my project. You've given me a lot to think about. I—I'll speak to my teachers, and see what I should do."

He goes still. "Your teachers know what you're up to?"

I glance around. There's no one on the road. No one in sight.

When he asks if my teachers know, it feels like having a guy in a white van pull over and ask if your parents know where you are.

"Yes," I lie. "They know exactly what I'm doing."

"And they've seen that list? They know who's on it?"

Oh, shit.

There is one very serious problem with going around Reeve's End inquiring after missing kids. Namely, that the person I'm asking could be the very one making them disappear.

"Yes," I say as calmly as I can. "They have a copy of the list and all my notes so far. I appreciate you pointing out potential issues with the project. I'll stop asking around and revisit it with my teachers on Tuesday. I'll let you know what happens."

I retreat cautiously, spouting apologies in my wake, as if

I'm just upset that I've angered him and I want to go before I make it worse.

I reach the top of the steps when McCall grabs me. My hand is already in my pocket, fingers wrapping around my switchblade as he's twisting my other arm up. I pull out the knife and hit the switch, and the blade flicks, and my brain screams *Now, what?* because Jude was right—I don't know how to use it properly. McCall will wrest it away from me before I can do more than blindly slash.

McCall sees the knife and flings me away—flings me hard. I'm at the top of the porch steps, and I fall straight backward, and there's no time to catch myself. I hit the paving stones flat on my back, head striking down with a crack, and then everything goes dark.

When I come to, McCall is holding me, saying, "Wake up. Please wake up." My eyelids flicker, and when I see his face, I scramble from his grip.

"You tripped," he says.

"Wh-what?"

"You were leaving, and you tripped down the steps."

I blink hard. I know that's not what happened, but I say, "R-right," and rub my face hard. "We were talking . . . I don't remember . . ."

"We talked about Susie. I showed you an article."

"Right." I push up. My switchblade is in the grass, and I manage to scoop it up discreetly as I fake more hard blinks. "I should go."

I get out of there as fast as I can. Only once I'm down the road and around a corner do I pause, heaving breaths as I run my fingers over my head. A bump is rising. I'll have to do concussion checks later, but that's the least of my concerns. Right now, I'm thinking of that bunker Susie and Cadence used to hang out in. The one McCall bolted up when he stopped growing pot. Which was about three years ago.

And most of the kids on my list? They left less than three years ago.

twenty-nine

I NEED TO GET TO THAT BUNKER. I NEED TO SEE WHAT'S INSIDE IT before he realizes he has to clear it.

I think of calling Jude. I should tell someone. But he's shut that door, and I can't bring myself to reopen it and ask for help.

I know where the field is. No one goes to great lengths to hide those around here. There's an unspoken rule in Reeve's End that you don't pilfer from another's pot or 'shine. Besides, if you did, it's a tight enough community that someone would rat you out.

I don't know this part of the forest, for good reason. Being riddled with pot fields, it's also riddled with booby traps. These aren't harmless alert systems; we don't have the technology for that. The devices are hard-core, everything from boards with nails to stake pits to bear traps, all covered in vegetation. I walk with a stick in hand, clearing my way, and only uncover a trip wire attached to a wildlife cam, which I avoid easily.

Once I reach Owen McCall's old plot, I need to be extra careful. If he's using it for what I fear, the traps could be more than boards with nails. I recall Cadence saying the bunker was smack in the middle of his field. As I pick my way through it, I uncover two bear traps. One is exposed and has been tripped and rusted, suggesting it's been here for years. The second, though, is covered, set and newer. Almost definitely laid out after McCall shut down his operation.

Bluegrass has grown up all through the field. On the hatch, though, the sod isn't thick enough for long roots and my penlight picks up the lower section of grass.

As I creep forward, I realize exactly how dangerous this is. I don't know what I pictured. Did I expect to see trails of blood? Hear cries for help? *Smell* people trapped below? Whatever my hopes, they were as stupid as this entire plan. The only way I'm going to know if someone's in that bunker is to open the hatch.

Just do it.

Open the hatch. Peek in. If something seems wrong, run and call Jude. If I think Lennon is down there, Jude will get help, even if it means having that Roscoe guy drive all the way from Lexington.

I reach the hatch and run my fingers along the ground until I find an edge. Then I follow it to a padlock hidden in the grass.

I'm not surprised that it's locked. If it wasn't, that'd have been a sure sign of trouble. *Hey, little girl, my underground lair is conveniently left open. Come take a look.*

I have no idea how to pick a lock. This one is rusted, but

when I give it a few tugs and twists, it does not miraculously pop open. Something creaks, though—the part attached to the wooden frame. A rotted wooden frame. When I twist the lock again, the latch twists with it, old wood splintering.

I dig at the wood with my knife and twist the metal latch until it comes free. Then I ease the hatch up an inch. It's pitch black inside, which I take as a good sign. Well, good in the sense Owen McCall hasn't beaten me here. As for Edie and Lennon, if he took them, it's not like he's going to leave a night-light on.

It's silent inside. I hesitate and then pull the hatch all the way up. Except it won't *go* all the way. It rises perpendicular, and when I try to fold it back, the rusted hinges refuse. I wiggle the hatch and the hinges squeal and I stop quickly, my heart hammering.

I crouch, propping up the hatch. The musty smell of old dirt wafts up. I focus on listening, and I'm about to stop straining when I hear the faintest sound of movement, deep underground.

I check over my shoulder. Then I bend and call, "Hullo!" I'm poised to drop the hatch and run at any sign of trouble. I hear a whispery scrabbling. Then there's a thump. Like someone gagged and bound, dirt scratching under them as they move, the thump coming as they pound their fists against the ground, desperate to make noise, any noise.

I push open the hatch, but it refuses to stay that way. I take the notepad from my pocket and wedge it in and that keeps the door propped up. Then I shine my penlight down into the hole.

Cadence called it a bunker and said it'd been dug by

McCall's miner father. I can see that in the construction, which looks not unlike the mine tunnel from this afternoon.

Was that really just this afternoon? It doesn't seem possible.

I pause one more second. Then I head in.

thirty

My second underground voyage in one day. At least this one comes with semi-proper stairs—a rope ladder that takes me down about twenty feet. At the bottom, it does indeed resemble a bunker. Like that mine shaft, it's blasted from the bedrock of the Appalachians. In this case, it's not a shaft but one big, empty room, with wooden braces holding up dirt walls and a roof.

I move around the walls, my penlight shining on every wooden beam and section of dirt between them. I don't know what I'm searching for. It's not as if I'd miss seeing a hatch or a hole big enough to crawl through. The room is no more than ten by ten. It's only on my second round that my beam catches a horizontal line between two support beams. I walk over and crouch and see that it's a wooden frame embedded in the dirt. The wood has even been painted reddish brown to match the surrounding soil.

I feel along the edge of the frame. My fingers find some kind of mechanism and a latch springs free.

The frame is a crawl-space door. Which makes sense. McCall would have stored tools in this open room, but the bunker isn't well enough disguised to risk hiding anything more valuable. Hence the secret door.

As I pull it open, I hear the whispery noise again.

"Hello?" I call.

The noise stops.

"I'm here to help," I say . . . because an axe murderer would clearly announce her intentions. Not surprisingly, the bunker stays quiet.

I crawl through the hidden doorway and find myself in a short hall with a low roof. It extends to a dead end. There are doorways to each side. I wipe my sweaty hands on my jeans. Then I take out my phone. My one bar wavers. I hold it as high as I can and the bar comes strong.

I pocket the phone again and call, "It's Winter Crane," and then "Edie? Lennon? It's Winter." Silence. I check the room on the left and then the one on the right. Both have old debris—pieces of crates and burlap bags and bits of dried pot. And that's all there is. The hall and these two rooms. Which is weird—why have the hall extend *past* the rooms? I shine my light over the end of the corridor. The top is dark. I keep going, and I see the hall doesn't end—it's been filled in. There's a gap at the top, as if the person ran out of dirt.

Or as if he intentionally left that opening so he could crawl through to what was on the other side.

I climb the dirt pile and push the penlight through the gap. When I hear a soft *tap-tap-tap*, I exhale, thinking it's whoever I heard earlier. Then I realize it's me pushing dirt down the heap.

I wriggle higher so I can see through to my penlight beam, and the whispery sound comes again, from the left, where another doorway leads into yet another room. I keep wriggling until I'm through and sliding headfirst down the pile of dirt. I come to rest at the bottom, arms outstretched. An awkward twist, and I get my feet under me and then rise.

I glance through the doorway on the right. Just more crap in there. I check my phone again. No service now. I hold it up. Still nothing.

I look at the pile of dirt and quickly calculate how fast I can get through to place a call if things go wrong. Then I start toward the left-hand doorway. I have the cell phone in my jacket pocket, switchblade in one hand, and penlight in the other. Two steps forward and then I can shine the light through the doorway and . . .

And nothing.

Broken crates and burlap bags. That's it. Just as my heart begins to sink, I realize there's more crap in this room—a lot more. There are a few whole crates and some stuffed burlap bags. Enough "garbage" to completely block my view of the other side of the room. Garbage deliberately arranged to block that view.

And the moment I think that, I hear the scratchy whispering sound . . . from the other side of that strategically piled debris.

I inch forward. And then I see a shoe sticking from behind a crate. A shoe topped by a sock and a slice of denim, the rest extending out of sight, hidden by the crate.

It's a white shoe. Dingy and dirt-streaked. But white.

"Lennon?" I whisper. "It's me. Winter."

The foot does not move. The sound does not come again. I creep forward, my gaze traveling up that leg as I circle wide to see past the crate.

A sheet. The legs are covered in a sheet, only that one foot showing. I keep moving.

The smell. God, the smell. It wasn't evident at first, as if the sheet stifled it, but it smells like . . .

No, I'm wrong. I must be wrong.

I pick up my speed and bend by that leg peeking out, and I grab the corner to pull and . . .

A snake slides from under the sheet. I jump back, my hand smothering a scream. It slithers out, making that whispery, scratchy sound as it moves over the dirt. It stops, head raised, fangs extended.

Brown snake. Light-brown body. Darker brown rings.

Copperhead.

Poisonous.

I back up until I hit the wall, and as my heart hammers, there's a little part of me saying to calm down, just calm down. I've encountered copperheads before, when they've come into the shack. I have a stick there for removing them.

But I've also helped Doc Southcott treat those bitten by copperheads. It isn't fatal. It isn't pretty, either.

And it's not just that. It's not just that at all.

I'm staring at this snake and I'm freaking, and part of that might be the poisonous snake hissing at me but most of it is . . .

Most of it is . . .

I look at the sheet. At that leg, not moving. I inhale the

smell and I know what it is. I've known what it is from the start. I smell it when I need to go into the basement at Doc Southcott's office and something has crawled in and . . .

My breath picks up, and I turn back to the snake, almost hoping it'll do something, distract me, make me leave without lifting that sheet. But it's already slithering off to a hole in the wall.

The snake disappears and my gaze shifts reluctantly to the sheet. I know what's under it. I just know.

Since the moment Lennon told me about Edie going missing, I have refused to acknowledge this possibility. I've thought about a madman, a psycho, a kidnapper. Never a killer. I've been so careful about even the terminology I use in my head.

Now I'm standing here, and I'm staring at what is clearly a man's shoe. At a white sock and blue denim. Like Lennon wore. All exactly like Lennon wore.

And the smell . . .

Tears fill my eyes.

I should leave. I can't do anything to help him. I should leave the scene intact. Instead I move forward, bending to grip the edge of that sheet.

It's a canvas tarp. Filthy, as if it'd been used for covering piles of pot from low-flying planes and it was repurposed for this, and when I realize that, rage fills me. Unreasonable rage, as if somehow this is a desecration, to throw a used and filthy tarp over a body.

I inhale and tug at the tarp. It doesn't come easily. I have to pull harder and then it slides down, over dark hair and a face and . . .

The face.

It's a corpse.

Yes, obviously, it's a corpse. But it's not someone who has just died in the last few days. It's decayed and desiccated, and that rage flares again, as I think that McCall has done something to Lennon's body to speed up the process, to hide what he's done.

Except . . .

It isn't Lennon. The dark hair lies straight and short. And there's enough left of his face that I can clearly see it's not Lennon. Enough left to identify the body.

Marty Lawson.

That's what McCall had seen when he spotted my list.

He knew Marty hadn't left Reeve's End.

I should run now. Hell, I should be gone already, tearing off the moment I saw a dead body. Racing away, heart pounding, a scream in my throat.

But I don't feel that scream. My heart isn't pounding. I'm staring down at Marty Lawson and every image I have of him—every moment when our lives intersected—rushes back. I remember how he always said hi to me, always stopped to talk to me even after Cadence broke up with him. I remember one time, when I showed up at school with a bruise on my cheek and told everyone I fell, he told me he needed some advice on trapping, and took me to dinner, and instead of talking about trapping, he talked about his mother, and how she used to hit him, and how he'd learned to avoid it as best he could. Passing on tips and sympathy without once mentioning my own situation, leaving my dignity intact.

That's the Marty Lawson I remember, but a few tears wash away those memories and my cold Winter self returns, the analytical one who does not run crying and screaming. I carefully tug back the sheet to see what I can of the corpse. To examine it. To analyze it. To accumulate answers before I leave.

Marty's neck is broken. I see that as soon as I get the sheet past his shoulders. The angle of his head is unmistakably wrong. I keep pulling the sheet. I see caved-in ribs and a compound fracture of the femur, the bone sticking out. Those injuries suggest a story. That Marty Lawson was struck by a motor vehicle.

I see something else under the sheet, tucked up against him. A wad of money. I don't touch it, but it's a thick wad, tucked under his body. Then I notice a pile of clothing, off to the side, partially hidden.

My imagination takes the clues and fills in the rest. Hit and killed on a quiet road. Body stuffed into the trunk. Hastily written note left in his empty house. Clothing grabbed. Money grabbed. Making sure it looked as if Marty just took off.

Marty went missing nearly three years ago. Right before Owen McCall declared he'd gotten out of the pot business. Right before he locked up this bunker to make sure his daughter wouldn't use it.

I haven't found whoever kidnapped Edie and Lennon. I've found another tragedy, unconnected.

I resist the urge to cover Marty's body. I will admit to the police that I pulled back the sheet.

I'm about to start making my way through the room, when a loud thump reverberates through the bunker. I go still for one second. Then I scramble around the crates, duck, and turn off my penlight.

No other sounds come. I stay still, knife in hand, eyes straining for any hint of light shining along the corridor.

After a moment, I creep, feeling my way in the pitch black until my foot tangles in a burlap bag and I stumble, hand striking a crate, the sound ripping through the silence.

Shit!

I crouch and try to control my breathing. Everything goes quiet again. I decide it's safer to turn on the light, then continue through the room and peer around the doorway.

Nothing.

I crawl to the dirt pile and carefully make my way to the top. When I'm close enough to peek through, I turn off the light again. Darkness falls. Complete darkness, which shouldn't be, with the hatch propped open and moonlight outside.

I realize then what I heard—the sound of the hatch shutting. I turn on the penlight and see my notebook on the floor.

Guess I didn't prop that open as well as I thought. I crawl through, recover my notebook, and shove it back in my jacket. Then I climb the rope ladder and give the hatch a push. When it doesn't budge, I don't think much of it—I'd broken the latch, so it can't have relocked. I push with both hands, a tremendous shove guaranteed to . . .

Guaranteed to do absolutely nothing. And that's when I realize someone has closed it, trapping me inside.

thirty-one

I'm overreacting. The hatch must be stuck. I push and I pry and I shake the hatch, fingernails digging into the wood to get a grip. I don't want to believe that someone has locked me down here.

Wasn't I trapped in another subterranean tunnel just a few hours ago?

Except there hadn't been any serious attempt to keep me down in that mine shaft. The dogs' killer hadn't even pulled up the rope.

I take my knife and work on pushing it around the perimeter to see where the hatch might be catching. There are a few places where it won't go in because the wood is too swollen.

The hatch creaks. And I'm not touching it.

I go still and watch, ready to drop at the first sign of the hatch lifting. It doesn't move. I hear a whisper behind me, but I know that's just the copperhead.

Just the copperhead.

I check my phone. The one bar wavers.

The hatch creaks again.

Screw this. My captor knows where I am, and going quiet isn't going to convince him I've somehow found a back exit.

He's playing with me. Cat with a mouse. Just like in the forest with Lennon. Just like in the mine tunnel. Yes, this could be McCall, but the way he's toying with me says otherwise. It says it's the guy who killed the dogs. The guy who's been stalking me.

I slam both fists against the hatch. "Hey! You! Open up."

Silence. I pound my fists on the wood.

"You want to scare me? How about facing me? Open up and face me."

After a minute of silence, I start to feel foolish. Am I sure someone's there? All I heard was a creak. Wood *does* creak.

"Hello?" I call.

When my phone rings, I jump and answer.

"It's Jude. Look, I'm sorry. I shouldn't have—"

"It's fine."

"I want to talk. Tomorrow over breakfast, maybe? Unless you're still up." He pauses. "The sooner the better, but if you've gone to bed . . ."

I look around. *Uh, not exactly.*

"There's no evidence Lennon got a call from Edie in the past week," he blurts. "That's why I cut dinner short and told you to stay out of it. His full week of calls is on the phone, and he didn't get any that could have been from her. Which doesn't mean she couldn't have contacted him another way. I just . . . I . . ." He inhales. "Are you still up? I could swing by."

"I found a body."

Silence. Then, "Sorry," he says. "It must be a bad connection. It sounded like you said—"

"Body, yes. I found a dead body. It's not Lennon or Edie. I was hunting for them and found a corpse in an underground storage pit and now I can't get out."

"What?"

"The hatch closed, and I can't open it. I don't think I've been locked in here, but I should still call the police—"

"Winter? Just tell me where you are."

I do. He hangs up as soon as I start telling him I'm fine. When the line goes dead, I call the sheriff's office. No one answers. I hang up. I redial. Still no response, which is not unexpected. The night dispatcher—Deputy Slate's wife—doesn't answer unless someone is free to actually dispatch. This makes perfect sense to her.

I send Jude a text message with more detailed directions, followed by a second one with warnings about the possible traps he could encounter. He replies with a simple "Got it." Then I push on the hatch. It moves but not enough to even peer out.

Ten minutes pass in complete silence. No whisper from the snake. No creak from the hatch. Maybe it wasn't even that creaking, but the wind in— .

The hatch moves. My fingers are against it and it shifts down and then, after a moment, rises again.

As if someone put his foot on it and then took it off again.

I push, sudden and hard. Nothing. Then, when I still have my hands against the wood, it moves up and then down, just that little bit.

I pound my fists against it. "Open this damn thing and face me."

I hear something between my pounding fists.

Laughter.

Just a chuckle, almost too low to catch, and then it's gone and I'm not sure I heard it at all.

No, I heard it. He wants me to be unsure. Wants me to question.

I pound on the hatch and then stop abruptly, hoping to catch that laugh.

Nothing.

I put my ear up to the hatch and listen. I can pick up the faint whistle of the wind, but there's no mistaking it for anything else. Then I hear an owl. A great horned owl.

I keep listening with my hands pressed against the hatch, waiting for that telltale push-and-release. Two minutes tick past. I bang my fist against the hatch, an offhand bang, more frustration than intent.

The hatch pops up and then falls shut with a thump.

Slammed shut? Or falling shut as my hand withdrew?

I press my fingers to the wood and flex them.

The hatch rises effortlessly as my fingers extend.

With one hand against the hatch, I flick open my switchblade. Then I slowly raise the hatch. I get it halfway up and shove as hard as I can, letting it fly open with a crack.

I pause, listening hard. Then I shift so I'm holding the hatch aloft with my shoulder, both hands steadying my knife as I scan the area.

There's no one there. Not *right* there anyway. Not close enough for me to see over the long grass.

I rise, my head swiveling, ears trained for any sound.

The owl hoots. The wind whispers through the grass. Then a twig cracks underfoot. A deliberate crack. A shoe poised over a stick and then crunching down.

I hear that and tears spring to my eyes. Angry tears. Enraged and frustrated tears.

He's baiting me, and there's nothing I can do about it. Nothing that won't put me in serious danger. Like Lennon I already tried to confront him—did something foolhardy in hopes of . . . of I don't know what. Just getting him to reveal himself. To say something. To show his face. To act.

Yes, even to act. He could have pulled up that rope in the mine tunnel. Could have pulled up the ladder here. Could have stranded me below either time.

He's taunting me.

I keep listening, but that single twig snap is all I get. Just enough to make me wonder if I really heard anything and then think I'm being paranoid and then be convinced of it and chastise myself.

Another crack. This one comes from the opposite direction, the quick snap of twigs underfoot. Then undergrowth crackles as someone pushes through, and I know that's not the stalker.

Jude.

I quickly text him a message to be careful, and in the silence I hear his phone chirp, but he just keeps making his way toward me as he texts that he's fine. I reply, warning him someone could be here. He doesn't answer.

I watch him edging along the field, getting parallel to me before cutting across. When he's as close as he can get, he steps away from the forest and slows, being even more cautious as he makes his way across the field. Then he's close enough to talk, his voice carrying on the quiet night.

"You called the cops?" he says.

"What?"

"You keep looking for someone. I'm guessing you contacted the police. I was going to suggest you report it, whether they come for you or not."

He didn't check the second message. Damn him. I send another. As I hit the button, a shadow glides behind him, stretching from the forest. A dark figure. Ten feet away.

"Jude!" I shout as I break into a run. "Behind you!"

He turns and the figure withdraws, but not quickly enough. *Intentionally* not quick enough, pausing just enough to let Jude catch a glimpse—and charge after the retreating figure.

"No!" I yell. "Don't—"

There's a tremendous crack as Jude stumbles. I run to him, hearing that crack over and over. The sound of gunfire.

I don't think. I don't look for the shadowy figure. I just run to Jude.

When I reach him, he's on all fours, breathing hard. His right leg is down in a hole. That's what the crack was—his shoe breaking through the branches covering a stake trap.

"Don't move!" I say.

I quickly look for the stalker, but he's gone. Jude is crawling forward, slowly lifting his leg out of the trap.

"Did I say *don't move*?" I snap as I jog to him, closing the gap.

"It's fine. I didn't fall in."

"I don't care. Stay—"

His knee slides on the dirt edge of the pit. He scrabbles wildly and I dive, snagging his jeans at the calf and stopping his foot an inch above the row of rusted nails lining the hole.

"Hold still," I say.

I yank off my jacket and put it over the nails. As I do, I see blood on one, and I notice more oozing from a hole in the bottom of his shoe, where he touched down before hauling himself up.

"Are your tetanus shots up to date?" I ask.

"I'm steady. I won't fall on them."

I don't tell him he already has, just say to slowly pull himself up. He follows my instructions. Once he's free, I say, "Sit."

"I'm fine."

"No, you're not."

He sighs. That trying-to-be-patient sigh. But he humors me, sitting down and tugging off his right shoe when I ask.

"I'm fine. See?" His lips purse as he pulls his foot up and sees the bottom, where blood soaks his white sock. "Huh."

"Yes, *huh*."

"I never even felt that."

"You will. Any idea when you had your last tetanus shot?"

"I got a booster when I went into high school. How long does it last?"

"Ten years, but I recommend you double-check your records. Better to get another shot than lockjaw."

I peel his sock down. Rust may have flaked from the nail, and I don't want to make the wound worse. When I get the sock off, though, it's only a gouge.

"Prognosis?" he says.

"In need of an actual doctor at some point, but the wound seems shallow."

He opens his mouth to respond. Then his head jerks up as he peers into the forest.

"Someone was—"

"That's what I texted you." I explain about the hatch and what I heard in the forest, and then I back up to Marty's body and my theories. My voice hitches when I talk about Marty, but I force myself past it. Deal with the circumstances first; grieve later.

"So it's possible this McCall guy came to check on his victim after you talked to him. He finds you down there and tries to hold you hostage and then thinks better of it."

"True, but—"

"But it seems more likely the same person who did the other stuff. I agree. Which means you're being stalked."

"And you got led into a trap for coming to help me."

He shakes his head. "He didn't lure me near that trap. I was coming to you. Coincidence, I think." He peers into the forest. "Did you get a good look at him?"

"I saw a figure. I could say male, but I may be projecting my assumptions."

"Okay. We'll go back to that bunker and wait for the police. . . . Wait, it wasn't the cops you were looking for."

"I tried. They weren't answering. Here, hold on. . . ."

I take out my phone, but he rises and waves for me to get into the field first. We walk maybe five steps in before he stops and says, "Okay, here we can see anyone coming." He looks around and adds, "And anyone can get a clear shot at us." He sighs with chagrin and a hint of annoyance, as if he really should be better at anticipating the dangers of psycho stalkers.

I motion for him to stand guard while I call.

"No one's picking up," I say.

"At 911?"

I shake my head. "We don't have 911 here. It's the sheriff's department," I explain. When he shakes his head, I say, "Yes, you really are in hillbilly country."

He makes a face at the term and then waves for me to start walking. "We'll stop at the station. If there's no one there . . ."

"We'll write them a Post-it note." When he looks over, he sees I'm joking, and I continue with, "If no one's there, we can contact the state police. Which won't win me any points with the local cops, but it's better than not reporting a dead body."

thirty-two

As we walk, I catch Jude wincing once or twice but when I ask if he's in pain, he says, "I'll survive." Not *I'm fine*. That would be a lie. I've already suggested we take the bike, which he's left just inside the forest, but he's worried it'll make too much noise, alerting our stalker. We'll come back for it.

When we reach the edge of the forest, he says, "Did you know him? The victim?"

"He dated my sister. He was a good guy. A really—" My voice catches again. "I don't understand how someone can do that. Stick his body down there and make everyone think he took off."

"I think it probably escalated. Hit a kid. Try to cover it up. Make it worse. Pretty soon, he doesn't see a way out."

"Which isn't an excuse."

"Course not. That's the problem with lies. They keep growing."

We walk a little farther, and I can see the lights of town in the distance when I say, "Did you contact Roscoe about looking into that call between Edie and Lennon? The one he erased from his records?"

There's a long silence. Then Jude says, "Lennon couldn't have accidentally deleted it. He'd need to clear all his incoming call records. Which he didn't."

I stop short and turn. "Are you suggesting Edie *didn't* call Lennon?"

"I . . . I don't know."

He tries to start walking again, but I get in front of him.

"What are you saying, Jude? Why would your brother lie . . . ?" I trail off and then stare at him. "The only possible reason to lie would be if he was involved with Edie's disappearance. If he was *responsible*. But someone did follow me in the forest when I was with him. I'm sure . . ."

Was I? Could I have misheard laughter in the forest and did Lennon then play along?

No, someone fired those arrows into my door while Lennon was standing right beside me. But it could have been an accomplice . . . or someone who knew what Lennon had done and came after him for *that*.

"You think your brother could have captured Edie?"

"No." He skirts around me to keep walking, moving fast, agitated. "I don't know what I think, Winter, just that I don't want to talk about it right now."

"Great. So if Lennon shows up at my trailer, I should just let him in, trust whatever story he tells?"

"Of course not—"

"You need to explain this to me, Jude."

"And I will. After you report the body. But I can't go with you to do that."

"You're worried that your brother is involved, and you're worried the police will realize it because you won't lie, even about that."

His face tightens. "Yeah. I'd put my brother in the cross-hairs of some small-town cop for some silly principle. I think we just proved that lying only makes things worse. My point is that I don't have experience with making up stories, so I'm not good at it. That'll show, and they'll think I'm covering up the fact my brother is some psycho—" He cuts himself short. "Can I ask you to report it yourself, Winter? Leave me out of it?"

"Lie, you mean."

That makes him go quiet. Then he swallows. "No, you're right. That's—"

"I'm not going to lie for you, Jude. But nor am I going to drag you to the station if you'll jeopardize Lennon. I wasn't going to tell the police about being trapped down in that bunker, which means I'm not telling them I thought someone else was there, which means there's no point telling them about you, either. The weirder I make the story, the more likely they'll question it. I'm sticking to the facts—I was checking into Edie's disappearance, asking about other kids who've taken off, and that led to McCall and the bunker and Marty's body."

I trail off as I look around.

Jude stops short. "What?"

"I just realized we'll walk right behind Owen McCall's place if we keep heading this way."

"You want to go a different route?" He looks at me and says, "No, you want to see if he's there. If you're planning to confront—"

"I'm not stupid. Yes, I'd like to see if he's there, but without actually going on the property. If he is, it's unlikely he was the person in that field."

"Good point. I'll check his vehicle, see if the engine's hot, peek in the house if I can."

"When I said I wouldn't go on the property, I wasn't hinting for you to do it."

"I know. But I will. Then I'll take off once you head into town."

We keep walking. We're getting close when a tree branch creaks. I stop. Jude looks over, his brows rising.

"You hear something?" he says again.

A tree branch. A creaking tree branch.

Uh, yeah, we're in the forest, Winter.

I know. It's just . . .

It's the way it creaked. A sound that makes my scalp prickle, makes me think of the feral alpha, One-Eye, hanging from the tree.

Except that's not really what I'm thinking of. I'm remembering a night when I heard a branch creak outside my shack.

I was sleeping there with Cady, for the first time in over a year. She'd told Colton she was going to college, and if he loved her, then he'd come to the city with her or wait back in Reeve's End. She never told me how the conversation went, but that night, she wanted to sleep in the shack, and I thought that was my reward—that I'd given good advice, been a good sister, and she wanted to spend time with me.

Then we heard that noise outside the shack—that creak— and she jumped up, and when I rose, she grabbed my arm and told me not to answer the door.

I'll fix this, Win. Let me talk to him. I'll fix this.

I'll fix this. That's what she said. Just like Lennon.

But there are some things you can't fix.

"Winter?"

I blink and for a second, I think I'm hearing Lennon, but the voice is pitched lower, more serious, and I look up into an equally serious pair of blue eyes. Jude stands in front of me, his hands on my forearms, holding me steady as if I was about to topple.

"Winter?"

I pull away, muttering something that isn't really words.

"What did you hear?" he asks.

I shake my head. It was nothing out of the ordinary. Just the normal sounds of a night forest and a night town.

"That's McCall's place," I say, pointing to a bungalow visible down the slope of the hill.

It's your basic single-story residence with a living room, kitchen, and a couple of bedrooms, a layout so standard I know the light I see comes from the kitchen at the rear.

I tell Jude all this. When I finish, he says, "You sure you're okay?" like he hasn't heard a word about the house.

"I'll be better once I've reported Marty's body. Just let me peek around the trees and see if McCall's truck is in the drive."

I cut through the forest. I've turned off the penlight—I don't want McCall spotting wavering lights in his backyard.

I stick to the darkest pathway, one foot in front of the other, my gaze fixed on the ground, being careful not to trip.

There's moss on the trees, thick and dangling moss, and I wind my way past a few strands and then go to brush another out of the way and my hand hits something solid.

It hits with a thump, and something swings and I duck, thinking it's a booby trap. A pale blur strikes my cheek and I grab for it, and Jude is letting out a cry, and then I see what I'm grabbing for.

It's a hand.

There's a hand dangling in front of me.

I fall back and my gaze swings up and I see . . .

I'll fix this, Win.

I'm back in my shack, on that long ago night, and I'm rubbing sleep from my eyes.

It's Colt, Cadence says. *He . . . he didn't take it well. He'll be fine. I just thought I should get away tonight, and I didn't figure he knew about this place. I'm sorry.*

It takes a moment for my groggy brain to realize what Cadence is saying. That the noise outside is her boyfriend, who has tracked her down to the shack. That she's been lying awake waiting for him.

She's afraid.

My sister is afraid.

That's why she came here with me. She's hiding. He's angry, and she's afraid of what he'll do.

Why didn't she tell me?

Why didn't I notice?

She's rising, but I push up fast, grab my switchblade, and run to the door.

"Winter! No!"

I ignore her. If Colt is pissy because she's going to college, he can take that up with me. I'm the one who talked her into it.

I yank open the door before she can stop me, and I race out and—

"Winter?"

"Get back in—" I wheel and see . . . not my sister. It's a guy. A stranger. In the forest.

"Winter?" The guy steps forward. It's Jude.

My brain stutters, like it's trapped between past and present. He's talking, but all I hear is the blood pounding in my ears.

Get Cady back inside.

Don't let her see . . .

Don't let her see . . .

I turn slowly. There's a body hanging in front of me. A body in a tree. I look up into its face. Into Colton's face, his tongue protruding, eyes bulging, rope around his neck, the over-weighted limb going *creak-creak* as his body sways.

Get Cady back inside.

Don't let her see this.

Colton wanted her to see it. Wanted her to step out in the morning and this to be the first thing she sees.

I spin, but it's not Cadence behind me. It's Jude, and he reaches for my forearms and says, "Let's go over here. Just step aside. I'll handle this."

I'll handle this.

I'll fix this.

Here, Cady, let me fix your problem for you. Tell Colton

you're going to college. If he loves you, he'll go with you or he'll wait. There. See how easy that was? Nothing to it. Problem solved.

"Just step over here," Jude says. "You don't need to look at that."

Jude's hands tighten around my arms as he steers me away, and that snaps me back long enough to look over my shoulder and see Owen McCall hanging from the tree.

I dig in my heels and pull my hands free and rub them over my face.

"Sorry," I say. "Sorry, sorry, sor—"

"Stop."

"I just—"

"And I'm asking you not to apologize. Come over here and sit where you can't see it."

"I don't need—"

"Yes, you do." He takes my arm, firmer now. When I yank free, he gives that sigh and says, "Winter . . ." like I'm a misbehaving toddler, and that evaporates the last of my memory fog and I say, "I'm going to ask you not to do that again."

A frown. "Do what?"

"Touch me."

"I'm not . . ." He trails off and when he looks at me, it's this deep, scrutinizing stare that feels like it's going straight into my brain, ripping off the cover to look inside.

"Okay," he says.

"I don't mean—"

"No explanation needed. If you're falling, I'll still grab your arm, but otherwise, no."

I mumble something before turning back toward—

"You don't want to do that," he says when I find myself facing the swinging corpse again. "Come on this way. Sit."

There's something white on McCall's shirt. I hurry over. Jude jogs up beside me and swings into my path, his hands raised to ward me off.

"Look," he says. "I'm not going to pry, but I will take a wild stab and guess this isn't your first suicide. You aren't going to make it better by pretending you're not freaked right now. I'm seriously going to ask you to—"

"There's a note."

"I see that. And if I can read it without disturbing the body, I will do so and tell you what it says. You will retreat behind those trees and call the police."

"Is that an order?"

"No. If you like, we can talk through your trauma and prepare you to deal with the body hanging behind me. You can tell me what happened before and—"

"Fine. Read the note."

I find a convenient tree to lean against as I wait.

"It's a confession," he calls after a moment. "He says Marty ran across the road in front of him. It was late, and there may have been alcohol involved—which he clarifies to mean the kid might have been drinking, not him."

"Bullshit."

"Agreed. He knows it's too late to prove it, and even in his confession he's lying to protect himself and dishonor the dead. Couldn't even confess properly, could you, asshole?"

Jude shakes his head, and when moonlight falls on his face, I see not anger but disappointment. As if he hoped for better, even from a stranger. As if he always hopes for better. As if he's always disappointed.

When he reaches me, he's stone-faced again. He glances at my hands, and I wonder why, and then remember what I was supposed to be doing.

I call it in. This time, someone answers.

"I've found . . . ," I begin. "I've found a body in the woods. Behind Owen McCall's place. It's—it's Mr. McCall."

Jude waits with me. I tell him the direction I expect the police to come and point out the best route for him to make his escape. When lights flash in McCall's drive, I say, "That's them." Jude grunts. A car door opens and slams shut, and I say, "You need to go." Jude starts walking . . . toward McCall's drive.

I jog after him. "Not this way," I whisper as Jude runs a hand through his hair, still walking. "You need to—"

Deputy Slate appears. He looks like he's been woken from sleep and is none too happy about it. He shines his flashlight on us. Jude picks up his pace, shoulders squared, hand extended.

"Jude Bishop," he says.

thirty-three

WE LEAD THE DEPUTY TO MCCALL'S BODY. MY TALK WITH SLATE gets off to a bad start when he calls for backup to help cut McCall down and I say, "You'll need a doctor, too."

"For what? To confirm he's dead?" Slate smacks McCall's corpse. "Yep, pretty sure ol' Owen's not faking it."

Jude stares like he's wondering if Slate has been drinking tonight. Sadly, there isn't so much as a whiff of alcohol fumes.

I tell my story, starting with the list. I'm not sure if Slate is even listening. He rips the note from McCall and reads it, lips moving, earning me an *Is he for real?* look from Jude.

When I finish explaining, Slate turns to Jude. "Did you put her up to this?"

"Up to what?"

"This story about finding Marty's body under Owen's pot field?"

"It's there," I say.

"Of course it is. Says so right here." He waves the note and then looks at Jude. "Bet that put a damper on your night, huh? Get one of our pretty girls into the forest, think you've hit the hick-town jackpot, and bam, dead body hanging from a tree. Really spoils the mood."

Jude's mouth opens just enough to say "Do you know who I am?" and there's strain there, as if it's a tactic he'd really rather not resort to but this is the only solution if we don't want to be here all night.

"Yeah," Slate says. "Some vagrant who's convinced Winter he's the governor's son."

"Congressman," Jude says, his voice tight. "Peter Bishop is a congressman. The state representative for Kentucky district six."

"Show some ID."

Jude goes still.

"I said, show me your ID. That's not a request. I'm an officer of the law, and if I ask for your ID—"

"I don't have to present it unless you're charging me with something."

"You *want* to be charged?"

"All right. Forget who I am. In fact, forget what Winter said. You don't believe she found that kid's body? Fine. She's officially reported it. Winter? Let's—"

"Hands against the tree," Slate says.

Jude sighs. Apparently I'm not the only one who makes

his life so very difficult. "There's no need for that, Deputy. I'm leaving, and I apologize for any misunderstanding—"

"Turn around. Hands up." Slate pulls his gun. "Now."

Jude does not sigh. His eyes narrow. His jaw tenses. It's only a split-second reaction before he relaxes, but it's enough for me to catch a glimpse of a very different guy. One who is not nearly so imperturbable, not nearly so inclined to respond with a soft sigh of resignation.

Then that calm look returns, and Jude raises his arms over his head and turns around.

Slate lowers the gun and reaches for Jude's back pocket, where I can see the bulge of a wallet.

"I presume you are checking my identification," Jude says. "It's fake. I'll say that up front. My birth date is actually correct on the ID, though, which means I'm not using it to sneak into bars. That would be illegal." He pauses. "Technically, so is the carrying of fake ID. As is the obtaining of it. . . ."

"Are you trying to be a smart-ass, son?"

"No, just honest. You'll realize it's illegal so I might as well admit to that. If you want to press charges—"

"You think you're clever, don't you?"

Jude purses his lips. "Not particularly. But if that's another way of asking if I'm trying to be a smart-ass—"

Slate cuts him off by waving Jude's ID in front of me. "Jude Hardy. Not Bishop. *Hardy*. And this isn't a fake ID. I know the difference."

"It's a *good* forgery," Jude says. "However, you'll note on the license that—"

Slate throws the wallet and cards at Jude. "Save your

stories for pretty girls. Girls from other towns. I catch you around here again, Mr. Jude Hardy, and I'll let Winter's daddy deal with you. And let me tell you, Robbie Crane is one ugly-ass drunk who don't like no one messing with his baby girls. So get the hell out of my town. And, Winter? Get home before I do tell your daddy what kind of trouble you've been up to."

"Jude Hardy?" I say as we loop back into the forest.

"It *is* a fake ID." He holds out the license. "See the—"

"I'm not questioning who you are. I saw enough photos online. But Hardy? Really? I suppose you thought you were being obscure."

He gives a snort of surprised laughter.

"Yes, I got the literary reference," I say. "It's not *that* obscure."

"Your deputy didn't get it."

"Our deputy can barely read the Sunday comics."

We circle past a stand of trees and he says, "I will admit, I thought you were exaggerating about the local law enforcement."

"And now you know."

"If you can give me a lift home," I say as we walk, "I'd be grateful. Normally I don't mind walking through the woods. . . ."

"Definitely not tonight. In fact, I'm going to strongly suggest you stay clear of them as much as possible."

"I will. The problem is that around here, it's all woods. So

I'd appreciate a lift. I can direct you down back roads if you'd rather not cut through town."

"I . . ." He checks his watch. "Oh. Yeah. It's late."

"Yep. If that means you don't have time to drop me off, I can walk."

"I'm not exactly running on a schedule. It's just . . ." He checks his watch again, as if the result has miraculously changed. "No, yeah, it's late."

"Spit it out."

"Okay, yeah, I was hoping we could talk, but your dad wouldn't appreciate you bringing a guy over at two a.m. Especially not after what that deputy said."

"That deputy is full of shit, in case you didn't figure that out. But no, bringing you home would be a very bad idea. My father might not be home, but if he is . . ." I shrug. "It isn't a good idea."

"Is he *likely* to not be there? You shouldn't be alone. I've got a motel room. You're welcome to stay with me. Call your father and tell him you're spending the night with a friend." He grabs the helmet from the bike as we reach it.

"Your motel room?"

"Right." He looks over, brow furrowing in genuine confusion as he sees my expression. "Oh. Yeah. I guess that might sound a little weird. I'm . . ." He gives a distracted wave. "I wasn't thinking."

"I know."

I can't imagine there are many eighteen-year-old guys who'd invite a girl to spend the night in their motel room and not realize that could sound suspicious. But Jude really is that guy, and maybe it's just because he's temporarily distracted, but I get the feeling he's been very distracted for a very long time. Or maybe not so much distracted as focused, like me. He has certain things on his mind and they preoccupy that mind to the exclusion of everything else.

"Let's go to your motel room and talk," I say. "By the time we do, it'll probably be morning anyway."

thirty-four

JUDE DRIVES ON BACK ROADS AND DROPS ME OFF WITH A KEY AT the motel rear, saying, "Go on in. I'll wait ten minutes. Make sure no one's watching."

I could tell him that I'm sure no one will see us at this hour and if they do, they'll be too wasted to recognize me.

I'm inside, sitting cross-legged on the bedspread, when he enters, sodas in hand.

"Is Ale-8, okay?" he asks. "The Coke machine's down."

"Thanks."

"And as you can see, two beds. So if you do want to shut your eyes, it's okay." He sets the sodas on the nightstand between the beds. "I'll ask, though, that you let someone know you're here. Just a friend or whatever, so someone knows where you are and who you're with."

I type a text. And then I send it to myself. His warning is

basic safety, but also reassurance that he's not going to knife me in my sleep. Not after he's told me to let someone know who I'm with.

After I hit send, I wonder if I was supposed to counter with "No, no, that's fine, I trust you." But his nod is genuine satisfaction. No games here. No need to read between the lines. I like that.

"Are we going to talk about Lennon?" I ask.

"Yeah." He's sitting cross-legged on the bed and he fusses, adjusting and getting comfortable, but mostly just fussing. He uncaps the Ale-8 and chugs it. Then he rubs his thumb over the label.

"Jude?" I say. "I'm not trying to invade your family's privacy, but for my own safety, I need to know why you would suspect your brother of lying about Edie."

"I know. I'm not trying to duck the subject again. I realize that was wrong. It's just . . ." He uncrosses and refolds his legs. "I've never discussed this. With anyone. And I should have. That's the problem. I had a responsibility to talk to someone about it, but I didn't know who or how. I'm the only person I can trust to understand Lennon, to have his best interests in mind."

"I would never share—"

"And then I left," he says, as if I didn't speak. "I decided I was the only person who could help him and I left. How does a brother do that?"

"You were dealing with your own issues."

He shakes his head sharply. "He's my brother. He was in trouble. I left. That's unforgivable."

I think of Cadence. Of all the times I've lain in my shack

thinking *How could you leave me?* and then hating myself for being so selfish. I know why she left. After Colton's suicide, she couldn't get away fast enough. Couldn't get me out of her sight fast enough.

But I needed you, Cady. I really was trying to help—if I was being selfish, I wouldn't have wanted you to go to college, right?

I need someone I could have sent that text to, the text that says where I am and who I'm with. But you left. And not just when you walked through that door. You left me long ago, on the first weekend you decided I was fine at home alone with Dad.

"I know there are millions of kids who'd gladly trade their lives for mine and Lennon's," Jude is saying. "But that doesn't mean there aren't problems. It just means we can't talk about them. Not with anyone except each other. We do have friends. Hell, Lennon has probably a hundred numbers in his contact list but . . . ."

"Lots of guys you'd hang around with on a Friday night. Not lots you can share your secrets with."

"Exactly. Sometimes, for me, it felt like being in the middle of this huge party, with all these people and all that noise and I'm in a bubble, and no one can really get to me and I can't really get to them. I—" He runs his hand through his hair. "Lennon. This is about Lennon. It's not the same for him. But he still has problems—real problems—no one else knows about because no one sees that side of him. They just see Lennon Bishop— the guy everyone wants to hang with."

"The charming side," I say. "He can make people like him, even if that's not who he really is."

"What?" He catches my expression. "No, it's not a front. It just . . . ."

"It doesn't go very deep. He can act like he cares about people, but it's superficial."

"No." Frustration laces his voice. "I know what you're getting at—suggesting he's a sociopath, the charming fake who doesn't give a shit about anyone but himself. He's not like that."

"Okay."

Jude shifts on the bed. "But he *is* charming. He can be manipulative—he knows exactly how to get what he wants. He's impulsive, too. Seriously, crazily impulsive. He doesn't think before he acts, and sometimes people get hurt, and he *does* feel bad about that, but it won't stop him. It's like he just can't help himself. He lies. A lot. Like you saw. I used to tell myself they weren't real lies. He's creative and exuberant, and he can't help twisting the facts if he can make a better story. But that's an excuse. He lies. Compulsively."

"Which is why you think he lied about Edie."

He says nothing, just takes another gulp of soda.

"Okay," I say. "Let's imagine the impulsiveness and the lying and the need for attention all roll together, and he decides to fake having been attacked. He could have somehow inflicted those injuries on himself. But Edie really is missing. So somewhere in that story, there's more than a grain of truth. There has to be."

He nods, his gaze on the green bottle as he rubs his nail over the label.

"Jude . . ."

"I'm afraid." He sets the bottle aside. "I'm just *afraid*. For him. For Lennon. To even be thinking . . ."

"Tell me about Lennon," I say.

He reaches for his Ale-8 again and then stops and folds his hands in his lap instead. "It's not as if he's ever done anything or I suspect he has or anything like that. Just things that . . . worry me."

"Spit it out, Jude."

"Okay, so . . . For example, horror movies. Say a new one comes out, one of those gory ones, and our friends want to go see it. Lennon won't. Absolutely won't. He avoids movies like that, games like that, books like that. But sometimes I've caught him watching, online or whatever, and he laughs it off, says he's trying to build up a tolerance. But . . ."

"You think he avoids them because he likes them more than he should."

Jude walks to the window and looks out. "I'm reading too much into it. I do that. An idea gets in my head, and I can't get it out."

I remember how Lennon stared at One-Eye strung up in the tree. I remember the look on his face, the one I mistook for shock. He'd been unable to pull his gaze away until I did it, and then he flushed, embarrassed. Not embarrassed at his shock. Embarrassed to need his gaze pulled away.

I also remember when I told Jude how Lennon had reacted. How Jude tensed, the reaction seeming odd.

"Your brother has a fascination with violence," I say. "He's afraid of what it makes him think. He—"

"Can we drop this now?" He turns, still at the window. "I've put the possibility out there. I feel like I'm betraying my brother by even suggesting it. This is a guy who's never even been in a fistfight. I have. I'm the one with a temper. Lennon isn't like that. At all."

"Okay. But we need to discuss—"

"No. I put it out there. I warned you. That's enough."

He pulls his keys from his pocket and strides across the room, saying, "This was a mistake. I'm sorry." He yanks open the door. "The room's paid for. Stay as long as you want. Just lock up behind me."

thirty-five

I SIT IN THE MOTEL ROOM AND STARE AT THE DOOR. I SHOULD GO after Jude. He's in pain, and I should have responded with a little human compassion.

I've screwed up. I handled it wrong. I failed to do something.

I failed to do *anything*.

Jude confessed his worst fears to protect me. And I sat here like he was lecturing me on motorcycle maintenance. No reaction. No empathy. No sympathy. When he wanted to take a break, I kept pushing. I required more data.

Analytical as always.

Cold as always.

I get up and go to the door. I heard the rev of the bike as he took off. Now I step outside and walk across the front lot, but I can't even see the taillight.

Long gone.

I head back to the motel room. I'll text him and apologize. . . .

I twist the handle and nothing happens. I try again. I left the key on the nightstand, but I didn't lock the door. I crouch and peer through the crack. It's definitely locked.

Because it does that automatically. It's just been a very long time since you stayed in a motel.

Shit.

I look toward the front office. It's dark. I could go see if there's a way to contact the manager, but . . .

Uh, yeah, sorry for waking you at four a.m. I left my key in the room. It's not actually mine, though. I think it's under Jude Hardy. Or maybe Jude Bishop. I can say for sure that the guy who checked in is about six feet tall, late teens, dark curly hair, and drives an old motorcycle. Is that enough?

I shake my head and head for the road. It's the main highway running through Reeve's End—Route 11—two lanes of blacktop winding and dipping through the hills and hollers. I'm walking along the dirt shoulder, hunched against the cool night. A couple of cars zoom past. Then one slows, an older male voice saying, "You need a lift, hon?" I don't look over. There's no leer in his voice, which probably means it's a genuine offer, but I can't take that chance, so I say, "No thank you, sir," and he continues on.

The next car that stops is a transport truck going the opposite way. The woman driving puts down the passenger window to say, "I hope you're not hitching a ride, sugar."

I walk over and shake my head. "No, ma'am. Just got in a fight with my friends."

"And they left you on the roadside at this hour? Not very good friends. Hop in, and I'll turn around and give you a lift."

"I 'preciate the offer, ma'am, but I'm almost home."

She gives me a hard look. "Well, I won't argue. Just because I'm a woman doesn't mean it's a safe ride. You got anyone you can call?"

"I got this." I take out my switchblade.

She chuckles. "All right, then, sugar. Pick up the pace and get yourself home and give those friends shit next time you see them."

"I will, ma'am. Thank you."

I think of getting off the road, but there's nowhere to go. Forest and rock line both sides. I pass a side road—dirt, with far less chance of traffic, but that feels even more dangerous than this dark and empty paved highway.

I'm still considering my options when a pickup squeals around a tight curve without slowing. I get as far on the shoulder as I can. It flies past. Then brakes squeal, and the truck goes into a slide, the stink of rubber filling the air.

It stops. Backs up.

"Well, hey there," a voice calls as the truck rolls alongside me. Male. Young. Drunk. I don't need to look to identify all three. I grip my switchblade a little tighter.

"You from round here?" another voice calls, a little farther away—the passenger, I presume.

"Course she ain't," the first says. "You see a third eye? A harelip? Definitely not from the local breeding stock. Or, should I say, local *in-breeding* stock."

They both laugh, their voices following as I keep walking.

The first says, "Well, actually, judging by those ratty

sneakers and the holes in that jacket, I bet she is local. She just got lucky and turned out purty. What are you? Fourteen? Got yourself a husband yet?"

They both snicker and the second says, "She's checking out her cousins but ain't ready to commit till she's fifteen."

More drunken snickering.

"I bet she's real keen to meet some boys who ain't blood relations," the first says. "How 'bout you slow down, girl. See what's on offer."

"How about you boys just keep on driving," I say.

"Ooh, you hear that, Jerry? She talks like a normal person."

Which is more than I can say for them. They're obviously from the area, given that dialect. They're just from a town with a higher median income than mine, which isn't hard to manage.

"I'm on my way to work," I say. "And I'm running late."

"My, my, you do sound all proper. Bet you think you're too good for us, huh."

I try not to give a sigh remarkably like one of Jude's.

"If you're looking for some fun, I'm afraid this is a dry county," I say. "But there's a bar 'bout five miles down. Not exactly open legally at this hour, but they'll serve you."

That seems reasonable, polite and friendly but not overly so.

"We want to have fun with you, girl."

"Sorry," I say. "I really do need to get to work—"

The squeal of the brakes cuts me short. The truck stops. I keep going, my breath coming a little harder.

Please don't. Please—

The truck doors open and slam shut. I turn. It's two guys,

maybe in their midtwenties. One is heavyset, wearing a too-tight T-shirt. The other swaggers like he's six four, though he's barely my height and not much heavier.

"Look, guys," I say. "I'm really just trying to get to work—"

"You want money?" The heavyset one yanks a twenty from his wallet. "What will I get for this?"

"If you continue on to that tavern I mentioned, it'll buy you four beers easy."

"You think you're smart, girl?"

My tone didn't hold a drop of sarcasm. But he's made up his mind and he's drunk. Reasonable isn't going to cut it.

"My boss is expecting me. He's at that gas station right down the road. My shift starts at five. He'll be watching for me."

"Then go ahead and run. See if you make it. We'll try to grab you in the truck, but we're a little loaded. Might hit you by accident."

I glance toward the forest.

"If you wanna play hide-and-seek, I ain't gonna stop you."

I squeeze the switchblade hidden in my hand and size them up.

The smaller guy lunges. I evade his grip as the bigger guy charges. I see him coming, and I hit the switch on the blade and slash. I catch him in the arm, and he staggers back, yowling as if I stabbed him through the heart.

The smaller guy snarls, "You little—" but the rest is drowned by the roar of an engine. A single headlight zooms down the road.

The larger guy takes a swing at me . . . using the arm I just cut. He yowls again, the strike aborted even as I duck.

I back up, switchblade ready. "Just let me get to my job. That's all I'm asking. You boys head to that tavern I mentioned—"

"Give me the knife," the smaller one says.

He makes no move to take it from me, just puts out his hand, like I'm going to shrug and pass it over. His friend edges forward, watching my blade, trying to figure out how to grab me without getting close enough to be cut again.

Jude skids the bike to a halt beside us, his foot going down to stop it as it slides. The helmet is still attached to the back and his hair is wild and dusty. He exhales as he rakes it back and swings off the bike.

"There you are." He walks over and puts his arm around me, pulling me over for a quick kiss on the forehead. "I'm sorry, babe. I shouldn't have taken off. I was mad and not thinking straight." He looks at the two men. "I'm guessing you guys were offering her a lift. Thanks. She shouldn't have been walking at this hour. Totally my fault. Being an ass." He gives a wry smile and extends his hand to them. "Thank you."

They stare like he's speaking Swahili. I carefully close my blade, pocket it, and say, "They were just asking how far I was going. I was going to let them drive me to the next town. But if you're not going to kick me off again . . ."

"I didn't kick you off, babe. You—" He exhales. "And we're not going to fight. Just grab the helmet and hop on. Thank you again, guys."

"That's a nice bike you got there," the smaller one says.

Jude laughs. "No, it's a piece of shit. But it does the job. Now, if you'll excuse—"

"Nice bike. Nice girl. I bet you get all the nice things, don't you, city boy? Just come here and start talking fancy and expect us to give you everything you want, including our pretty girls."

Five minutes ago they were mocking my background, and now we're kith and kin.

The guy keeps talking. "We're going to take the girl, and we're going to take the bike, and you're going to call your daddy to come get you."

Jude shakes his head. "No, guys. Just don't, okay? If I've insulted you somehow, I apologize. I just want to get her some breakfast and win back the boyfriend points I lost by being a jackass—"

The smaller guy takes a swing. Jude yanks me out of the way, sidesteps the blow, and grabs the guy by the wrist, and then he's got the guy twisted around, arm pinned behind his back. In the same amount of time, I get as far as pulling my blade from my pocket. The bigger guy doesn't even manage to move.

"Let's not do this," Jude says, and his tone is so calm that the smaller guy stops struggling and gapes over his shoulder.

"I can break your arm with one twist," Jude says. "I'd rather not."

"You smug—" The smaller guy lunges forward to get free. Jude yanks his arm and there's a crack. An actual crack. The guy screams and stumbles around, cradling his arm.

"That was your wrist," Jude says, still calm. "You'll need to get a cast, but it's not as bad as a broken arm."

"You—you broke—"

"I warned you." Annoyance prickles in Jude's voice, like when I gave him hell for tossing me around in the shack. *Attack me, and that's what you'll get. Ignore my warning, and that's what happens. If you start something with me, don't complain about the consequences. I don't have time for that shit.*

Out of the corner of my eye, I see the bigger guy run at Jude. I lunge to stop him. The next second, I'm falling, my hand empty, and Jude's in front of me.

"Stop right there," he says to the bigger guy.

The guy roars and charges. I see Jude swing. I see the blade flash in the moonlight. I see it go in and fly out and blood flicks from the blade and the guy falls, yowling and gripping his leg, blood soaking through his fingers.

"You're fine," Jude says. "It only hit fat and muscle." He turns to me. "Get on the bike, please. Take the helmet."

The bigger guy is on the ground now. The smaller one stands there, holding his wrist, saying, "What the *hell*? You crazy son of a bitch."

Something flickers in Jude's eyes, but he only gives this weird nod, like acknowledgment. Then he waves me toward the bike. I take an unsteady step toward it and then another, and I'm nearly there when the smaller guy makes one last attempt—this time running at me. I'm turning fast, ready to defend myself, but Jude's already sending the guy flying with one perfect punch. It's then, as he hits, that Jude's mask cracks and I see rage, honest rage. But he blinks it back, and by the time the guy strikes the ground, Jude's face is expressionless again.

"You've had too much to drink," he says to the two. "You're not in any shape to fight and trying only makes this worse. We're leaving now. You'll want to get to a hospital for a cast and stitches."

Their eyes flash, as if in insult, but Jude's only being rational. Still trying to talk them down, to avoid prolonging the altercation even when it's clear he'd win.

He waves me to the bike. I hesitate. I'm trembling, and there's part of me screaming to run, just run. But I take the helmet and when he climbs on, I get behind him.

He starts the bike. The guys stay on the ground as we ride off.

thirty-six

WE TURN ONTO A SIDE ROAD AND PULL TO THE SHOULDER. DAWN is breaking, but it's still quiet.

"I think I should go home," I say.

Jude turns off the ignition and twists to look back at me. "I scared you."

I climb from the bike and remove the helmet. "I'd just—"

"You can say it. I did. I could see that. I have a temper."

"That wasn't a temper."

"Yes, it was." He climbs off the bike and puts up the kick-stand. "The first time I reacted like that, I was eight. I went off on a guy at school. I can't even remember why. We got into it, and I lost my temper. He had to go to the hospital."

I tense. "What did you do to him?"

"Cracked a couple of ribs."

I relax. "A schoolyard fight."

"Just because I didn't put the guy in traction doesn't mean I'm okay with what I did, Winter. Ten years later, I still can't look him in the eye, even if he's long over it. I lost my temper. Totally lost it, and if no one had intervened, it could have been a lot worse. My mother freaked. She pulled me from school for a month, had all these assessments done. When shrinks tried to shrug it off, she'd find another one until she was absolutely convinced I wasn't okay."

Had she seen signs of trouble with Lennon, even then? Signs that made her worry about Jude?

"She didn't want me embarrassing the family," he says, as if I asked the question aloud. "Considering where we came from, me and Lennon, sometimes I think she's always watching."

Watching for signs that the boys' biological parents came from a place not much better than Reeve's End. As if Mrs. Bishop adopted children who weren't quite as high up on the evolutionary scale as she was, and perhaps even after pouring all that money into smoothing their rough edges, it was like putting a Neanderthal in a fancy suit and teaching him proper English, and underneath it all lurked that half-wild creature.

I hate his mother for that. Which isn't fair—I've never met the woman and might be totally misjudging. I still hate her.

Yet something is wrong here, at least with Lennon. And it's a lot more disturbing than a propensity for violent outbursts.

"So lots of therapy," Jude continues. "The upshot being that two counselors recommended martial arts for self-discipline. My mother said no—she didn't consider those real sports. But for once our father argued. Mom finally agreed I could get training. Just me; not Lennon. I was good at it. Really good. When my coach suggested I compete, though, my mother fired him. I kept training on my own. It taught me discipline, how to control my temper. Also taught me how to defend myself without going off like I did on that kid in school."

"Okay."

He eyes me. "You think I went too far with those two tonight."

"I didn't say—"

"You do. You think I shouldn't have broken his wrist. I shouldn't have stabbed the other guy. And this is where we're going to disagree. I tried to avoid a fight. When it happened, I ended it quickly. And the truth, Winter, is that I'm okay with that. I don't regret what I did to them. Which is probably why you're wondering if Lennon is the only brother you should be scared of. Maybe you're right. But I'm not going to apologize, and I'm not going to say I'll never do something like that again. If you want to leave, I understand. Hop back on the bike, and I'll take you home."

When I hesitate, he says, "All right. I'll call you a cab, then. I'll cover the fare."

He just broke a guy's wrist. Stabbed another guy in the leg. That should be a clear sign to run, as fast as I can. But his "victims" were threatening me with worse, and while I think I could have gotten away if Jude hadn't shown up, my attempts to defend myself had only riled them up. He'd stopped them.

I still reel at the suddenness of that violence, the almost perfunctory way he handled the situation. Face a threat; put it down. It's the same part of me that still bristles recalling how he threw me aside in the cabin. He had no compunction about hurting me. Not if I came at him.

I don't know how to handle that.

I'm accustomed to Bert, someone who lashes out in anger, needing no provocation. Someone who'll blame me after the fact—*you should know to stay out of my way when I've been drinking.* Someone who'll deny the damage—*stop giving me that look, Winter, it was just a tap.* Endless blame and denial. *I'm trying here, and you need to understand that.*

When I don't reply, Jude says, "I need to make sure you're okay, Winter. That means I'm a little stuck here. If you don't want me around, I should leave you alone. But that isn't safe. So either you let me drive you to town or you let me call you a cab and wait until it comes."

I want to find Edie. I want to find Lennon, whatever he may have done.

And I want to stay with Jude. Even if I felt I could pursue this alone, I don't want to. That's the hardest part.

Jude is a puzzle I have to solve. A puzzle I feel, uncomfortably, that I need to solve. I don't understand him, and I want to.

That's not because he's a cute boy. Lennon is the kind of guy who, if he went to my school, I would have a bit of a crush on. Nothing I would ever act upon. But I would sneak glances at him, and I would think he was cute and funny and charming and sweet and smart, and that it would be nice to get to know him better.

Jude is more. He *is* cute. He is smart. He can even be sweet. But he's more than all of that and it's the rest that I want to get to know better. I just want . . .

I don't even know what I want. To solve the puzzle, I guess. It goes back to that, and I don't know if that's reducing him to an enigma I need to crack. I have never in my life met someone I want to understand the way I do Jude.

"I know you don't want to discuss Lennon," I say. "You want to just throw the possibility out there and consider me warned. But we need to discuss exactly what we're saying when we say he might have lied. Exactly how he could be involved. If you think he took Edie—"

"No," he says. "I absolutely do not. No matter what's happened since I left, it can't have gotten that bad."

"Which means things *have* gotten worse since you left."

He flinches.

"I'm not blaming—" I begin.

"No. Honesty, right? Yes, he's been different. Secretive. He was never like that with me. We had an agreement—no secrets. So I thought he was trying to get my attention. I've always been the one who gets him out of trouble, and the surest way to bring me running back is to make me worry."

"You thought he was manipulating you into coming home."

He nods. "It's been hard on him. Me leaving. He doesn't understand. I'm not sure I understand. But yeah, I thought he was acting secretive, knowing that's the one thing that would get me home: him needing me."

Except he did need you. He always needed you. That's the problem. You feel responsible, but at some point, you need to step away. Yet if you do that and something goes wrong, you'll never forgive yourself. Which is why you came back, guns blazing, to do whatever it took to find him.

I don't say that aloud. He already knows it.

"You don't believe Lennon could have hurt Edie," I say. "But his story about helping her is clearly a lie, and she is missing. So the alternative is . . ." I think it through, piecing the clues together, and then say, "A middle ground. He's involved but not the perpetrator. He's gotten mixed up in something. Mixed up with the person responsible."

"The person . . . ?"

"What if Lennon knows the person who did this. Maybe a friend who shares his . . ." I struggle for the right word. "Proclivities," I say, and I think it's the best one, but Jude flinches again so I say, "His interests, impulses. Someone who recognizes that in him and got Lennon mixed up in something he didn't condone."

As I say the words, those pieces clunk into place, backfilling the story. "Which is why he ran. Why he was beaten before he escaped. Why he said he could fix it. Because he knows the guy responsible."

Jude blinks, mouth slightly ajar.

"It makes sense, doesn't it? As a theory."

"It does." He takes time to do some thinking himself and says, "If he made a new friend, another guy who shares his . . . his issues. Someone who was ready to go further. Lennon meets him, and it's like . . . like meeting a girl you know is no good for you but you can't stay away. You keep it a secret from everyone."

"The other guy sees the connection he's looking for. If you're messed up, you want to believe others are, too—proof you're not a freak. He thinks Lennon wants what he does. So he kidnaps Edie. Tells Lennon to meet him."

"Lennon finds out what this guy has done and he freaks. They fight. Lennon escapes. You find him and he has to make up a bullshit story."

"Which convinces me not to go to the police or your parents. He's afraid of anyone finding out he was involved. He wanted to save Edie and fix it as much as he can."

"Then he realizes he's endangering *you*. So he leaves to go resolve it alone."

And after that? Well, neither of us speculates about after that. Lennon goes back to "fix" the situation and then two days pass and we hear nothing from him. Then someone starts stalking me.

Is Lennon still trying to find Edie?

Has he been taken captive himself?

Or worse?

If it played out as we think, then Edie is still alive. She is the first person this guy has ever taken. He was waiting until he had a partner, only to have that partner reject him.

"That's why he's coming after you," Jude says, in that uncanny way of his, as if he's answering an unspoken question. "Because he saw you with Lennon," he continues. "This guy saw that and if he's pissed with Lennon, he's going to target you." He goes quiet. Then he says, "But it fits, doesn't it? It fits everything we know."

I nod, and he smiles. A smile so real it startles me, as I catch a glimpse of the guy I saw in older pictures, the ones when they were children, ones that caught him off guard, talking to his brother or scoring a touchdown or backstage after accepting an award. Those rare, real grins from a rare, real boy.

This theory doesn't mean Lennon is okay. If he got caught

up in this, he has problems. He needs help. But he's still the person Jude knew him to be, under all the shadows and the confusion.

"All right, then," he says as he gets to his feet. "So the next step is to investigate this theory. First . . ." He checks his watch. "First, you can get some sleep while I talk to his friends. Okay?"

I'm not sleeping anytime soon, but I can't accompany him to talk to their friends—it'd raise too many questions. I agree and he drives me back to Reeve's End.

thirty-seven

BERT'S NOT HOME, THANKFULLY. THAT'S NOT SURPRISING, though—he rarely comes home Saturday nights. I head into my room and doze fitfully for a while. Then I'm up, lying in bed, working on my case notes, trying to unravel everything I've learned. It's past noon when Jude texts.

On my way. Talk?

I reply that I'm going to shower and change, and I'll meet him in the forest behind the trailer. I give directions, but ask him to please stay out of sight. I finish my notes and then I'm heading for the bathroom, when the trailer door opens.

"Winter."

Bert stands in the doorway.

I try not to tense, and say, "Hey. I'm just going to shower and head out."

"Eli Slate stopped me this morning. He says you found Owen McCall's body." Bert advances on me, and I sidestep as he says, "Eli told me there was a boy. But there is no boy, right, Winter? You swore there was no boy."

Jude's right. Lies do escalate. Time to stop this one.

"Yes," I say. "There's a boy—"

He slaps my face. I reel back, head thumping into the wall.

"I was trying to explain," I say.

"I asked if there was a boy and you said no."

"Because it's not like that. There's a boy I've been talking to. He's trying to find his brother, and it may have something to do with Edie Greene, who's missing, and I thought it might even have something to do with Cady."

His eyes narrow. "So this boy tells you something happened to your sister—"

"No, I just . . . I'm worried. I've been worried for a long time. That's why I asked about her yesterday. I thought if his brother and Edie disappeared, then there could be others."

"Like what? Owen McCall ran over more kids?"

"Of course not. Marty's death isn't connected. We just found that out while we were digging."

"Digging for what? A serial killer? I've seen those shows you watched with Cady, Winter. The books you read. Filling your head with garbage when you're supposed to be studying. Now this boy tells you there's a killer in Reeve's End, and you fall for it?"

"I didn't say—"

"You fall for the lies of some city brat who's only looking for some fun? That's what you are to this boy, Winter. A bit of fun. A chance to make up wild stories he can share with his buddies at college. A chance to get lucky with a hick girl too dumb to make him wear a rubber."

"I'm not—"

"Do you want to end up like your sister? Throwing her life away because some pothead says he loves her? Turning her back on her little sister because she tried to help?"

I blink. He's never acknowledged that I was trying to help Cadence.

"You are going to get out of this town, Winter. You're going to college, and you're not letting anything stop you. Not some loser local kid. Not some jackass college brat."

"It isn't like that. Jude and I aren't—"

"But that's what he wants. What he expects. And you'll convince yourself he loves you and you'll end up like your mother, married to the loser who got her knocked up at seventeen."

My mouth opens. It stays open as I stare at him. Then I say, "Mom . . . ?"

"How else do you think she ended up with me?"

"But . . . you . . . you had an engineering job. I remember—"

"I hauled garbage. So-called sanitation engineer. That's what your mother got. Her big prize in life. She was headed into college. Going to be a lawyer. Smartest girl in her class. Then she fell for me, the dropout who told her a thousand lies. She got pregnant. Her parents kicked her out. The loser boyfriend steps up, marries her, gonna do right by her and their kid." He waves around the trailer. "See how right he does?"

I stare at him. I don't know what he expects me to do, how he expects me to react.

"I told her I'd take care of you," he says. "I promised her that."

"Then why don't you?"

He comes at me. I dodge, but his hand catches my shoulder, shoving me back into the wall. When I try to get away, he grabs my arm and I yank and he releases me so fast that I skid, falling to one knee. I stay there, breathing hard, not daring to rise, not daring to look up, just measuring the distance between me and the door.

"She had no right to *ask*," he says. "I screwed up her life. I dragged her down with me. And then she expects me to take care of you girls? I could barely take care of myself. She looked after me. She kept me straight. She kept me clean."

Don't respond. Just don't respond.

I can't do it. I look up at him. "Then you should have told her that."

He lunges and I cringe, but he just feints my way, his face twisted in rage. "You don't think I did? I wanted to call her parents. They had money. They'd tried to get in touch for years, to see you girls, but she wouldn't let them. When she got sick, I wanted her to contact them. To at least let *me* contact them. Let them take you girls. She *begged* me not to. *Begged* me. What was I supposed to do? I made her that promise. What could I do?"

"Keep it," I say, and my voice is so cold that he doesn't lunge at me this time. He just stands there, teetering. Then he runs his hands over his face and through his hair, and when he lowers them, his expression is as cold as mine. "You don't think I tried? I screwed up. Again and again. Everything we'd saved went to trying to save her. She was the one who looked after the money, kept the bills paid. I never knew how. I told myself that was fine, I'd get us on our feet again. Only I couldn't. It just got worse and worse until we ended up in this shit hole, and do you know the only good thing about that, Winter?"

"What?"

"That you're never going to stay here. You aren't like your sister. You won't get comfortable and settle in. I made a mistake with her. I was too soft. I won't make that mistake with you. The minute you graduate, you're going to run as far as you can and you're never going to look back."

Silence falls. I stare at him. Then I take a slow step forward. "Is that your excuse?"

"It's not a—"

"You tell yourself this is for my own good? Hitting me is for my own good?" I stop in front of him. "You fell into that damned bottle and you gave up being a father and you hate your damned life and you hit me because it makes you feel better. What would Mom say if she saw that? You think she'd be proud of how you *motivate* your daughter?"

He slaps me. Slaps me so hard I stagger, and when he goes to grab me, I lash out, knocking him off me. He grabs my wrists, and I hurl myself away from him, and he lets go and I fly into his stack of bourbon bottles by the door, and they crash around me as I fall.

He comes at me, and I don't see his face. I just lift my hands to ward him off and the door flies open, Jude charging in. He sees me and puts his hands out, saying, "Don't move. There's glass everywhere. Stay where you are."

"Get away from her," Bert says.

Jude turns to him, in that slow way that makes me tense.

"I was going to say the same to you, sir," Jude says, his voice unnaturally calm. "Step away, please."

"I'm her father."

Jude looks from Bert to me, his gaze traveling from the broken bottles to my nose, dripping blood. He turns to Bert.

"Then maybe you should act like it," he says.

Bert charges. I say, "No!" and start to scramble up, but Jude only grabs Bert's arm and wrenches him around. Then he says, "Don't move, Winter. It's okay."

"Let me—" Bert says.

Jude flips him into a headlock before I can do more than inhale. Then he says, "I'm holding you until you agree to back off, sir. We are not going to fight, because your daughter is sitting in a pile of broken glass and if we fight, she will try to stop us, and she'll get hurt a lot worse."

Bert gives an experimental twist.

"Don't," Jude says. "If you give a shit about your daughter, you'll back away and let me clean up the glass."

"Don't you give me orders in my—"

"It's not an order. It's a plan to protect Winter from further harm. You might be okay with smacking her around, but I don't think you want her bleeding out. If you'd like to help me clear the glass, do that."

Bert grunts something. Jude takes it as agreement and carefully releases him. I brace, ready for Bert to swing or shove Jude, but once he's free, he stands stiffly, marches into the bathroom, and shuts the door.

Jude comes over and crouches in front of me. When I reach for a piece of glass, he says, "Uh-uh," and catches my sleeve, and I see that my hands are trembling. I remember when I brought Lennon, how ashamed I'd been. That was nothing compared to this. I feel as if I'm crouching here naked, completely exposed, and I want to sink into the floor.

When Jude's fingers touch my chin, I jump, and he steadies me and I see a tissue in his hand. He wipes the blood from my nose and murmurs, "Does that hurt?"

I shake my head. "It's not broken."

His lips compress, as if realizing this means I know what a broken nose feels like. And I want to say it was just once, but that sounds like I'm making excuses for my father.

"Hold it and tip your head back," he says.

"That's an old wives' tale," I say. "The proper way to deal with a bloody nose is to pinch the nose and lean forward."

"Ah, right. Forgot who I'm speaking to." He gives a faint smile and then starts clearing away the glass.

After a moment, he says, "I'm sorry for interfering. I heard a thud and raised voices, and I worried it was your stalker."

"Thank you for not doing anything to him."

"Doesn't mean I didn't want to," he says, his gaze on the glass as he moves it aside. "But that wouldn't help you."

And that, I realize, is the difference between Jude and Bert. Jude has a violent temper. He acknowledges it. He's learned to control it. It's a tool he can use, only when absolutely required.

He's still clearing glass when Bert comes from the bathroom. He has a box of bandages in one hand and a wet towel in the other. He hands me the towel and says, "I didn't push you into those bottles, Winter."

I say nothing.

"I slapped you. I got mad, and I slapped you. But then I was trying to catch you, to say I was sorry. You panicked, so I let you go, and you fell onto the bottles."

Jude looks up at him. "Does it matter?"

Bert scowls. "I wasn't talking to you, boy. I'm letting you clean up that glass because I don't want Winter getting cut. Then you're leaving. Walking through that door. Never seeing my daughter again."

"I believe that's up to her, sir."

Jude speaks in his usual calm tone, and Bert snaps, "Don't talk to me like I'm five."

Jude rises. "I will if you act like it."

I tense, ready to intervene, but Jude only says, "Is there a dustpan? So I can sweep up the glass?"

"I've got it," I say. The pieces are cleared away enough for me to get to my feet, and I'm steady enough to step over the rest. I clench my hands as I head for the kitchen, so Bert and Jude won't see how badly they're shaking.

Keep it calm. Like Jude. Calm and collected.

I get three steps before Bert advances and I stumble, Jude catching me.

"I wasn't—" Bert begins. Then he turns to Jude. "Get out of my house."

"Let's go," I murmur.

"Don't you dare, Winter," Bert says.

I swallow, hoping it smoothes my voice. "I'm helping Jude look for his brother, as I explained. His brother and Edie Greene. That is all we're doing."

"I said no."

For years there's been one principle I've lived by in this trailer—never turn my back on my father. And now I do.

At a snarl from Bert, I wheel to face him, but he's stalking in the other direction. Jude grabs the door and ushers me out.

thirty-eight

WE MAKE IT AS FAR AS THE EDGE OF THE FOREST.

"Stop right there," Bert says behind us. "Or I pull this trigger."

I turn and see the shotgun pointed at Jude. I start to leap forward, but Jude's fingers wrap around my elbow and he says, in a low voice, "You don't want to do that, sir."

"I won't. All you need to do is walk away. And, Winter? You come inside."

"It won't work," I say.

"Oh, I'm pretty sure it will. That boy doesn't want a chest full of shotgun pellets."

"I mean the gun," I say. "I jammed it. Edie taught me how."

"Why—?"

"So you can't use it on me."

His eyes widen. "I would *never*—"

"I can't take that chance. I'm going to leave and help Jude. I may not be back today. But that's all it is—helping him."

"No boy just wants to talk to you."

Jude clears his throat. "That's a little insulting—to Winter, to me, and to guys in general. I'm perfectly capable of controlling myself around her. I'm just very grateful that she's agreed to help me. The local police aren't interested, and she knows the area and the people."

"If you—" Bert begins, and Jude says, "I won't," before he can finish, but he can't resist adding, "Though I think any such choice would be your daughter's to make, not yours."

Bert's face tightens, but he only says, "You better come home tonight, Winter," and stalks to the trailer.

Once he's gone, Jude whispers, "Is there a place nearby where we can talk?"

I consider options and then say I have an idea and lead him along the forest's edge.

We walk into the local Baptist church. It's one of four—yes, four—churches in town, along with United Methodist, Presbyterian, and the Calvary Temple. There's also a second Baptist church just outside town, for those who split off when the local pastor opined that he wasn't convinced playing cards on Sunday was truly a sin, at least not on the same level as stealing from your neighbor.

"Services ended at noon," I say. "And they never lock the door."

"You know all the hidey-holes, huh?" Jude smiles and then falters, as if realizing *why* I know them all.

"Can I ask if you're okay?" he says, his voice low.

I manage a wry smile. "You can ask . . ."

"But you'd rather not talk about it."

"Yep."

He nods, and we move into the cool, dark building. He runs his fingers across the back of a pew, stirring the dust motes to dance in the colored light. There's exactly one stained-glass window, donated by a family nearly a hundred years ago. Otherwise, the church is like everything else in town—decently maintained but simple.

"So, church, huh?" he says. "You go?"

I shake my head. "You?"

"Used to. Kinda necessary for a politician's family in Kentucky."

"I suppose so. What denomination?"

He turns, a faint smile on his lips. "Now there's the question, and it's not as easy as one might think. My mother was Catholic, but that doesn't always play well. My father was Baptist, which was a little too fire-and-brimstone for his taste. So they chose something else. The question was, which? Definitely not evangelical. And it can't be too rare a denomination"—he switches to a stronger accent—"or folks'll reckon you're mixed up in some kinda weirdo cult, sacrificin' babies and such."

I laugh softly.

"They settled on Methodist, the second most common Protestant faith in Kentucky, making it a decent political choice."

"I take it you're not a fan of religion."

"No, I was fine with it. I like the sense of community. Our church was progressive in a lot of ways—none of the anti-this and anti-that bullshit. It was all about doing good works, being good people. I'm not looking to go back right now. But someday? When I have kids? I'd consider it, at least."

"A reasonable answer."

"I'm a reasonable guy."

Silence falls, and it grows awkward fast. I'm about to ask what he found out, talking to their friends. Then I see his gaze has fallen on the piano.

"I hear you're good at that," I say lightly, trying to lift the mood.

He shrugs and moves away to check out the stained-glass window. I watch him standing in the shards of light. Then I work up the courage to ask, "Could you play something?" As soon as I do, I regret it, because he tenses so fast you'd think he'd heard that shotgun click.

"Sorry," I say, words tumbling out. "That was rude. Presumptuous. We need to talk about the case, and I'm stalling."

"No. You're trying to forget. . . ." He clears his throat. "A distraction would be good, and I'd be happy to help. I just don't . . ." He looks at the piano. "I just don't. Not anymore."

"I'm sorry for bringing it up. As for your earlier question, I *am* fine. What you saw at the trailer? It happens."

"It shouldn't."

I realize my hands are shaking again and shove them into my pockets. "But it does. To lots of people. Usually worse. They deal. I'm dealing. So let's just move on and talk about—"

"Do you play?" he asks, pointing at the piano.

I can't help giving a choked laugh. "I am one hundred percent *not* musically inclined. I could barely manage the recorder. I'd love to play an instrument, but I don't have a lick of talent."

"Want a lesson?"

"That wasn't a hint."

"I didn't take it as one." He waves me to the piano. "Come on. Ten-minute lesson. Pick a song, any song."

He wants a distraction for me. I understand that—it's why he's had the sudden change of heart—and telling him no denies him the right to do something nice. So I pick a song. When I do, he's the one laughing, a sudden, startling whoop of laughter.

"No," he says, shaking a finger at me. "Absolutely not."

"You don't know it?" I say, biting back a smile.

"I can't help but know it. Every freaking word and note. And no. Never, ever, ever. Any song but that."

"Okay," I say. "Any other song. Your choice."

He opens the piano and sits on the bench. Then he pats the spot next to him. I take my seat. He shifts closer, bumping against me.

"I'm not flirting," he says.

I smile. "I know."

He puts his hands on mine. "Still not flirting."

"Still know."

"Okay, so we'll do the F major scale." He moves my fingers. "This is F."

He takes me through, his hands guiding mine. His touch is careful, gentle and light. I remember when Lennon took my hand in the forest. Later I realized that was the first time a boy ever held my hand. I didn't think of it at the time, and I wondered if it should have felt like some big milestone, to be commemorated in my mental diary. It wasn't, because it didn't feel any different than if a boy took my hand in gym class for a game.

When Jude takes my hand, I notice it. All of it. The way his touch feels, the warmth of his fingers, and I know it isn't meant to be *like that,* but I don't have the urge to pull away, as I usually do when someone touches me. Maybe it's because of what happened at the trailer. Maybe I still feel exposed, open in a way I haven't felt in so long. When he lays his hand on mine, there's a feeling of connecting with someone, of taking comfort in something as simple as a touch, and tears prickle at my eyelids.

He doesn't notice the tears as I blink them back. He's completely rapt in what he's doing, and when I see that, I'm completely rapt watching him. His face . . . I won't say it lights up. It isn't like that. But his expression is both relaxed and focused, in a way that mesmerizes me as I listen to his voice, leading me through the scale, as I feel his fingers on mine, watch his profile as his gaze sweeps over the keys. Then he turns and smiles, and my cheeks heat, but again he doesn't notice, only says, "Got that?"

"I . . . I think so."

He takes me through the scale one more time, and then says, "Now a song?"

I nod.

He guides me through the notes. It takes a second\to figure out what I'm playing, and when I do . . .

When I do, I feel . . .

The tears threaten again, and that's silly, because it's just a song, but I hear those notes and I'm thinking about him and . . .

When he looks over, he's grinning, waiting for a reaction.

"I—" I swallow fast and force a smile. "I thought you said any song *except* that one."

"Yeah, but you asked so nicely, I couldn't resist." He bumps my shoulder with his. "Just don't tell anyone. I have refused to play it since I was ten, and I get really cranky if I'm asked."

"I can tell."

He grins at me—a grin that makes my insides do things my insides have never done before. But if there's any sign of that on my face, he's oblivious to it, and he just leads me through a complete rendition of "Hey Jude." When it's over, he says, "Don't ever say I never gave you anything," and swings off the bench.

I play the first few notes again, just to see what he'll do, and he turns, making a face at me, and I feel that twist inside me again, but I cover it by sticking out my tongue and that makes him laugh. It's a wonderful laugh, and his face *does* light up then, as if he's accomplished something—made me forget what happened in the trailer. Even if it meant acting out of character and goofing off, it was worth it.

Only he hasn't just distracted me. In that laugh and that grin and even that face he makes, he shows me another side of himself. And to distract me, he did something he's obviously conflicted about—playing the piano. He was so sweet and considerate doing that, he's shown me yet another side, the same one I saw in the trailer, the guy who insisted on cleaning up the broken glass.

I could fall for you, Jude Bishop.

Maybe I already have.

But it doesn't matter. There's no harm in it, no danger that anything will come of it. I can blush and stammer, and he doesn't even notice. He's not his brother, the charming flirt, waiting for his chance to steal a kiss. Jude is a guy with a mission, everything focused on that mission. He's rock-solid and safe.

"Now, the story of my day's investigation," he says as he plunks down on the floor. He reaches into his jacket and pulls out a Hershey's and a Mars. "Candy bar?"

"Sure. Thanks."

He holds out both.

I shake my head. "You pick."

"Ladies first. We *are* in the South."

"They're your candy bars."

He sighs—I'm being difficult—but there's a smile with it. Then he closes his eyes, mixes them up, and tosses me one. It's the Hershey's. I tear it open and settle in as he starts to talk.

thirty-nine

WHAT JUDE LEARNED FROM THEIR FRIENDS SUPPORTS OUR HY-
pothesis, while not adding much to it. Lennon has been
sneaking around. He has been seeing someone. Their friends
assumed he'd just met an unsuitable girl. One, though, has a
different hypothesis.

"I saw him getting picked up last spring," he'd told Jude.
"After school, when he told us he was going home to study.
Only it wasn't your driver who picked him up. It was, uh, a
guy."

The friend didn't see much, just that it was the kind of car
he expected Lennon would get into—a luxury sedan. Tinted
windows meant the friend didn't get a good look at the driver,
but he was dark-haired and definitely male.

The friend's theory, then, was that the unsuitable lover
was male, which explained the secrecy.

So we had that much. Confirmation Lennon has been meeting someone. Confirmation that person seems to be a man.

"You need to go home," I say when Jude finishes. "See if you can find anything in his room."

When he hesitates, I say, "Yes, that's an invasion of his privacy. But under the circumstances . . ."

"Under the circumstances I don't give a shit about his privacy. The problem is that I, uh . . ." He fusses, uncrossing and recrossing his legs. "I can't go home. I've been barred. That's how my mother is handling this. I left, so the household staff is under strict orders not to let me back in. Which doesn't mean they won't, but if they're caught, it'll cost them their job."

"But you have an invitation."

He looks up. "Hmm?"

"Your mother *invited* you home tonight."

"Yeah, for a party. What she's really asking, though, is for me to clean up and come home, the prodigal son bowing his head at the door and asking for forgiveness. Publicly."

"Okay. I can see why you wouldn't want to do that."

"No, I would. For Lennon. I just . . ."

He inhales and he's clenching his fists, like I was earlier at the trailer. Trying to control trembling hands. This is more than *I feel like I was raised as a photo op.* That's a big deal—huge, I'm sure. But there is more to his decision to leave. I see that as I watch the turmoil in his face.

"Yes," he blurts. "Okay. Yes. I'll do this. We need to get into his room, and it's just a party."

"It's more than that. To you," I say, my voice low, and I expect him to balk. Before, he would have balked. Withdrawn. But now he gives a wan smile and says, "Yeah, but I'll survive."

"Do you want me to come along?" As soon as I say that, I flush, shaking my head. "No, that doesn't help, does it? Sorry."

"Actually, it *would* help. It'd be an excuse. Or it could be, if you don't mind, uh, playing my date."

"As long as you don't call me babe again."

He exhales in a whoosh, part relief, part laughter. "Deal. So I met a girl, and I want to take her home." He shifts. "Which is partly true, I guess."

"We'll make the story as close to the truth as we can. And, yes, I know you don't want work-arounds, but any dishonesty is for Lennon."

"You won't have to play a role. Not even 'girlfriend.' Just someone I met and I'm trying to get to know better, maybe even impress."

"That'll take some of the pressure off you, too. You're there with me, not to socialize or hang with your parents. It also gives us an excuse to poke around the house."

"Exactly."

"I suppose wardrobe is a factor, though."

"Hmm?" He seems lost in thought, his brain racing ahead.

"You said they expect you to clean up and come home. I'm guessing that means this is not proper party attire." I wave at my jeans.

"Shit. Right."

"I have Lennon's money. We can hit a thrift shop in the city."

"Good idea." He rises. "Okay, then. Let's go shopping."

* * *

Jude texts his mother to say he'll be there and he's bringing someone. His mother replies with, "Don't embarrass us," and I'm not sure if she's referring to how he'll dress or how he'll act or who he'll bring. All three, I suspect.

By the time we finally get to Lexington and find a consignment store open on a Sunday, it's five o'clock. The shop is just about to close, but Jude explains we have a party that night and it's "kinda an emergency." The shopkeeper takes pity and says she has work to do in the back and we have thirty minutes.

Jude finds two possible suits with a mere scan of the racks. Another five minutes to try them on and he's done.

"How's it going?" he says as he wanders over and sees me staring at the rack of cocktail dresses. He chuckles. "Yeah, it's a whole lot easier for guys. Black jacket. White shirt. Tie. Can't really go wrong. You girls . . ."

He trails off as he catches my expression. I have absolutely no idea where to even begin. I wouldn't know if a dress is out of style. I wouldn't know if it was appropriate for this type of party. I'm not even sure what size I wear.

He quickly says, "Way too many choices, huh? How about I butt in with some unwanted advice? Because that's what I do."

I nod wordlessly.

"Go with a dark color. Not black—everyone wears black. Dark blue, maybe? Or green? Above the knees, because you're not seventy. Maybe not sleeveless, because it's fall—or we can grab one of those little sweater things. And girls complain the sizes are always screwy, but you're probably about here. . . ."

He scans the rack and starts pulling off dresses, saying, "Reject all the ones that suck, which is probably most. . . ."

I manage a smile. "No, choice is good. Thank you."

I take an armful and try them on as fast as I can, though I'm so nervous I can barely get the zippers up. I narrow it down to two. I emerge, holding them, and he says, "What? No fashion show?" and I feel my cheeks go scarlet as I mumble something, realizing that's probably how girls usually do this—wear the dress out and say "How does this look?" like I've seen in movies.

"I'm kidding," he says quickly. "The only person you need to please is yourself. So which is the winner?"

"I . . . I couldn't decide. I . . . guess I should try them on again and let you see. . . ."

He takes them from my hand and holds them up in front of me, saying, "I have no idea what I'm doing, but this is what I see others do." I laugh and he says, "Yep, still no clue."

"Close your eyes and throw one at me."

He smiles. "They aren't candy bars."

"Close enough. Just do it."

He does. I take the dress.

We go out for dinner and then change and clean up in the restroom. I really regret missing that shower now. I bought hair clips and pins, though, and I have a brush, so with some water and careful work, I coax my hair into a style Cadence and I used to do for each other when there was some dressworthy occasion. Then I apply makeup to my scrubbed face. And by *makeup* I mean the mascara and tinted lip gloss I picked up at Rite Aid. I also bought blush, but only put on a touch, terrified of looking like a ten-year-old who got into her mom's makeup drawer.

Hair done. Makeup on. And then I realize that I really should have donned the dress first.

Dress on. Shoes next. They're also from the consignment store, low heels because anything else would be a recipe for disaster. I stand in front of the mirror and tug and tweak the dress, having no idea what I'm actually doing, just trying to make it look more, well, normal.

I don't feel magically transformed into a princess. I feel like the servant girl who stole a party dress from the clothesline. It does fit me. It just doesn't . . . fit me. The image, that is, and as I stare in the mirror, I want to yank it off and tell Jude I can't do this. Everyone will know I don't belong at that party. They just will.

"You look very nice, dear."

The voice startles me, and I turn to see an elderly woman. She catches my expression and says, "Young people don't dress up as much these days, so it feels strange, doesn't it?"

I nod. Then I blurt, "I think I'm missing something."

She passes a critical eye over me. "Well, if you have a necklace or earrings . . ."

My face reddens. Jewelry. Of course.

"Frankly, I wouldn't bother," she says. "Leave the glitter for us old ladies." She winks. "We need an advantage somewhere." She pats my shoulder. "You look lovely. Now, I believe there's a young man waiting outside for you."

forty

JUDE STANDS IN THE HALL, LOOKING THE OTHER WAY. I DON'T know enough about men's fashion to say more than that his outfit isn't a tux, but it's fancier than guys wear to prom in Reeve's End. It fits him far better than the stuff he's been wearing, and I see the boy from those photos—the confident stance and athletic build, the clean-shaven angular jaw, the black curls, tamed and dampened and pushed off his face. He looks more himself, the way I feel less myself.

This is the guy I'm about to walk into a party with. Walk in on his arm. Walk in like I belong with him.

I step back toward the restroom, ready to retreat and say I can't do it.

Then the still-closing door creaks. He turns and sees me. I move forward, one careful step after another, even the low heels feeling precariously high. In the silence, I manage a nervous smile and say, "Do I clean up okay?"

"I was resisting the urge to say you look nice, which would imply that you didn't before."

My smile relaxes. "Okay, then I won't say it about you, either."

"On second thought, it's fine. The alternative implies that we don't look any better after having clearly taken the effort to do so."

"True."

"On that note, while being clear that I thought you looked very nice before, I will say that the dress was an excellent choice and you look awesome. But I'm still not flirting."

"I know."

The newspaper articles I read called the Bishop home an "estate." Given the rural location, I expect that means the stereotypical Kentucky horse ranch—a stately home on acres of rolling bluegrass.

When Jude pulls into a dirt laneway with a gate, I hop off to open it, but he beats me there, pointing to the muddy ground.

I lift the helmet visor.

"A mildly trespassing shortcut?" I say with a smile.

"Nah, we're here. Just coming in the back way."

I crane to get a look at the property. It's what I expected—rolling bluegrass and white fence. The house is obviously beyond those rolling hills.

Jude navigates the bike through the gates and then guns the engine on the short grass. I look over those acres of grass and think, "Who cuts all this?" A gardener, obviously, but I mean what kind of person *pays* to have acres of grass cut?

Jude revs again as we climb a slope. When we near the crest, I see the top of buildings and then . . .

The house goes on forever, white buildings stretching across the horizon. In old books, they talk about homes with "wings"—the north wing or the east wing—and I've never really been sure what that means. Now I know. The Bishop estate looks like a plantation house from the photos at that Civil War reenactment site. I cannot comprehend this as a single-family home. I just can't.

I've heard the cliché that someone comes from a different universe. Now I see what it means. These aren't just people who don't need to hunt and trap for their dinner. That applies to the average person in Reeve's End, and I'm accustomed to that level of disparity—seeing kids throwing away a sandwich because they hate egg salad and wondering if anyone would notice if I snagged it from the trash bin.

I knew what Jude came from, but it wasn't obvious. He dresses like me. Rides a beat-up motorcycle. Checks his wallet before ordering dinner. Even Lennon—with his expensive sneakers—didn't seem more than upper-middle class, like kids I met at science camp.

But I see this house and I realize that what separates those city kids from Jude and Lennon isn't a few social rungs—it's a whole ladder. And me? For the first time in my life, I actually feel like a hillbilly. Like someone who doesn't just live in Reeve's End but belongs there.

I want to leap off the seat and run. Just run. Get away before I make a fool of myself.

Jude guides the bike toward the house and stops beside what looks like a garage. Through trees and bushes I can see a circular front drive with a steady stream of cars, men in suits and women in dresses getting out as valets rush to drive the vehicles away.

I've read about valet parking but never even been to a restaurant that has it. I clutch the seat so hard my fingers ache.

Jude turns off the engine. Then he twists and waits. After a moment, he motions, and I realize he's waiting for me to remove the helmet and slide off the bike. I dismount and edge closer to the garage wall, where I can't see that endless line of cars. I run my hands through my hair. Jude moves closer and leans down, his voice lowering.

"We'll go in the side," he says.

"No, the front door's fine. I'm just . . . a little nervous."

"We'll take the side. My mother might complain about that, but she'd also bitch if I came through the front like a guest instead of family. Damned if I do, damned if I don't, so I vote for the side entrance and a bathroom stop to make sure I don't have bugs in my teeth."

When I don't smile at that, he squeezes my elbow. Just a quick squeeze to get my attention.

"It's okay, Winter."

"I . . . This isn't . . ." I swallow. "I know your family has money, but this . . . this . . ."

"It's not mine."

I shake my head. "You might have walked away but—"

"The money is not mine. The money is not even theirs. It's family money. No one here has earned it."

"But—"

"This isn't where I come from. I saw you reading the articles. You know ..." He rubs his mouth. "I don't want to sound like a thoughtless jerk, saying hey, we're from the same place—the same *kind* of place. Obviously I haven't lived there since before I can remember. But it's still ..." He looks at the house. "*This* isn't mine. I'm very aware of that. That's what I'm trying to say. I've always been aware of that."

He looks at the house, and I realize I'm not the only one who doesn't want to be here. And I realize how much worse it is for him.

What I'm feeling is pride. Pure and simple. The fear that I will embarrass myself. That people at that party will sense where I come from and turn up their noses. That's it. In Jude's eyes, I see genuine fear. Coming back here is a move he isn't ready to make.

Before I can speak, he does, his gaze still on the house. "I had a good childhood. A really, really good one. Money buys you that. But money ..." He swallows and I realize he's no longer seeing the house, no longer seeing anything. "People like this can buy anything they want. *Anything.*"

"Maybe there's another way to Lennon's room," I say. "We can sneak in."

The corners of his lips lift. "Believe me, if there was a way to sneak in, Lennon would have found it years ago. I have to do this. But if you don't want to ..."

I square my shoulders. "The only thing I'm going to hurt is my ego. And sometimes I think maybe it could use a little bruising."

"No, I'm pretty sure it doesn't need that at all." He moves closer and leans down, his voice lowering. "It's money, Winter.

Just money. It doesn't make them good people. Doesn't make them bad people either. Don't ever let anyone make you feel worse about yourself. Don't give them that power."

I nod. "I can't change how others treat me, but I'm responsible for how that makes me feel."

He moves in front of me, catching my gaze. "No, I didn't mean it like that. Of course it hurts."

I know he's talking about Bert, and I inch back.

"Not the time," he says. "Yeah. Sorry. Feel free to tell me to shut up when I do that."

"No, you have good advice."

He brushes his hair back. "I don't mean to." A wry smile. "I mean that I don't intend to give unsolicited advice, not that I'd rather give *bad* advice. I'm serious, though—tell me to stuff it when I pry."

He takes out his phone and calls a number. Someone answers and he says, "Hey, Roscoe. It's Jude."

Pause.

"Yeah, I wasn't sure if my mother mentioned I was coming to the party and—"

Pause.

"Anyway, we're by the boathouse and—"

Now the pause comes with an added eye roll for me.

"Yes, I brought a girl. Just don't make a big fuss and scare her off. It's not exactly a done deal and—"

He squeezes his eyes shut and shakes his head as I hear someone giving a laughing reply on the other end.

"I don't mean *that* way. Just help me look good, okay?"

He listens and then hangs up and says to me, "Roscoe likes

to talk. So be warned. I apologize in advance for any off-color comments."

"Don't worry. I remember the porn links."

He snorts a laugh and then leads me between the detached building and the side of the main house.

"So . . . garage?" I say, gesturing to the smaller structure.

"Nah, boathouse. For all those big bodies of water we have in Kentucky. We call it the boathouse, but it's mostly a giant shed."

"Storage for that pool I saw?"

"No, that has a pool house."

"Of course."

The side door opens. A man pokes his head out. He's in his early thirties and looks like a security guard—or a cop or soldier. A big guy, maybe an inch taller than Jude and thirty pounds heavier.

"Hey, Jude," he says. Then, "Oh, sorry, did that wrong," and he sings the words, getting a good-natured "Yeah, yeah," from Jude, who then says, "Roscoe, this is Winter."

"And the young lady's surname?" Roscoe says. "Because you know I gotta ask."

Jude says, "Crane," and I'm thinking *whoa, that is some serious security,* when Roscoe bows and says, "Miss Crane, pleased to meet you," and I realize he didn't ask so he could run a background check, but because he's expected to address me that way.

We head down a back hall, past closed doors.

"Have you heard anything from Lennon?" Jude asks.

Roscoe sighs. "You still on about that, bud? I know you

worry, but I was hoping maybe a little time apart would be good for both of you. Lennon's always leaned on you. Relied on you. With you gone, he had to get into the world by himself. Explore his own interests. With you gone, he's really been coming into his own. Doing his own thing. Cutting those apron strings, which, as we both know, your momma ties damned tight."

Jude nods, but he doesn't say, *That's good.* In general, yes, independence is a fine thing. But from what we suspect, getting into the world and exploring his own interests doesn't mean Lennon has joined the Peace Corps.

Roscoe must sense Jude's unease and he says, "It's been good for him, Jude. It really has."

"Any idea what he's been up to lately?" He tries to say it casually, but the guard eases back a step, saying, "Your brother's business is his own, Jude. I don't interfere."

"I don't mean that. I've just been having trouble getting hold of him this week, so I was concerned."

"As a good big brother should be, and you're always a good big brother," Roscoe says with a smile. "I'm not going to say he's keeping his nose clean, but with you boys, getting into trouble means having a couple of drinks before you're twenty-one, maybe hooking up with a girl from the wrong zip code, if you know what I mean."

I tense, but he doesn't even glance my way, just continues with, "If Lennon's taken off, he's just doing something he shouldn't be. But it's nothing serious. You boys don't get in that kind of trouble."

"Okay," Jude says. "I was just concerned."

"You don't need to be. It's Lennon. And if you don't mind my saying so, I might suggest you take a note from his book, Jude, and find a bit of trouble yourself. Young men need to cut loose. You'll be tied up with responsibilities soon enough—job, kids, wife. Get as much as you can, while you can." He glances at me and clears his throat. "Trouble, I mean. Get in some trouble, preferably the kind that won't leave a criminal record."

Jude nods and says, "I'll take Winter from here. I'd rather not walk into the party with a security escort."

Jude lets Roscoe leave and then murmurs, "We'll go this way," and leads me through a door into a room. It seems to be a library. There are chairs that look old but not terribly comfortable. And shelves of books—leather-bound first editions. I long to detour over and read those spines, but we're on the move.

When I tear my gaze away, I see old family portraits. One guy could pass for Lennon in period dress, and I'm about to comment on the resemblance when I remember this isn't Jude and Lennon's birth family. I notice the same dark hair and blue eyes and basic facial shape on a few other portraits and I wonder if that's one reason the Bishops were so quick to adopt the boys—they looked enough like the family that they wouldn't stand out as clearly adopted.

When Jude opens the door across the room, I hear sounds of the party at last, strains of music and laughter. I glance back, tempted to find some excuse to linger.

"Is this the library?" I ask.

"The small library."

My brows arch. "There's a bigger one?"

Spots of color touch his cheeks. "Yeah. You know your house is too big when you have duplicate rooms."

"Actually, I was drooling at the thought of an even bigger library. With even more books."

He smiles then. It's a little uncertain, and it reminds me of taking Lennon to the trailer—the discomfort of bringing people to your home, knowing how they might judge you for it. Given the options between having money or not, there's really no choice, but either way, there's a stigma attached. Either you're poor and worthless or rich and unworthy.

"You know what I'd like best about living here?" I say.

A faint smile. "The books?"

"Close. The best part would be all the places to hide." As soon as I say that, I realize how it'll sound, given what he knows of my home life, and I hurry on with, "Places to be alone, you know? Just grab a book and find a quiet spot where no one can track you down. I bet it doesn't matter how many people are in this house, there's always a corner to hole up in."

The smile touches his eyes then. "There is. And I know all of them." He glances down the hall. "In fact—"

A loud laugh from the party stops him and he says reluctantly, "We should get going. I don't mean to stall."

"But I'm not arguing if you do. Were you going to show me one of those hiding spots?"

He hesitates. He's off-kilter here, a place that's so familiar and comfortable, yet no longer his home. Having me along doesn't help. I'm the same—familiar and yet not, someone he's just getting to know; he's uncertain whether to let his guard down or stick to the mission. He's not sure what this is yet—what we are. Personal or just business. I'm not sure either.

"You're right," I say. "We need to get to Lennon's room as soon as we can."

Jude shakes his head. "We'll have to circulate at the party first anyway. We've got time. Come on."

forty-one

WE ENTER ANOTHER ROOM, THE FUNCTION OF WHICH I DON'T dare guess. It's small and utilitarian.

There's a second door. Or it looks like one, but there's no handle. When we reach it, Jude pushes aside a painting to reveal a panel with an LED screen. He punches in a code and that knob-free door slides open.

I laugh. "Now *that* is a secret room. I don't think I've seen anything like that outside of spy movies."

"Nah, if it was a real secret room, you wouldn't see a door at all. Lennon says we should put a wall hanging over it. I say there's not much point hiding the security panel if you can obviously see a door requiring one."

I smile at that. The solutions fit them perfectly—Lennon wanting more creative and elaborate subterfuge, Jude arguing for candor.

Jude leads me into the room, and when I step inside, I have to laugh again.

"Oh, my God," I say. "Is this a panic room?"

He chuckles. "Yep, they exist outside of spy movies too."

I walk in, marveling. It's exactly what I've read in books. There's a landline phone. Food and water. Flashlights. There's even an armchair and a couch. Jude plunks onto the sofa, reaches into the cushions, and pulls out a thick, dog-eared novel.

"It's still here."

I grin. "This is your reading room?"

"Privacy guaranteed. No one ever figured it out."

I take the book. "*War and Peace*?" I check the bookmark, which is past the three-quarter mark. "Impressive."

"Far more impressive if I don't admit how long it took to get that far. It's more a goal than a pleasure, as you might have guessed by the fact I 'accidentally' left it behind."

"Well, you're farther than I am, and I've been working on it for three years."

He smiles at that and finally relaxes, tucking the book into the cushions and then saying, "So this is my hidey-hole, and if the party gets unbearable, you are free to use it."

"I'd need the code for that."

"It's 252423. But if you escape back here, you need to read the next chapter and secretly move my bookmark."

"It's not a secret if you tell me to do it."

"I'll conveniently forget. Like I've managed to forget half the damn novel."

"*Les Misérables* is almost as impressively long and far more entertaining."

"I know."

We share a smile, and I'm turning to go when I see a pistol hanging behind the door.

"Yep, a fully furnished panic room," he says. "Not that Lennon or I have the faintest idea how to use that. Like martial arts, shooting and hunting were not on our mother's list of acceptable sports."

I look at the gun and remember Lennon skinning the rabbit for me.

This city boy is still a Kentucky boy.

I open my mouth to comment and then shut it. Jude's already worried, and this doesn't add anything new.

As we head into the hall, I say, "Did you mention a bathroom pit stop earlier? I'm trying not to think what that helmet did to my hair."

He smiles. "Yours looks fine, but I suspect the *lack* of a helmet totally ruined any work I did taming this." He tugs a curl of his hair. "It's just down here."

We tidy up in a bathroom that is roughly quadruple the size of my bedroom. Jude's mood stays high, and that calms me, and as we walk down the halls, we're comparing our must-read lists of classic literature. I've always been rather proud of mine, along with the fact that I'm often the only person who has ever checked half of them out of the Reeve's End library. Jude's list puts mine to shame, in both what he wants to read and what he's finished. I'm telling him I want recommendations, and he's promising me that and—

"Jude," a voice says.

We look up and . . .

We're in the party. There's no grand entrance. I'd never even noticed we walked in, and from Jude's expression, he hadn't either. We were too busy talking, and now we're about ten paces into a room filled with partygoers who've stopped what they're doing to watch the prodigal son return.

A woman makes her way over, the crowd parting for her. I've seen photos of Elysse Bishop. I know she's not what I would expect. In movies, the wives of powerful men seem to come in two varieties: the well-dressed and commanding first wife or the glamorous and young second wife. Parting that crowd with her very presence, Mrs. Bishop is the very definition of *commanding*. With dark blond hair and hazel eyes, she wears a tasteful and conservative gown that still makes her, quite possibly, the most beautiful woman in the room. From everything I've heard, I expect a chill. While I don't sense warmth, her expression reminds me of Jude—absolute control rather than arctic frost.

She puts one arm around Jude's shoulders and pulls him into an embrace that is neither stiff nor overtly maternal.

"It's good to see you," she says, and her voice is just loud enough that others can hear while quiet enough to seem as if the words are for Jude only. A woman who does nothing impulsively, nothing by accident, every move considered and measured. Like her son.

She pulls back and when she looks at me, I try not to quail. Should I have worn more makeup? Less? Is my hem too high? Too low? Is my dress too young for me? Too old? Is—

"And this must be . . . ," she prompts.

I open my mouth to answer, but Jude beats me to it, and I remember that it's correct for others to introduce us. At least it is in Victorian novels. Which may still apply in this house.

"Winter," he says. "Winter Crane. And this is my mother, Elysse Bishop."

"Winter," she says. "That's an interesting name."

Not pretty. Not nice. *Interesting.*

I'm reading too much into that response. I know I am. I can't help it.

"Oh, it's a lovely name," says an elderly lady, moving forward from the crowd. She gives me a smile not unlike the old woman's in the restroom—sympathetic and encouraging.

"I know a Summer and an Autumn," says the elderly man with her. "But not a Winter. Always nice to have parents with imagination."

"So, Winter," Jude's mother cuts in. "Are you a college student yet?"

I know I look young for my age. Is that what she's suggesting—that I'm too young to be with Jude? Or that I'm another dropout he met in the city?

Jude opens his mouth to reply, but I say, "I'm in my senior year, getting ready to submit my applications."

"Where do you plan to go? Penn? Cornell?"

Ivy League schools. She says them as if they're the only possible choices. Waiting to see me blush and stammer a response? Pretend I can afford them?

"I've applied to Penn," I say. "But that will take a bigger scholarship than I dare hope for. A state school will do for my undergrad. I'll save Penn or Stanford for med school, though Johns Hopkins ranks higher on my list. I know the connections you make at Ivy League schools are important, but personally, I feel the program is better at Hopkins."

Mrs. Bishop doesn't respond. I've thrown her, just a little. She recovers quickly with, "Medical school? That's quite a goal."

"I've been working for a family physician for almost five years now. It's not as much experience as I'd like, but it's helped me know it's the career I want."

The elderly woman says, "That's the way to do it. So many young people pick a career like they're choosing a dress from a shop window. You need to try it on for size first. So, tell me, Winter, do you have a specialty in mind? Family medicine?"

And with that, the elderly couple engage me in conversation, effectively shutting out Mrs. Bishop. She murmurs, "I'd like a word," to Jude, but he replies in that same voice she'd used earlier, loud enough to be heard but not so loud that it seems intentional, "Later. I don't want to abandon my guest," and I swear the elderly woman's lips twitch in a smile. Mrs. Bishop takes her leave, and I exhale as she departs.

It isn't until I've been talking to the elderly couple for about five minutes that Jude remembers to introduce them . . . as his grandparents. His father's parents. I'm actually glad that introduction came late, because by then I was relaxed enough not to be intimidated. They talk to both of us for a while, and I notice they're careful not to ask Jude what he's been up to. I know from dinner that he has a noncommittal answer ready—working, exploring his options—but I think he's glad not to need it for his grandparents.

We circulate a bit. I try not to gawk at the house, at the people. At one point, I hear a laugh and it reminds me of Edie, and I think of what she would have said about this place, this party, which only makes me anxious to get through it, get to Lennon's room, keep investigating. But we can't rush out or people will notice.

As we circulate, we catch a glimpse of his father across the room. I recognize Peter Bishop from his photos too. He's not as strikingly attractive as his wife but he's handsome, with graying dark hair and blue eyes. When he sees Jude, I expect a polite nod, maybe even a distant one, given how Mrs. Bishop has implied Jude's behavior upsets him. Instead, those blue eyes light up, and he grins and lifts a finger to say he'll be over in a moment. I glance at Jude, whose gaze shoots to the buffet table, as if looking for an escape.

Mr. Bishop starts making his way toward us, his face still alight as his long strides cover the distance. A woman steps into his path, motioning to a man at her side, as if wanting to make an introduction. The congressman hesitates, his gaze lifting over the man's shoulder to Jude, as if he wants to make an excuse and continue on his way. But it seems important and he makes a face for Jude, one that reminds me of Lennon, a faint grimace that wryly says *Duty calls,* and he motions for us to stay right where we are.

"Let's get a drink," Jude says. "They won't fuss with ID."

I shake my head. "I'm fine."

"Just because I don't drink . . ."

"I only do if I can't say no without being rude. But your dad seemed to want to talk to you."

"He'll find us."

As we get our drinks, he says, "I'm going to grab a plate of food, too. You?"

I chuckle and shake my head. "I'm still feeling dinner. Go get something. I'll hang out in that very cozy corner over there."

He still hesitates, and I have to shoo him off. Then I take my spot in the aforementioned corner and wait while Jude fills a small plate from the buffet. As he's turning to come back, an older man puts a hand on his shoulder and traps him in what doesn't look like will be a short conversation.

I glance around. Should I keep standing here or join Jude?

"It looks as if my son has been waylaid," a voice says, and I turn to see Jude's father walking toward me, smiling. He extends a hand. "Peter Bishop. And, yes, I'm sure you figured that out, but I'll say it anyway."

"Winter Crane," I say, shaking his hand.

When he catches me glancing toward Jude, he says, "Don't worry. He'll be back the second he can escape. I'm sure he doesn't want to be pulled away, but my son is nothing if not conscientious about his responsibilities. Perhaps a little too conscientious. And a little too responsible."

His lips quirk in a smile, and I can't help returning it. I know he's a politician, so I expect him to be engaging, but I expect it to be false charm, a little smarmy. Yet there's a warmth there that reminds me of Lennon—even when you know he's going out of his way to be charming, it doesn't feel phony.

"Did I hear this is your first date?" he asks.

"We've known each other awhile, but this is our first time 'out' together."

Mr. Bishop talks to me for a few minutes. Like his parents,

he doesn't pry, just expresses an interest while skirting around specifics.

"I also hear you're applying for scholarships," he says. "I know the state ones can be complicated, so if you have any questions or problems, contact my office. I'll give them a heads-up to expect a call."

"Thank you, sir."

My gaze slides toward Jude, who's now talking to an older couple.

"Yes, everyone wants to speak to him," Mr. Bishop says. "Hoping for grist to feed the gossip mill, find out exactly what scandalous things he's been up to. Which I know are not scandalous at all. He just . . ." A shadow passes behind Mr. Bishop's eyes. "I don't know how much he's discussed with you."

"Not much."

"If you can get him to talk, please do. I'd like to think he has someone to speak to. I'd love to do it myself, but . . ." His fingers tighten around his wineglass. "I hope he's making a good impression. I know Jude can seem distant, but he has a good heart. Possibly the best I know. That doesn't always make life easy. A good heart plus a sharp mind means a very busy head and a very deep conscience."

A rueful smile, another hint of Lennon, as he lifts the glass. "Yes, this is actually my first, and I'm already probably not making any sense. I'm much better at sticking to the issues. Ask me my views on needle exchanges and I'll do a much better job."

I smile. "What's your view on needle exchanges, sir?"

He laughs. "Oh, you'd better *not* ask unless you really want to know, or you'll get a half-hour lecture on balancing public health concerns with the need to get prescription opioids off our streets. I'll just say that I'm in favor of the exchange centers. I'm also in favor of my son, as fine dating material, in case you couldn't tell."

"I could. And you did make sense—I know what you mean about Jude, and I agree."

His face lights up again, as if I've paid his son the greatest compliment. Then he says, "All right. I'll stop monopolizing you and go wrench your date from the clutches of the busybodies. In fact, I'll suggest he take a break and show you the conservatory. You can wait for him in there." He gives directions and then heads off to free Jude.

forty-two

I FIND THE CONSERVATORY EASILY. WHAT I CAN'T FIND IS THE light switch. But there are huge windows, and while night has fallen, the front yard is lit enough that I'm able to see my way around.

The first thing I spot is the piano. A grand piano? A baby grand? The terms are only words in books, and I have no idea which this is, only that it must be a *grand* of some variety. It's beautiful, with black wood that gleams like glass, a curved lid propped up, and impossibly white keys. I stand behind the bench and put my fingers over the keys. I don't touch them—I don't dare—but I'm remembering Jude's hands placing mine and the sequence of notes, the first strains of—

"Do you play?" a voice asks.

A man walks into the room. He's tall, with curling dark hair, broad shoulders, a black suit and tie. He's in shadow, only his silhouette clear, and there's a split second where I think it's Jude. He's going to tease and ask if I remember the notes, maybe even make me play them. I smile as the figure steps in.

Then I realize it's not Jude. While I can't see the man well with the shadows, he's at least in his late thirties.

"Mr. Bishop told me to wait in here for Jude," I say. "I couldn't find the light switch."

He pats the wall and says, "Looks like they've hidden it. Peter sent me to tell you Jude will be a few more minutes. He's speaking to yet another old family friend."

"I'm Winter," I say, extending a hand.

He doesn't seem to see my hand. His teeth flash. It's a smile, but in the dim light all I see are those flashing teeth set against a shadowy face.

"Yes, I know," he says. "And I am yet *another* old family friend, in what probably, by this point, seems an endless stream of them, and an equally endless stream of names you can't possibly remember." He waves at the piano. "Do you play?"

I shake my head. "I was just admiring it."

I'm glancing at the piano, when I see a grouping of picture frames. Photographs of a boy at a piano.

"Jude," the man says, following my gaze.

I walk over and bend to look at them. Then I notice the awards on the wall. *Covering* the wall. Framed honors for Jude's musical accomplishments.

"Sorry," I say, turning my attention back to the man.

"No, go ahead. Take a look, if you can manage to read them in this terrible lighting."

I can, and when I do, I'm stunned. There are many levels of talent. You can be the best in your school, the best in your community, the best in your city, and so on. When I'd seen articles calling him a prodigy, I'd taken that with a grain of salt. But these awards aren't from school competitions. They're statewide, countrywide, even worldwide.

As I read, the man moves up behind me, and I say, "I knew he was good, but I had no idea."

"Jude is special. You won't see a room like this dedicated to any talent of his brother's."

I must stiffen, because the man says, "I shouldn't say that aloud. It's just that I know Lennon leaves the better impression on young women, and I want to give Jude his due."

"I haven't met Lennon."

"No? Well, if you do, you'll find him very charming. But it's superficial. Shallow waters. A disappointing lack of substance."

I bristle. I'm fine with people singing Jude's praises, but insulting his brother to do it is wrong.

"Does that make you uncomfortable, Winter?" the man says. "I only speak the truth. I've known the boys for a very long time. They both take after their father, in their way. Do you know him?"

"Congressman Bishop?"

That flash of teeth, now not seeming nearly so innocent, makes me steel myself against inching back. "Yes, of course. Who else?"

I start to say that I only meant I know the boys are adopted, but he continues with, "At first, Lennon seems to more closely resemble his father. It's an easy mistake to make. I made it myself, unfortunately. But with Lennon, that charm isn't a mask. It's really all there is. His father is deeper, far more complex, far more . . . dangerous. Not a man you want to underestimate."

"O-okay."

"And that is Jude as well. A boy with hidden depths. A boy with incredible intensity. You can see that here." He waves around the room. "Talent and intensity and passion, the likes of which his brother cannot match."

My gaze shoots to the door.

"Do I make you nervous, Winter? Truth is uncomfortable. Ask Jude. He knows all about truth and lies. I only wanted to warn you that the apple does not fall far from the tree. He is his father's son. Remarkable in a way few can appreciate."

"I—"

"I know that may be hard for you to understand. You're nothing like your family, are you, Winter? Particularly your sister."

My head jerks up. "My sister?"

"Yes, your sister. You are nothing like her."

"You know my sister?"

He frowns, the shadows of his face rearranging. "I thought I did. Are you not . . . ?" He glances toward the party. "Someone told me your family was . . ." A sharp shake of his head and a laugh. "I see now that wires have been crossed. You are not the girl they think you are." His gaze swings to me. "Are you, Winter?"

I freeze. His gaze cuts into me, and I can't breathe. I know I'm being foolish. I can smell alcohol fumes as he moves closer. He might wear a fancy suit, but he's no different from the drunken idiots I met on the road last night, offering insults and invitations.

"I'm sorry," I say as firmly as I can. "I really should go find Jude."

"Are you sure that's wise?" He moves closer. "Are you sure you're good enough for him? Granted, you are a very pretty girl. . . ."

His fingers caress my cheek. I don't see it coming and can't move away fast enough. I stagger back and stumble over the piano bench. I hit it hard and twist, and then crash to the floor, the bench falling with me.

"Winter!"

It's Jude, his footsteps thumping down the hall. The man strides through the doorway while Jude is swinging in, Jude snarling, "Hey!" as the man brushes past.

I push up. Jude rushes over, saying, "Did he—?"

"I fell."

His eyes narrow, and I hear, *Tell the truth, Winter.*

"He touched me." Jude's face flushes with fury as he spins on his heel, and I scramble over to grab him. "My *cheek*. He touched my cheek. It startled me. That's all."

"He shouldn't be touching you *anywhere*. Who is he? Did he say?"

"Just that he was a family friend. You didn't recognize him?"

He shakes his head. "It's too dark, and he barreled past me. But I don't care who he is. I'll have him escorted—"

"He's been drinking. Which is no excuse, but it's a party and I don't want to make a fuss."

"I don't care. Touching any guest without her permission—"

"If he'd done more, I'd agree, but he didn't. Creepy drunk

friend. Every family has them. Your dad sent him to tell me you were delayed, talking to another old friend."

Jude frowns. "I was speaking to my father . . . who didn't tell anyone to come find you." He glances toward the door. "I really should have him escorted—"

"I didn't mean to leave the party," I cut in to distract him. "Your dad said I could wait for you in here."

"I'd say I'm glad he did . . . if it hadn't led to a run-in with a drunken perv." He looks at the door again, and I know he still wants to pursue it. I don't. I really don't. We need to search Lennon's room, and that'll be a lot harder if I raise an alarm about a drunken guest.

"I couldn't find the light switch either," I say to divert him again.

"Hmm? Right. There's no overhead light in here. It's just the lamps." He flicks one on and looks around, stiffening as if just realizing which room we're in.

"Is that a baby grand or a regular grand?" I ask.

"Baby." He makes a face. "It's a fancy showpiece. Looks better than it sounds."

I smile. "Don't worry, I wasn't going to ask you to play it."

"Yeah, the moment I hit a few notes, my parents would have the entire party in here to listen."

"I mean I wouldn't ask at all. I know you don't like playing anymore."

He rubs his chin, his gaze sliding to the piano. Then he pulls his gaze away and follows mine to the wall of awards. "Obviously my father wanted to show me off by sending you in here."

"He's proud of you. Very proud of you."

It's the wrong thing to say, and as Jude looks away, I hurry on with, "Rightfully so. These awards . . . I had no idea . . ."

"Can we go?" he says gruffly. "Sorry, I'd rather not . . ."

"I know," I say.

He glances toward the door again. "I really think we should do something about that guy. At least look for him. It bugs me."

It bugs me, too, but I don't want to let on that it does. I already feel like I've overreacted to what was just, as Jude said, a drunken pervert. So I say, "What about Lennon's room? Shouldn't we go check that?"

Another hesitation. Then he reluctantly says, "I guess so," and leads me out.

forty-three

THERE'S NO OBVIOUS SECURITY PREVENTING GUESTS FROM snooping in the family's private quarters, but the two guards *are* watching. Jude finds Roscoe posted at the back patio exit, ostensibly playing doorman while making sure guests don't wander too far into the yard.

"I'm going to show Winter my room," Jude says. "There are some books I said she could borrow."

"Uh-huh." Roscoe's wink isn't exactly discreet, but Jude is already heading back inside. Roscoe taps his arm and leans in to whisper, "Do you need anything?"

"What?"

Roscoe mouths, *Protection?* and Jude says, "*No.* We're getting books."

"Okay, but if you do, call, okay? Even if you just think you might. Better safe than sorry. And I'll make sure no one bothers you up there."

Jude sighs softly but says "Yes" and "Thank you."

We step inside and see another guard on his Bluetooth. His gaze swings to Jude as we walk in and he gives us a subtle thumbs-up. Jude sighs again, and I can't help smiling. It's not that Jude is naive—he just didn't stop to think that taking his date to his bedroom might lead to certain seemingly obvious conclusions. As always, his mind is completely focused on the matter at hand.

As we walk, my mind keeps wandering back to the man in the conservatory—the encounter still bothers me—but I tell myself I'm overreacting. Just a drunk, middle-aged creeper. It happens. Unfortunately.

Jude leads me up a flight of back stairs. We reach a section of closed doors. He opens the first, but not enough to let me see inside, and I stay where I am. He's gone only a moment before he returns with a book. He said he was taking me to his room to get books, so that's what he's done. Because, honesty. Or as close to it as he can manage under the circumstances.

I stuff the book into my purse as he pauses at the next door and looks around, his hand on the knob. Then he opens it, motions me inside, and eases it shut behind us as he hits the light switch.

At first, I think maybe he heard someone coming and ducked into a different room to wait until they pass. There's no bed in here, which would suggest it's not Lennon's room. Then I get a better look around and see that it's not his *bedroom*—it's part of his bedroom *suite*. This area looks like a teen's dream entertainment center, beanbag chairs and four theater-style seats arranged in front of a projection TV screen with three different game consoles.

Jude opens one of two interior doors, and through it I see a bathroom. There's a glassed-in shower with a head the size of a dinner plate and more jets on the walls and a touch screen to operate everything. I can't even imagine what that would be like, with guaranteed hot water in unlimited amounts, no one banging on the door, and enough room to turn around in.

Jude sees me looking and says, "Yeah, ridiculous, huh?" and shakes his head and walks to the other door. He opens that, and I pull myself from the sight of shower nirvana and peek into the bedroom. It's what I'd expect. A huge bed—king-size, I'm guessing. Dresser, nightstands—not a lot of variation in bedroom furnishings, at least not when you have an entertainment depot attached to it.

There's a set of weights in one corner and a small desk in the other. Otherwise, it seems a place for sleeping only. Which is not to say I wouldn't love a night in that bed. By myself, of course—just to clarify.

Jude heads to another door, presumably a closet, saying, "His secret spot's in here."

"Secret spot?"

"For stashing stuff he doesn't want the maids to find. And, no, I don't snoop through his things. He told me where he keeps it."

I arch my brows. "He told you his *secret* hiding spot?"

"Yeah, long story. Basically, in sixth grade, he caught me passing notes to a girl. Just typical stuff at that age. Asking about the homework. Saying her hair looks nice today. You know."

I never received any notes like that, but I nod as if I know exactly what he means.

"Lennon flipped because I was keeping a secret—that I liked this girl. So the next week, I caught him smoking . . . which was apparently payback." He shakes his head. "Anyway, big fight, as I explained that liking a girl and smoking cigarettes are very different kinds of secrets, only one of which is likely to kill you. In the end, we agreed we wouldn't keep secrets, so he showed me his hiding spot."

"And you showed him yours?"

He shrugged. "Don't have one. Well, not one where I stash secrets."

Just the panic room, where he hides himself. Which doesn't surprise me at all.

"So what about the girl?" I tease. "Did it work out?"

"Sure. I kept passing her mash notes until she asked if she could come over for homework help . . . and spent the whole evening trying to hang with Lennon."

"Well, that was stupid of her."

A wry smile. "Thanks. It happened now and then. I got used to it. And then girls had to get used to me being paranoid when they *did* like me, which didn't help." He makes a face. "But it's not as if I had time for that anyway. Between school, lessons, sports, whatever." He turns to the closet. "Dating was Lennon's thing. No idea how he found the time. Probably because I'd do his homework so he wouldn't catch hell."

There's no rancor in his words, not unlike me with Cadence, rolling my eyes at her social calendar, too caught up in my schoolwork to imagine having the time.

He walks into the closet, climbs onto a stepladder, and lifts a ceiling tile.

"Still there?" I ask.

"Yep."

He brings down a metal box and opens it on the bed. It's overflowing with papers.

"Lots of secrets," I say.

"Hmm."

There's a manila envelope on top. He shakes the contents onto the bed. A handful of Polaroids fall out. Shots of a girl in various states of undress.

Jude scoops up the photos, cursing under his breath. "I've told him not to do that."

"He likes taking photos, does he?"

"Girls used to text them to him. I never understood that. What if he lets someone use his phone? Or if he was the kind of guy who'd pass the pics around?" Jude shakes his head. "I told him he shouldn't keep them on his phone and should tell girls not to text them."

I point at the pile of pictures. "Loophole."

"Yeah, apparently I wasn't specific enough." He looks in the envelope and then passes it and the photos to me. "Can you check them? Just make sure none are Edie. Those top ones are an ex of his."

I flip through. There's only one other girl in the collection and when I show Jude her face, he shakes his head and says, "Another ex."

I put the photos back and set the envelope aside. There are condoms in the box, including one in an odd package that makes Jude take a closer look. He sighs and tosses it aside. I pick it up.

"Strawberry flavored," I say.

He takes a tube, reads it, and his sigh deepens. This time, he just passes it to me.

"Chocolate body paint," I say. "I bet it goes well with the strawberry."

He chuckles and shakes his head. There's no hint of embarrassment that I'm seeing this stuff, no awkward jokes or excuses made. Refreshingly honest, as always.

There's a dime bag of weed in there. It looks a few years old, as if it was shoved in and forgotten. Another bag holds two small yellow pills etched with happy faces. They're chipped around the corners, as if they've also been in there a while.

"Ecstasy," Jude says. "It wasn't his thing, so he started saying he was allergic. Because 'no thanks' aren't words in Lennon's vocabulary."

At the bottom there's an envelope. It's as big as the box and flattened into the base. Jude wedges it free and pulls out papers inside. The top one is a printout of an article about their parents' car crash, with words and phrases highlighted. Jude picks it up, stone-faced, while I check the page beneath. It's their parents' wedding notice. Then the boys' birth notices. Again, Lennon has highlighted information—names and dates and places.

"He's looking for information on your birth parents," I say. "Has he shown an interest in that before?"

"No." Jude's voice is flat and he's still staring at that page.

"Did you know this?" I say softly. "How your parents—?"

"Yeah," he cuts in. He abruptly puts down the paper. "We always knew we were adopted. We were about seven when someone mentioned how our birth parents died. Our mother explained it then. She said . . ." He trails off, that distant look again. "She told us . . ."

Anger flashes in his eyes. He squeezes them shut and when he looks again, that stone face has returned. He flips through the pages. I sit back and let him. From what I can see, it's the same thing: Lennon gathering details about their birth family.

"He wants to know more," I say. "That's understandable—"

"No." Jude snaps the word. Then he grabs the papers and shoves them back into the envelope. "He did not want to know more. He made that very, very clear and—"

He stops, and he's breathing hard, his eyes shut again. I resist the urge to say something placating. I'm only making things worse.

Jude opens his eyes and the anger crackles there. "All he had to do was ask me. But no. He didn't, and he told *me* not to look. *Just relax, Jude. Chill, Jude. Stop making such a fuss, Jude. Christ, Jude, you can be such a damn drama queen.*"

He takes deep, ragged breaths. Then he pushes up from the bed and strides across the room and stands there, staring out the window. I watch his shoulders shake with rage, and I remember in the motel room, when he walked to the window and I did nothing. I thought it was because I felt nothing. That's a lie. I feel impotent. I'm watching him fall apart again, and I still have no idea how to react. No idea how to help him.

"I . . . ," I begin.

He wheels. "Do you want to know why I left, Winter? The real reason?"

I want to know anything you'll tell me.

Anything that can help me understand might let me do something for him. But I only nod mutely.

"How much did you read about our adoption?" he says. "How it happened? Why we ended up with the Bishops?"

"The articles said you had grandparents. Maternal grandparents. But they weren't able to care for you. Health issues, I think? You would have been put into foster care—"

"Lies."

I hesitate. "Which part?"

He strides toward me. "All of it. There were no health issues. There would have been no foster care. Those articles only say that *after* we were adopted. Backfilling the story. Our grandparents were going to raise us. Then they changed their minds. Changed their minds and moved out of their trailer and into a nice home in a better town. Courtesy of the Bishops, who 'just wanted to help.' The Bishops felt so bad about the tragedy, about the fact our grandparents—sadly—could not raise us. Not bad enough to allow any contact with them, but that's what our grandparents thought was best. Or that's their story. The Bishops' story."

"Are you . . . Are you suggesting . . . a payoff?"

"Payoff?" He gives a bitter laugh. "That's one way of putting it."

He's furious, and he's warned me about his temper. I don't want to spark it in my direction. But I need to say this. He needs to hear it.

"It might look like that," I say. "But . . . raising two boys wouldn't be easy. It's . . . well, it's possible they did have health issues, minor ones, and they may have exag—emphasized them as an excu—rationalization for finding better homes for you and Lennon. Better than they could provide. And the Bishops may have bought them that house in gratitude, understanding how difficult a decision—"

"I overheard my mother last year," he says. "She was talking to our biological grandmother on the phone. Our grandmother needed money. Our grandfather had died—not that anyone let us know. Our mother said they'd paid enough. They kept arguing, and I heard the whole story. The Bishops *asked* to adopt us. They read about the accident, and they saw the perfect way to circumvent the adoption system while looking like heroes for saving two po' white trash babies."

"I . . ." I swallow. "I don't know what to . . ."

"They *bought* us, Winter. The Bishops bought us like they bought this damned bed." He thumps it. "Like they bought that fancy shower. Nothing but the best, and that's what Lennon and I were to them. Healthy, white, American boys. Not easy to get a pair of those, you know, especially brothers, both still young enough for the damage of poverty to be undone. You buy them and then you raise them to be model sons. Media-ready sons. You give them tutors and trainers and teachers and make sure they know they damn well better put in the effort after you've given them all these amazing opportunities. You push them until they fall asleep exhausted from work and from stress because they know if they don't do well enough, their parents will be *disappointed*. And that's all they have. Their parents' approval. Their father is a busy, busy man, and they may not get to see him much, but they need to know how disappointed he'll be if they don't do well. He won't show it, but *she'll* tell those boys all about it. As for her? Well done, boys. Now run along and get some ice cream from the kitchen. Don't actually run, though—you might knock something over. And don't make a mess in the kitchen or you'll upset the cook. And once you're done, it's time for more lessons. Now run along. Quickly, please. I have things to do."

He stops to catch his breath. I can't move. I can only think of what it would be like to discover you've been bought and paid for, and you'd damned well better be worth the price paid and the effort invested.

"I told Lennon what I heard," Jude says, his voice so low it's almost inaudible. "I told him everything. Do you know what he said? That I was making too big a fuss. So what if they paid for us? We got a good life. I should just . . ." He heaves a breath. "I should drop it. Be happy for what I had. But he never . . . It wasn't . . ."

"It wasn't the same for Lennon," I say. "He didn't push himself the way you did. He didn't worry the way you did. Didn't stress about his grades the way you did. If he wanted to hang with his friends, he would. And then he made you do his homework."

He shakes his head. "He never asked. He'd give me shit for doing it. But I didn't want him to get in trouble. I wanted them to be proud of both of us. With the piano . . . Lennon didn't have anything like that, and he acted like it was fine, but I worried."

"Worried you'd pull too far ahead. That your parents would be prouder of you, and he'd resent you for it."

He nods. "And then . . . This . . . Finding out . . . It was huge. Unbelievably huge. Everything was a lie. *Everything*. And he told me to chill. Just chill. I couldn't handle that. So I left."

He looks away and silence falls, and when he glances back, tears are streaming down my face. I want to wipe them away, before he sees, but it's too late and I can't do it. I can't do anything but sit here and feel . . . so many things. Too many things.

I'm imagining what that must have been like. To hear such a horrible truth, and share it with the only person you really trust, the only person who really cares . . . and have him tell you that you're overreacting. Your world has crashed, and the only person who's ever given a shit brushes it off.

I don't think Lennon meant to be cruel. He just doesn't feel things the way Jude does. Like Mr. Bishop said, like even the man in the conservatory said. Jude runs deeper. Feels deeper.

In that moment, when Lennon must have been trying to make Jude feel better—*come on, it's not that bad*—he betrayed his brother in the most painful way.

I can see Jude through my tears. He stands there, watching me, his head tilted, as if trying to figure out what I'm doing.

I wipe my cheeks. "Sorry. I cry easily. I don't know why. I'm not really the type."

"The type?" he says, and his voice is soft, and he's still watching me.

I rub my bare arm over my face. "I'm sorry. I just . . . It . . ." I swallow. Then I lift my gaze to his. "I don't know what to say. I should. I know that. Nothing seems . . . enough." I shake my head sharply. "I'm making this worse. Can we . . . walk outside? Or something? I don't know. I'm sorry. I'm just not very good at . . ."

I have my head down, gaze lowered. I hear paper rustle, as if he's taking the envelope. He's standing by the bed, his hand out. When I don't move, he takes my hand and says, "Come with me," and leads me from the room.

forty-four

JUDE KEEPS HOLD OF MY HAND AS WE HEAD BACK THE WAY WE'D come. Then he opens a closed door to steps leading up. I follow him to the top and emerge in a room that belongs in a castle. A circular room set in the rear corner like a turret.

"The guy who built the house made this room for his wife," Jude says. "She came from England, and she had a room like this at home. No one uses it much anymore. Just me, when I lived here. For . . ."

I follow his gaze and see a piano.

He turns to me, the moonlight from the window casting him into half shadows. "You wanted to hear me play."

I shake my head. "No. I didn't understand. I do now, and I won't ever ask again. That's your choice."

"It is. And I choose to play for you. What I said down

there . . ." His gaze slides toward the door. "I didn't mean to upset you."

"I really do cry easily. I don't know why. It's embarrassing and—"

"You felt bad for me."

Another shake of my head, vehement now. "Not like that."

"I'm sorry I unloaded on you, Winter. I didn't mean to go off."

"You didn't. You explained. I understand now. That's what I wanted. To understand."

He's watching me and I can't read his expression—it's too lost in the shadows. But after a moment, he says, "I explained this wrong. I just want to say thank you. For listening. For . . . for caring." He rubs his face. "That doesn't sound right either. I just . . . You wanted to hear me play. I'd like to do that. For you."

"You don't have to," I say.

His lips curve in something not quite a smile. "I know."

He sits on the bench. This piano is smaller than the other one, and not nearly as fancy. There's a layer of dust on the keys, which he wipes off with a brusque stroke. Then he hits a few experimentally and glances over, making a face and saying, "Needs tuning," and I'm going to say again that he doesn't need to play, but he's already turned back to the piano. He flexes his hands. He gets into position. And then . . . he plays.

If anyone asked, I would say I couldn't tell good piano playing from great. As long as the notes sound right, that's all I know. It isn't. I hear Jude play, and I cannot believe what I'm hearing comes from a single instrument, from a single pair of hands. It's a quiet song, melodic but not slow, his fingers moving so fast that I can't even begin to follow the notes. And I don't try. I close my eyes, and I listen, and I feel tears trickling down my cheeks and that song is so beautiful, so incredibly perfect that I cry, even as I feel myself smiling.

And then . . .

And then it's over, and it takes a moment to realize that, the notes still lingering, and I open my eyes and he's standing in front of me. I start to wipe away the tears, to apologize again, but his arms go around me, his hands in my hair, and he lifts my face and he kisses me.

That kiss is as perfect as the song. As achingly beautiful, seemingly gentle and light, but not light at all. There's more, just like the song. Passion and longing and something that touches me and all I can do is follow it, rise onto my tiptoes to get closer to him, my hands going around his neck to bring myself closer, lose myself in that kiss.

It seems like an eternity passes before he pulls back . . . and yet it seems like a heartbeat, too, not nearly long enough, and I chase after the kiss before stopping myself. I ease away, but he stays there, his face over mine, eyes half closed, breathing softly, catching his breath. Then he blinks. Another hard blink and his hands fall from my hair fast, and he shoves them into his pockets as he steps away.

"I'm sorry." He pulls out his hands and runs them through his hair. "That was—I can't believe I—" He turns away fast and walks to the piano. "I got offended by your dad suggesting I'd make a move on you, and then what do I do?"

He turns to face me. "I'm sorry, Winter. I'm confused. It won't happen again."

I steel myself and look up into his face and it takes every

ounce of courage I have to say, "Not even if I'd like it to happen again?"

His mouth opens. Nothing comes.

"Okay, I get it," I say. "There's a lot going on, especially tonight. Like you said, you got confused. You didn't mean anything by it."

"No, I . . ." He trails off as if searching for words. "I *did* mean it. That is, if you . . ."

I walk toward him. "So, not confused?"

He lets out a choked sound, not quite a laugh. "Um, yes, right now, very confused and making a huge mess of this— and possibly a huge fool of myself—but no, I wasn't confused about . . . I wanted to . . . I definitely wanted to . . ."

He swallows, and I stop right in front of him. I look up. Then I rise on my tiptoes, bringing my face up to his, and I say, "May I?" and he nods, and I can see his pulse, beating fast, and I swear I can hear his heart thumping as I put my arms around his neck and he leans down, and I rise to meet him and—

And his hand tangles in my purse strap. He's trying to put his arms around me and catches the strap, and he doesn't notice right away, as his hands keep going around me, fingers hooked on the strap until he yanks it clear off my shoulder. That wouldn't be so bad if I hadn't only half shoved in the book, and now it topples out and everything inside follows, clacking and scattering across the floor.

We jump apart, startled at the noise, and then stare at the mess.

"Well, that was smooth," Jude says, and he looks so chagrined that I burst out laughing.

"Yep," he says as he crouches to gather my lost items.

"At least now you're warned that I'm not very good at this. I started strong—played you a song, followed it with a kiss. And then made a stammering idiot of myself and dumped your purse when you tried to kiss me." He sighs. "If you want to reconsider, now's the time—" He stops as he picks up a piece of cloth. It's baby blue and bloodstained and filthy, and as soon as I see it, my throat goes dry.

"That's . . . That's from . . . It's Mange's," I say.

"Mange." A moment's pause and his eyes widen. "The dog you—"

"Stabbed. The last time I saw him, he was alive, right before the others . . ."

My head jerks up, and I try to form words—to form thoughts—but I can't. I dimly notice Jude is unknotting the kerchief. There's something tied to it, and he's tugging that off.

When Jude rises, he's dropped the dog's kerchief and he's holding up a golden band. It's a ring. A narrow ring with a tiny diamond, little more than a chip.

"Is this yours?" He sees my expression. "Winter?"

"It's . . . it's my mother's promise ring," I say. "From my father."

"Does he keep it at home, in the trailer?"

I shake my head. "He gave it to Cadence on her sixteenth birthday. She was wearing it when she left Reeve's End."

forty-five

SOMEHOW I MAKE IT TO A WINDOW SEAT. I DON'T REMEMBER moving there. I don't remember lowering myself onto it. One second I'm staring at that ring and standing in the middle of the room. The next I'm sitting on the window seat, and Jude's crouched in front of me, one hand holding mine, the other supporting me as I sit.

And then I'm crying, so hard it physically hurts, like someone reaching into me and wrenching my insides out. It's the worst kind of sobbing, my body starting before the tears do, and it's dry, ugly, racked sobs as my whole body heaves. And then Jude's not crouched there. Not holding my hand, and I think he's gone. He's retreated. Left me to my grief. *Fled* my grief. But it's only one split second from when he lets go of my hand until his arms are around me and he's holding me tight.

And then I cry. Really cry. The tears come and they keep coming, and I can't say a word, can't think a thing, can only cry.

Cadence is dead.

My sister is dead.

I have refused to consider this possibility since the moment I considered that Edie might not be the only one who'd disappeared from Reeve's End. I've told myself Edie and Lennon are a separate case and we don't have someone kidnapping and killing teens from Reeve's End. Edie's case just made me think of Cadence. That's all. Even when I let myself think something might have happened to Cadence, I would not allow myself to even consider the possibility she wasn't alive.

And now I have the ring she wore when she left. The ring she never took off. Bound in a dog's bloodstained kerchief.

Your sister is as dead as that dog.

I killed that dog. And I killed her.

So I cry. I cry and I cry and I cry, until I'm raw and I'm empty, and when I move back, Jude crouches in front of me again, holding both hands now, tight in his.

"We are going to the police, Winter. I am going to *make* them listen. I swear I am."

It takes me a moment to respond. I don't want to respond. I want to say thank you and hug him, and maybe break down a little more, if I have any of that left.

But I can't. No matter how broken I feel at this moment, I'm still Winter Crane. Logical, pragmatic Winter Crane.

"How will we make them listen?" I say. "That ring isn't proof. I'm the only one who paid enough attention to know Cadence was wearing it when she left. We still have no proof Edie was taken. They'll say she was eighteen and free to leave.

Then there's Lennon, who apparently texted your mother yesterday. The police will talk to the Reeve's End sheriff's department, who will say I'm making the whole thing up, as I have been from the start, and now I took my sister's ring from the trailer and planted it in my purse. This psycho knows what he's doing. He knows *exactly* what he's doing. He's made damned sure no one believes us, and now he's watching us run about in a panic while he laughs at us."

Jude is quiet for a moment. Then he says, "Someone planted that ring. When's the last time you looked in your purse? When I gave you the book?"

"No, I just shoved that in. The last time I looked was in the bathroom before the party."

"Right. You couldn't find your lip gloss so you dumped everything. The dog's kerchief wasn't in there. Someone put it in your purse at the party. But I was right beside you the whole time. No one else got . . ."

He trails off as we both realize the answer.

"That man in the conservatory," I say, and my heart starts pounding hard. "He mentioned my sister. He said I wasn't like her. Then he acted as if he'd thought I was someone else. He was taunting me. Telling me he . . ." I swallow.

"And now we have something," Jude says. "We finally have something."

I grab tissues from my purse and clean my face as best I can. Then Jude has my hand in his and he's moving fast. We don't slow until we're in the main room. The party is still going. I can't believe it's still going. My sister is dead. The world has not stopped turning. Even a party did not pause.

Mr. Bishop sees Jude and he starts to smile. Then he catches Jude's expression and strides over to us.

"Jude?" he says. "Is everything—?"

"Can I speak to you? It's important."

"Of course."

Mr. Bishop leads us toward the conservatory, but Jude says, "Out here, okay? We could use some air," and takes us through an exterior door that opens to a front patio garden. There are wrought-iron chairs, set up bistro style, as if for morning coffee, but when Mr. Bishop pulls out one for me, Jude shakes his head and we stay standing.

"Something happened with Winter earlier," Jude says. "In the conservatory. A guest made a pass at her."

"What?"

"I walked in as it happened. She handled it. He stormed past me before I realized what I'd seen. I wanted to go after him. Winter asked me not to. She didn't want to raise a fuss. We went upstairs to talk about it, and I've convinced her that we at least need to identify this man, so he's taken off the guest list."

"Absolutely. And I'll do more than strike him from the list. You didn't recognize him, Jude?"

Jude shakes his head. "Winter couldn't find the light switch, and the guy certainly didn't offer to help. The room was too dark for me to know if I'd recognize him."

"Can you give me a basic description?"

I tell him everything I can remember, and Jude adds what

he can. As we're talking, I think I hear the patio door open. But when I glance over, no one steps out. A minute later, I look again to see Mrs. Bishop, halfway hidden by the shrubbery. She hesitates only a moment before continuing forward, saying, "Is something wrong?"

"One of our guests cornered Winter in the conservatory," Mr. Bishop says. "Jude has convinced her to come speak to us."

"The man had been drinking," I say. "I didn't want to raise a fuss."

I expect her to say I'd misunderstood. Or, worse, I should be flattered. But instead she looks . . . Shocked? Dismayed? Even a little horrified? Then she says, "No, you certainly should say something, Winter. I heard you describing someone. Was that him?"

I nod.

"Would you know him if you saw him again?" she asks.

"I think so."

"Then let's look around. Peter? I was coming to say that Clive Wilson just stopped in after another engagement. I know you were hoping to speak to him."

When Mr. Bishop hesitates, Jude says, "We're fine, Dad. Thanks for taking Winter seriously."

"Of course. I'll go speak to Clive, then, and your mother will help with this. When you find the man, I want a word with him before he leaves."

forty-six

MRS. BISHOP TAKES US BACK INTO THE PARTY AND DISCREETLY mentions possibilities. As we walk, she points out pictures or antiques, as if that explains why we're talking on the move— part conversation with her son and part tour for his guest. I don't have a moment to think about Cadence; I'm too busy trying to keep up.

"And this painting is Eugène Delacroix. A very minor one, obviously."

"It's gorgeous," I say.

"I like it. The play of light always impressed me. My grand-mother found it too . . . active. Too intense. She kept it upstairs, but I had to bring it down. To your left, Winter, the gentleman seated?"

"No, the man in the conservatory was thinner."

"He had more hair, too," Jude says. "No sign of balding."

"Jude, do you remember Mr. Cleaver? Your history teacher? He retired this year. I'm hoping he'll take a spot on the historical society board. Now, if you head left, Winter, there's another painting there, one I'm not nearly as fond of but Peter adores."

And so it goes. She finds four men that roughly match my description. None are the guy from the conservatory. Of course I doubted he would still be here—I only hope comparing him to others has helped refine our description, Jude's memory and mine tweaked as we compare my assailant to other men.

After we make the rounds, Mrs. Bishop speaks to both guards. Neither recall seeing a man matching our improved description.

That's when Cadence slams back to the front of my mind, and I'm overwhelmed by the need to get away from this party.

Jude notices and says, "Mom? I think Winter's had enough. I'm going to take her home."

Mrs. Bishop blanches at that, and I feel a pang of guilt. She's gone out of her way to help, and I know that's for Jude. He's worried about me, and so she's taking it seriously. And now, despite her efforts, he's about to leave again. I'm not surprised when she says, "I need to speak to you, Jude."

"Can I call later? I really need to—"

"It's important, and it will only take a few minutes. We'll go into the kitchen and make Winter some tea. That might help her feel better."

He sighs, softly, and glances my way.

"Tea would be great," I say, though it's the last thing I want. This is how I'll repay Jude's kindness—prodding him, just a little, toward reconciliation with his family.

We go into the kitchen, where staff scurry about. Mrs. Bishop says, "I'd like tea for Jude's guest when you get a moment, Maria. We'll be on the back side patio."

As it turns out, the back *side* patio is different from the back *main* patio, where guests are mingling. The side one is off to the east, hidden by bushes.

"You can sit here, Winter," Mrs. Bishop says. "Jude and I will be right—"

"I'm not leaving her alone after what happened earlier, Mom."

"Yes, of course," she says quickly, as if she'd forgotten, and there's an uncharacteristically anxious note in her voice as she says, "I'm sorry. I wasn't thinking. You absolutely should not be alone, Winter. I'll ask Maria to sit with you. I just need to speak to Jude about his brother." She turns to him. "You're concerned, and I've been ignoring those concerns. I want to talk about them."

Jude goes silent before saying, carefully, "You mean my concern that he's missing."

"Yes. He texted to say he couldn't make the party. I texted him back earlier and he hasn't replied, which isn't unusual, but . . . after what you said, it makes me uneasy."

"Then there's no need to speak away from Winter. She was the last person to see him. She was trying to help him when he disappeared."

Jude tells a pared-down version of the story.

"Why—why didn't you tell me?" she says when he finishes.

"I tried. You wouldn't even entertain the possibility Lennon was missing. If I told you the whole story, you'd have just jumped to the drug-induced-psychosis conclusion even faster."

"I . . ." She trails off. Then she says, "Have you gone to the police?"

"We've tried."

He's halfway through that explanation when Maria brings tea, and Mrs. Bishop seems about to wave her off and then forces herself to wait until it's served, and watches the woman go before telling Jude to continue.

When he is done, she seems to barely be listening. I can tell her mind's already elsewhere, like her son again, thoughts racing off ahead of her. She rises and starts for the house, as if forgetting we're still there. Then she stops and turns abruptly.

"You'll stay here tonight. At the house. Both of you. Winter? If you need me to speak to your family to do that, I will. I'm going to make some calls."

"If it's the police, Winter—"

"Not yet. You're right that we need more. I'm going to telephone Lennon's friends and make sure he's not with them."

"He's *not*. I've already—"

"He's made other friends since he finished school. You know how he is. I'll also double-check that my texts definitely came from Lennon."

"They didn't. They couldn't. I have Lennon's phone. I've had it since—"

"I'll get this sorted," she says, as if not hearing him. "Please don't tell your father just yet. He'll worry himself into a state.

294

Let me look into this. Your brother will be fine. Just fine. This missing girl . . ." A sharp intake of breath and she comes back, shoulders poised, more herself as she says firmly, "She will be fine. This is all a mistake."

"Mistake? Mom, what—?"

He doesn't get a chance to finish before she's gone, door shutting behind her.

"She doesn't believe me," he says. "She *still* doesn't believe me."

"She's . . ." I shake my head. "I'm sorry. I don't know your family, and I shouldn't presume."

"No, go on." When I hesitate, he says, "I need more data here, Winter. Give me your opinion."

"She's been telling herself you're overreacting about Lennon. Now she hears the whole story, from your lips, and she realizes she was wrong. Very, very wrong. Which means her son has been kidnapped for days and she's brushed it off. She can't deal with that, so she's *still* telling herself there must be a mistake. You just said you need more data. So does she. That's what she's getting, and we have to let her do that." I meet his gaze. "It's a start."

He shakes his head. "We needed a *start* three days ago. Now we need answers."

"Hey, here are the lovebirds," says a voice, and Jude winces as Roscoe comes through the door.

"Not now, Roscoe. Please. Winter and I need—"

"Miz Bishop says some perv bothered you in the conservatory, right, Miss Crane?"

My head jerks up. "Yes. Did you remember seeing him?"

"Nah, sorry. But I thought I'd do a little detective work, so I went in and poked about, see if he"—a wry smile—"left a clue or something. Instead, I found something you left. Looks like a bus ticket. But it's a different first name. I figured either you bought it for someone or Winter is your nickname."

"What's the name on the ticket?" Jude asks.

"Cadence. Cadence Crane."

I snatch it so fast he jumps, and I apologize. Or I mean to. I'm not sure I even get the words out. I'm busy reading the bus ticket. From Lexington to Reeve's End. Dated this afternoon. With Cadence's name.

My hands shake as I look up, and Jude's already escorting Roscoe to the door, saying, "Thanks for bringing that. Winter thought she lost it, and she was freaking."

"Where did you find it?" I say, getting to my feet.

He looks at me like this is a trick question. "Uh, the conservatory?"

"She means exactly where?" Jude says.

Roscoe looks confused. "On the piano. In plain sight. I figure you took it out and then forgot it when that guy came in. Can't blame you. Asshole. I've been going through the security footage, hoping to see him, but there's nothing so far."

"Keep looking," Jude says. "Please." He lowers his voice and says, "I want Winter to feel comfortable here, and that encounter left a really bad impression."

"No, sure, totally get it. I'll keep at it."

Roscoe leaves, and Jude comes back.

"He bought a ticket for her," I say. "A ticket for Cadence to come home." Angry tears fill my eyes and I fling the ticket. "Why is he doing this? Why taunt me? Why torture me? I didn't do anything to him. I don't *mean* anything to him. If he wants to take me, just take me. It's not like I haven't given him enough chances."

"Don't say that."

"Why? Because he's lurking in the bushes, waiting for an invitation? Because I'll give him an idea he can't possibly have considered? *Hey, that's right, I could just kidnap her. Kill her, like I killed her sister. Why didn't I think of that?*"

Jude puts his arms around me, and I try to fling him away, but if Jude doesn't want to be flung, he isn't going to be. He just hugs me and says, "I don't want you to say it because I don't want to think it. That's all. As for why he's doing this? I have no idea, Winter. But I'm going to ask you to do something for me. Call your father."

"What?" I back from his grip as it loosens. "Why? You know what he's going to say when I tell him? *Well, that's what she gets, taking off like that.*"

Jude shakes his head. "I don't think so, and I don't think you do either, but I'm sure as hell not defending him. Nor would I ask you to call and tell him she's gone. That has to be done in person. What I'm asking . . ." He trails off and seems to consider. Then he says, "May I have his number? Please?"

"What for?"

"Do you trust me, Winter?"

I don't answer that—I just rattle off Bert's cell number, and Jude says, "Can you step inside, please? Just past the door, where I can see you, okay?"

I want to argue, but he's using his just-being-reasonable voice, and as upset as I am, I know this time he really is just being reasonable. I lean against the window, arms crossed. When I hear him say, "Mr. Crane? It's Jude Bishop," I realize this glass isn't going to block the conversation. But when I move away, he taps the glass, motioning for me to stay there.

So I listen.

"It's about Cadence," he says. "Please don't hang up, Mr. Crane. This is important."

I tense. He wouldn't tell— No, he said that had to be done in person.

"I believe Winter asked if you knew how to contact her. You said you did not. However, you also know Winter is looking for my brother and Edie Greene, and that the reason she'd be asking is because she's worried about Cadence. I think you still care, at least a little. Maybe enough to find out how to contact Cadence and tell her Winter's worried. Tell her to get home and speak to her sister."

I stop breathing. I just stop.

"Yes, sir, I understand. I'm going to put Winter on, and I'd like you to tell her that. Just a second."

He opens the door, and I nearly fall. I right myself, and he's holding out the phone and I'm backing away, my eyes filling with fresh tears, those tears flying as I shake my head vehemently.

"Winter, I need you to speak to your father."

I keep shaking my head. He hits a button and says, "Sir, please tell Winter what you just told me."

There's a pause, and I keep backing away, but Jude catches my hand. He doesn't hold it tight. Just catches it.

"Winter?" Bert says.

"Please go ahead, sir. You're on the speakerphone."

Bert sighs and says, "Okay, fine. Win? You asked if I had contact information for Cady. I didn't. But I figured Cady's friends would know. One gave me the number. I called. Cady hung up on me. I called back and left a message saying you were really worried because Edie Greene might have been kidnapped, and of course that got you thinking about Cady, and she needed to contact you somehow, tell you she was all right."

"And when was that, sir?" Jude prompts.

"I started calling her friends right after you left."

"So you spoke to Cadence this afternoon."

"Yeah. It might take a while for Cady to figure out how she'll get in touch, but she will, Winter. I'm sure she will."

And she did. She hopped on a bus to come see me. She just never made it home.

forty-seven

THE MOMENT JUDE HANGS UP, HE'S MOVING, HIS HAND STILL lightly gripping mine. He takes me outside and starts walking into the yard, circling wide around the main patio and the partygoers.

I don't ask where we're going. I can't even form the question. All I can think about is Cadence, coming home to see me. Cadence, never arriving home. Cadence, grabbed somewhere by a psycho who . . . who . . .

I can't finish that thought.

As we're circling the patio, I catch sight of Peter Bishop. He's outside, talking to an older man, and he sees Jude and stops mid-conversation. Jude gives an *everything's fine* wave as he keeps moving.

We reach the bike. Jude starts talking then, a stream of

words, almost babble, as if he's been running through his plans as we walk.

"He got the ticket from her after she got on the bus. It's been stamped. That's why I called your father. She almost certainly got off the bus. I don't see how he could grab her on it. I don't see how he'd even know she was *on* it, but I can't worry about that. He did. So she got off in Reeve's End. That means we need to get there and retrace her steps, figure out what happened."

I'm not sure that's possible. Especially not at midnight on a Sunday. I don't think he believes it either—he's just taking action for the sake of taking action, and that I *do* understand.

He texts Roscoe, asking if he can trace Cadence's phone. Then he's on the bike, and I'm waiting for him to start it so I can hop on the back. He cranks the ignition. Gives it gas. Cranks again. Nothing happens.

"No," he says. "No, no, no. You piece of shit, do not do this now."

He's off the bike, and he's checking it, and he's talking again, that babble to fill the space and the silence. "I should be able to get it going. I usually can. I'm no mechanic, but I've learned a few things. Had to, with this thing. It—" He stops, and he's holding something, and he lets out a string of curses.

I see what he's holding. Two pieces of wire. I'm no mechanical expert either, but as someone who can't afford to call a service person if the fridge goes on the fritz, I've learned a few basics too. The wire he's holding hasn't come loose or frayed and snapped. It's been cut.

"Jude?" Mr. Bishop's voice precedes him as he turns the

corner. He gives a soft laugh. "That sounded like you, but I don't think I've heard you say those particular words."

He stops as he sees Jude's expression. Before he can ask, Jude says, "My bike's not working, and I need to get Winter back fast. Problem at home. Can I take one of the cars? I'll return it tomorrow."

"Of course. Take mine." He leads us into the garage and over to a box, punches in a code, and removes the keys. "Take it for as long as you need. I mean that. It's not like I don't have backups."

He motions at the garage, where I count four cars, and he gives me a wry smile and an eye roll, as if embarrassed by the excess.

I don't hear the rest of Mr. Bishop and Jude's conversation. I don't notice anything about the car once I'm inside. I'm too numb to process until, once we're on our way, I can't help wishing Jude would drive faster. Then I glance at the speedometer and see he's doing almost a hundred miles an hour.

"We don't have proof this guy's hurt anyone," Jude finally says, his voice soft.

By *hurt* he means *killed*. He's just not going to say the word.

"He's taunting you," he continues. "I don't know why. But that gives him even more reason not to hurt Cadence. He'll want to hold on to her. Use her against you."

"For what?"

"I don't—" He stops short.

"You thought of a reason. Tell me."

"To lure you in."

"Which means we could be running straight into that trap. But he's *had* chances to take me, Jude. In the forest. Down the mine shaft. In that bunker. Three times when I was alone and vulnerable and he could have hauled me off and no one would ever know. I couldn't have given him better opportunities if I tried."

He runs a hand through his hair. "I'm missing something. Maybe it's just the game. You're a challenge, and he can't resist prolonging the chase."

"A challenge? The girl who repeatedly ends up in situations custom-made for kidnapping? More like he's waiting for me to actually *present* a challenge. I'm making it too easy."

He glances over, sees I'm giving a twist of a smile, and returns it. "Maybe we're looking too hard for a reason. He's a psychopath. Does he need an excuse to fixate on you? He just has."

I still feel like we're missing something critical, but I don't know what. I settle back in the seat, watching the scenery pass. We're roaring along the back roads, not another car in sight, and I look and I think of all the nights I'd sat in a backseat, my father driving, Cadence asleep beside me.

Come on, girls. We need to go.

But it's the middle of the night, Daddy.

And that's the best time to drive. When you can sleep.

I suspect now that wasn't the reason at all. We'd been fleeing bills he couldn't pay.

Everything we'd saved went to trying to save her.

When he said that this afternoon, I'd brushed it off. Yes, treating my mother's cancer couldn't have been cheap, but neither was bourbon, and that's where the trouble came from.

Except it wasn't like that in the beginning. The drinking came later, after those endless nights of running to some new town, that ever-disintegrating parade of new residences.

We fled our home—our real home—in the middle of the night too. We had a house then. Heavily mortgaged probably, right at the time of that housing market crash. We were fleeing debt he couldn't repay. Debt so staggering all he could think was to leave the house, leave his job, leave the bills, grab us and run.

There were other ways. Declaring bankruptcy, for one. But did he realize that at the time? He said our mother managed the finances. She was the college-bound one. He'd been a high school dropout. Maybe the only solution he knew was to run and start over and hope things would get better.

I squeeze my eyes shut. I don't want to make excuses for him. No excuses justify the bruises.

I won't make that mistake with you. The minute you gradu-ate, you're going to run as far as you can and you're never going to look back.

Not an excuse. A rationalization. A stupid, idiotic—

I take a deep breath and glance over at the other side of the seat, half expecting to see Cadence dozing there. It's Jude, of course, his gaze on the road, focused on doing what I asked, what I need—getting me home.

"I have to tell you about Cadence," I say. "I've barely men-tioned her and then I get the ring and I freak, and you don't ask what happened. You just listen. You just accept."

"I pieced enough together, and it wasn't the time to ask more. I knew you have a sister. I knew she wasn't around and I figured she left, and I knew there was something about a boy-friend."

"She took off over a year ago. We didn't question why she never made contact. I know that sounds weird."

"I've met your dad. I think I know why."

"He wasn't like that with Cady. He wasn't a good father, by any stretch. Drank too much. Neglected us. Sometimes lost his temper and smacked us. The physical stuff, though, was mostly after she left. I think he blamed me . . ." I swallow, remembering what he said about trying to scare me off, so that he wouldn't make the same mistake he made with Cadence.

"My sister had a boyfriend. Colton. She got into college. He didn't want her going. I told her that if he really loved her, he'd either go with her or wait."

Jude gives an abrupt nod, as if this barely requires agreement at all, it's so obvious. Others tell me I did the right thing, but in their eyes I see doubt, the sense I'd interfered, that maybe a *girl* should be expected to wait, but not a boy, never a boy. Jude only gives that *well, obviously* nod and when I see that, I don't regret the kiss. I don't regret anything.

I continue, "She told him she was going. That night we slept in my shack. I thought she wanted to spend time with me, but I think she was hiding from him. That she was scared of what he'd do."

Jude makes this noise. It's not quite a growl. More of a grunt. But his eyes narrow. After Colton's death, I told Deputy Slate that I thought Cadence was afraid of Colton, and he'd told me to shut my mouth, not go talking against the dead. He never even asked Cadence about it. I didn't either. By then, she already wasn't speaking to me, and I think if I'd raised the subject, she'd have denied it.

Cadence bore the weight of Colton's death, the albatross around her shoulders, for all the town to see. She could put none of that weight onto a dead boy. A little, though, might be shifted to the person who started it all, the sister who'd given her that bad advice.

"We woke up in the night," I continue. "I heard something. She was afraid it was him. I went to confront him. He . . . He'd hanged himself in the tree outside my shack."

Jude glances over so sharply the car veers onto the shoulder, and he has to steer it back.

"Yes, that's why . . . ," I begin. "Colton told enough people about the college thing that they blamed Cadence for breaking up with him and me for telling her to. She left town and didn't look back."

A moment's silence. Then, "You know that's bullshit," he says quietly. "He didn't kill himself over her. He *wanted* her to blame herself. Wanted both of you to. Hanging himself outside your shack said he was a thoughtless bastard who wanted to hurt someone he claimed to love. To hurt her in the worst possible way, because he couldn't come back and tell her it was okay. Couldn't ever absolve her. That's a shitty, shitty thing to do. And, yeah, I shouldn't blame the dead. The guy obviously had other issues. I get that. They don't absolve *him*."

I say nothing.

"You did nothing wrong, Winter," he says. "I know you must be sick of hearing that, but you made a rational argument. The smart argument. If he hadn't killed himself, and she'd gone to college, in the end, whether they stayed together or not, she'd have been thanking you."

I say nothing and he shifts, the leather squeaking. "I'm doing it again, aren't I? Poking my nose in. I don't mean—"

"No, it's okay." I glance over. "Really. You aren't saying

anything I don't try to tell myself. It's a lot better hearing it from someone else."

He reaches for my hand, fingers entwining with mine until a curve comes, and even then he doesn't let go, but the car does a little jiggle, and I release his hand and manage a smile as I say, "At this speed, better keep both hands on the wheel."

He nods, and I loosen my seat belt enough to lean over and brush my lips against his cheek and say, "Thank you, Jude."

"I didn't do anything."

"Thank you for being you. That's enough."

His cheeks flush in the moonlight. I pull back and tap the dashboard. "I'd turn on the radio but I have no idea how to operate this thing."

He taps one dial and then jiggles another. When an NPR announcer's voice comes on, he spins the dial, saying, "Tell me when to stop."

"Keep going."

He tries, and then says, "Reception's crap out here. I'll see what he has on CDs."

He hits more buttons and the sound of eighties pop music fills the car.

"Uh, no . . . ," Jude says as I sputter a laugh. He changes CDs and the next is classical piano, a piece even more beautiful than the one Jude played earlier, and I say, "This. Please."

Jude's finger stays on the dial. He's gone very still.

"Wait," I say. "Is that you playing?"

"It's a piece I wrote for a competition. I didn't know he'd recorded me playing it. . . ." He trails off. "You really want to listen to this?"

I smile at him. "Yes, please."

I lean back and listen to the music, focusing on that to stop the screaming in my head that tells me Cadence needs me and we have so far to go. Jude glances over and says, "When did you know you wanted to be a doctor?"

The non sequitur startles me. But I realize that's intentional. I'm sick with worry, and he can't fix that so he's trying for a distraction.

"When my mother was in the hospital, I kept asking what cancer was and getting the usual answers people give a seven-year-old. I wanted more. I wanted to really understand, and the nurses kept putting me off, and my father and my sister told me to stop bugging the staff. So this young doctor took me aside and explained. She showed me books and used the proper terminology and said that if I wanted to know anything else, I should ask for her. I figured she was just saying that, like grown-ups do, but afterward, whenever something new came up, she'd ask if I wanted an explanation, and I always did, and she always gave it. Mom found out and started asking to hear it with me, and I'd crawl up on her bed, and it'd be just the two of us and that doctor, and I don't think Mom really cared about the explanations—she just wanted that time with me, something the two of us could share. That doctor didn't save my mom. No one could. But the doctor gave me—gave *us*—something. I decided that's what I wanted to do when I grew up, and it never changed." I glance his way. "And you? What do you want to do with your life, Jude Bishop?"

"I have no idea. Never have. Which sucks, because everyone asks—all the time. In my case, they all presume . . . Well, with my piano . . ."

"You don't want that. You do seem to enjoy . . . I mean, I thought maybe it was one of those things that parents push on you, and it doesn't matter how good you are at it, if you're not interested. But you seem to like it."

"I *love* it. I really do. No one ever needed to push the piano on me. But a career in it?" He shudders. "I hate performing."

"So I shouldn't ask you again."

"What? No. Not at all. That's *playing* for someone. Performing is a totally different thing." He eases back in the seat. "Lennon used to come up to the turret room when I practiced. He'd hang there—doing homework, playing a game. Dad would do the same when he was home, working in there while I practiced. I liked that. No pressure. No obligation. They were there because they wanted to hear the music, not because they shelled out two hundred bucks to support the arts and are trying not to check their watches or their cell phones, because the music's very nice, but after ten minutes of it, really, they have better things to do."

"It'd be a whole lot more *comfortable* curled up in one of those window seats listening to you play. But I don't think your mother would appreciate a steady stream of traffic through her house for private performances."

He chuckles at that. "True. Maybe I'll become one of those old-time bar players, just there to provide ambience and take the occasional request."

"As long as it's not 'Hey Jude'?"

I get a genuine smile for that. "Only for you. But, yes, I shouldn't have given up the piano. Thank you for that."

"For making you play?"

"For giving me a reason to."

We settle into an easy silence. When it starts to chafe again, I say, "Do you mind if I look through that envelope from Lennon's room? Maybe it has something we can use."

He nods. I take it from the backseat, pull out my notebook, and set to work.

We knew Lennon was researching his biological parents. It isn't until I evaluate the whole collection that I notice more.

"He's focusing on your father." I wave a collection of small-town news articles, dating back to their dad's—Matthew Lowe's—high school days, when he'd been quarterback on a state-championship football team. "Which might seem a matter of circumstance—he's the one who got the ink, but Lennon only collected his yearbook photos. And in the articles about their deaths, he's highlighted your father's background."

Jude makes a noise to tell me he's listening but doesn't interrupt.

I pick up my notebook. "The man in the conservatory kept talking about your father. I thought he meant Peter Bishop. I tried to confirm that, and he seemed to agree. But I wonder if he was being snide. *Of course that's who I mean. Who else?* There must be a reason Lennon was looking into Matt Lowe. Something set him on that trail. Something that happened *after* you left home. Maybe when he met someone who knew Matt." I pause. "If it's the guy from the conservatory, the age is about right. It'd explain why Lennon wouldn't tell anyone—it'd be easy for the guy to convince him to keep their meetings quiet, so he doesn't upset your adopted parents."

Jude keeps driving as I continue working it through aloud.

"What if Lennon's problems are hereditary?" I say. "What if it came from your biological father? Maybe this guy knew Matt Lowe, shared these interests, and hoped you inherited that?" I shake my head. "But what would that even mean?"

I lapse into silence. After another mile, I say, "You said you and Lennon don't hunt, right?"

"Our mother wouldn't allow it. Our dad used to, but she wouldn't even let him talk about it in the house."

"Well, someone taught Lennon. He cleaned a rabbit for me and did a decent job of it. I still don't know what that means. How it would tie into your biological father or the guy in the conservatory or Cadence or Edie or anything."

This time, when Jude doesn't reply, I prod him with, "I'm grasping at straws, aren't I?"

"There's ... something, but— Let me work it through. We're almost at the spot and we need to focus on that. I'll think about this."

forty-eight

As we near Reeve's End, I direct Jude to the bus stop. I don't know what he expects to find there. Signs of a scuffle, like Lennon did with Edie?

When I tell Jude to pull over, he stops at the side of the highway. I get out and he follows.

"What are we doing here, Winter?" he says in a careful tone, as if I'm upset and he doesn't want to question.

"The bus stop," I say, pointing at the sign. I don't blame him for missing it—the metal is rusted and riddled with pellets; locals use it for drive-by target practice, as if by obliterating the one sign of public transit they can forget that there *is* a way out of Reeve's End.

"Wouldn't she get off at the terminal in town?" he asks.

I look at him. He turns toward the town lights, less than a half mile away.

"Why is there a stop right outside . . . ?" He squeezes his eyes shut. "Shit. This *is* the stop. I'm sorry. I didn't think—" He shakes his head. "I didn't *think*."

"You expected a bus station? Like in the city?"

"Yeah. I figured she'd get off at a terminal, and the clerk on duty might have seen her or . . ." He looks at the empty highway, the forest closing in on both sides.

"She'd get off here and walk along down the highway, which as you've noticed isn't exactly a busy expressway. She'd have turned off down there to take the back way to the trailer park. There's no need to even pass through town."

"Shit. I wasn't thinking. Okay, so plan B. Is there anyone she might have called as soon as she got to town? Maybe for—"

His phone rings. He looks down at it and murmurs, "Thank God." Then he answers with, "Tell me you've got something."

Jude jots down numbers on his notepad. They look like GPS coordinates.

Please let them be coordinates.

He thanks Roscoe profusely, hangs up, and flips screens on his phone. "Cadence made a call. Or she tried to. I'm guessing she managed to start dialing, and her captor realized what she was doing. But Roscoe's contact could get rough coordinates. He's confirmed that the phone is shut off now, so it can't be tracked, but he knows where it lost signal. The call coordinates and final coordinates are about a quarter mile apart. Like her captor took the phone and then walked farther before he realized he should shut it right off. But the trajectory between the points shows the direction they were heading." He turns and gestures. "The first set is about a half mile that way." He pauses. "That's the direction of your cabin, isn't it?"

I nod, and I'm holding myself so still, against every urge to run to my cabin and save Cadence. That's not how this works. That can't be how this works.

"This is bullshit," Jude says finally. He walks to the car and climbs in, and I'm left standing there, staring, and there's part of me that thinks he's done, just done, had enough and is ready to give up. But I know better. I know *him* better. So I stand there and watch as he starts the car and hits buttons on his phone. Then he says to me, "It's not 911, right?"

"What?"

"You said the local police number isn't 911, right?"

I give him the number. He punches it in, and when it connects, I hear the answer over the car speakers.

Jude says, "To whom am I speaking?" in a tone straight from his mother's playbook. Not cold or loud, but sharp, each word snapping off.

"Sheriff Ronald Slate," the respondent says, with no small amount of superciliousness himself. "Reeve's End sheriff's department."

"This is Jude Bishop. My father is Congressman Peter Bishop. I met your deputy last night—"

"You're that boy that's been bothering Winter Crane, selling her that cock-and-bull story. Well, I'm sure Congressman Bishop's office would like to speak to you, son, about a little issue of misrepresentation."

"I *am* Jude Bishop. My father is Peter Bishop. If you would like to notify him, I will happily provide you with a number. His *direct* number. Here. Write this down." He rattles it off. "Would you like that again?"

"I don't know who this is—"

"I just told you, sheriff. I'm calling to report an abduction. Winter's sister, Cadence, returned to Reeve's End late this afternoon. I can provide the details so you may verify that she purchased a ticket online. She hasn't been seen since, and Winter received a message indicating she has been abducted."

The sheriff snorts. "Of course she did. The message went to Winter—the same person who's been part of this mess all along. First your brother, now her sister . . ."

"No, first Edie Greene. Then my brother. Then Winter's sister. My father's security team managed to track Cadence's last call to the woods west of Reeve's End. We have two sets of coordinates, providing a trajectory."

"Providing a what? No, never mind. You're telling me that your daddy's security people tracked this, but you want *us* to investigate?"

"You are the local police. If I go over your head—which you will not appreciate—you still must be involved, and the delay in sorting jurisdictional issues will endanger Cadence Crane's life."

"Is this a prank, son? You get bored and dream this up with your brother? Convince poor Winter that her sister's missing, when the truth is that her sister just doesn't want nothing to do with her?"

"Sir?" I say. "It's Winter. This is not a prank. My father contacted my sister this afternoon. He can confirm that. I can provide the bus ticket and her ring, both of which came from the man who has abducted her, which proves—"

"Which proves nothing but that your new *boyfriend* has deep pockets and a good imagination, enough of both to carry out this crazy scheme. Tell him I don't care who his daddy is, if he keeps scaring you with these crazy stories, I'll have him charged with obstruction of justice."

"That would require me stopping you from investigating a crime," Jude says, his voice brittle. "The problem, *sir*, is that we can't get you off your ass to investigate one."

The sheriff hangs up. Jude drops his face into his hands and shakes his head.

"You tried," I say. "You did the responsible thing, and it failed. Now I have to do the irresponsible thing, and go after my sister."

forty-nine

WE SOON REALIZE THE TRAJECTORY DOES NOT LEAD TO MY CABIN.
And we know where it does lead: the mine shaft.

"The mine is just up there," I whisper after a few minutes,
and Jude has me turn off my penlight and then . . .

Darkness. The moon has slid behind cloud and even overhead I can see nothing except the outline of tree branches, black
against black, visible only by the faint movement of leaves in
the wind, the limbs like gnarled claws hiding in shadow.

Jude finds my hand, and his fingers entwine with mine, and
it is such a simple thing, but it feels so *not* simple. It feels like
comfort and warmth and guidance in the dark, someone saying, *You're not alone.* He squeezes my hand and I lean against
his shoulder, just for a second, and that small gesture isn't
simple either, not for me. I don't lean. I don't accept kindness

easily. But I will admit that I need him, and that's okay, because he needs me, too.

To say my eyes adjust to the darkness would overstate the matter, but they adjust enough that, holding hands, we can guide each other over the rocky terrain, saying not a word as we strain for signs of trouble. Or signs of hope. We hear neither. The forest is as the forest always is at night—the scamper of tiny feet, the cry of a bird, the musky smell of fur, and the sweeter smell of leaves. Nothing out of the ordinary. Which is as reassuring and as disappointing as hearing none of those signs we're straining for.

We reach the hole into the mine shaft. It's exactly as we left it. I even find that old footprint, the one that told me it wasn't Jude. No others have joined it, but that one is off to the side, in a pocket of sandy soil. The rest of the ground is rocky, barely sprinkled with dirt.

Jude crouches by the hole and reaches in for the rope. He whispers, "I'll go first. Wait until I tug it."

We reach the bottom, where it's pitch black. We turn on our lights. Jude bends at the hole into the shaft and looks and listens. Then he goes through. I follow.

The shaft proper looks untouched. Jude shines his light around. I motion that I'll lead and when he hesitates, I whisper, "I know what's in here," which he accepts with a nod.

I reach the cave-in. Just enough rocks have been moved to pick through to the other side. Someone's been here. I don't say that. I don't dare even think it or I'll run, tripping and stumbling and shouting my sister's name.

We make our way over the rubble. On the other side, the edge of my beam catches something on the wall. It's a dark green tuft of yarn, caught on a splintered wooden support beam. I look down and see a scuffle of footprints. Large footprints. That shade of green, though, suggests a woman's sweater.

I picture the man from the conservatory carrying Cadence through this tight passage. Her sweater catches, just enough to make him stumble and scuff the ground. Then the fibers break, and he carries on.

Jude checks the clues as I pass them. He doesn't ask what I saw. Doesn't ask what I'm thinking. Observes, draws his own conclusions, says nothing.

Another step, and I hear a sound that makes me stop short.

I don't even know how to describe the noise. It's a hoarse, guttural sound, harsh and insistent, over and over, but barely loud enough to hear. The sound makes every hair on my neck rise. It isn't human. It isn't beast. It's a nightmare sound, harsh and urgent and voiceless and raw.

I back up, and Jude's there, his hand gripping my shoulder.

"A gag?" he whispers. "Someone gagged?"

I want to say yes. Yes, that's exactly what it is. But it's not, and the question in his voice tells me he knows.

I want to run, and I am shamed by the impulse. I grip my open switchblade, and inch forward toward the sound. It doesn't get louder. It's almost like a gagging now, but hoarse and rasping and urgent.

I'm moving with my right hand on my penlight, the left against the wall, and when the wall vanishes, I falter that way. Jude grabs for me, but my foot slides, and I hear Jude's "Shit!"

I have the weirdest sensation of my foot sliding into nothing, and then Jude is hauling me away, and my light bounces as the penlight falls from my hand and keeps going, keeps dropping. Jude's holding me tight as his heart pounds against my chest. I pull away, carefully, and turn.

Behind me is an alcove along the left wall. And on the floor of that alcove? A hole, half-covered with rotted and broken boards. I move closer, Jude holding my arms like I'm going to topple at any moment. I look down into the hole . . . and I can't even see the beam of my penlight.

fifty

I SHIVER. IT'S JUST A CONVULSIVE SHIVER AT FIRST, BUT ONCE IT starts, it doesn't stop, and it's not just how close I came to falling down that endless hole. It's as if the shot of fear disintegrates the walls I'm holding up, the walls that keep me calm when a madman has my sister—my *sister*—and . . .

Jude pulls me closer, and I fall against him as I shiver. He takes off his suit jacket and tucks it around my shoulders.

"I'm not really—" I begin.

"I know. Keep it anyway."

He shines his cell phone light down the mine shaft, and the beam bounces off the walls. It's a straight passage for at least twenty feet, before the tunnel veers left, in the direction of that hoarse rasping sound.

As he pulls the beam back, it trips over the floor. I notice debris ahead, and I'm processing that—wondering if it's significant, when he says, "Huh? Is that . . ." I follow the light to a spot halfway between us and the debris. It glints off something metallic.

When Jude starts forward, I grab his arm. I'm waiting for this whole scenario to turn into a trap, so when I spot metal on the ground, I think of a literal trap. But then I realize what it is, as he already has, and I let go. He continues forward and then crouches as I join him.

It's a knife. A hunting blade, half out of a leather sheath. Jude checks it from all angles. Then he prods, as if thinking it could still be a trap, a conveniently placed weapon that will launch a cave-in.

He pokes at it. Examines it again. Then lifts it and turns it over in his hands.

It's a knife. Nothing more. A big one, though, too big to have dropped from a pocket. There's a hook on the sheath, for hanging it from a belt, and while it seems possible that it *did* fall off, we look at each other for an alternate explanation, a more sinister explanation. Yet neither of us has one.

Jude takes the knife. When I step into the lead, he only hands me his phone for light.

I shine that light on the walls as we go. I can still hear that sound, coming from around the curve in the passage. There's the debris on the ground too, as if from an old cave-in.

I'm stepping over the debris when I notice a red dot on my leg. My first thought is blood. But it's not. It's a red dot of light, and my foot is already in motion, moving past it. I spin, grab Jude, and stop him. When I look down, I see a small red laser beam nestled in the debris.

Jude crouches and goes to move a piece of rock so he can

see where the beam originates, but before he can touch it, there's a crash from down that left-bending corridor. A crash and then the thump of running feet. No, running *paws,* the particular rhythm of four legs, and I hear that sound, that rasping and hacking sound, and I turn, yelling, "Run!" as I shove Jude.

I know what that sound is, what it *should* be. Barking. Frenzied barking. But it's much too soft for that, and all I can guess is that the beast has been barking so long it's lost its voice.

I shove Jude, and we start to run, but I forget about the debris and stumble over it and face-plant in the dirt.

I hear Jude's sharp intake of breath as he wheels and I see the look on his face, the horror on his face. Something jumps on me. Jaws clamp on the back of my neck, and I don't have time to react, don't have time to think. All I see is Jude's face, that horror turning to rage as he charges, hunting knife drawn.

The jaws around my neck disappear. The weight vanishes too, as I hear what must be a yelp, but it's as terrible and unnatural as the bark. I scramble up, and I see Jude stabbing something brown. There's flashing fur and there's spraying blood, and it happens so fast that I don't register what he's attacking until it's over and there's a dog lying on the ground. It's Mange. And I don't have a split second to process that before Scar leaps at Jude. I lunge at him, my switchblade ready, but Jude's faster; he's already spinning, already slashing.

Another shape appears behind Scar. It's Reject, the omega, and I race between them, ready to fight her off, but she's cowering and she's making this horrible noise, like raspy crying, and I can see blood on her throat and her eyes burn with pain and terror. She's covered in blood and patches of missing fur.

I keep watching her, ready for attack, praying she doesn't

because I don't want to do this—I really do not want to hurt her—but she only cowers there, and then I hear Jude say, "Is she . . . ?" and my eyes fill with tears. I can't help it. I look at her and I want to cry.

"He drugged them," I whisper. "Drugged them and damaged their vocal cords so they couldn't bark. Then he locked them up in here, and between the drugs and the dehydration and imprisonment, they went mad. They turned on her and . . ."

I start to look toward the other two dogs. Jude stops me with, "Don't. I had to—" and I say, "I know," and I look anyway. Scar and Mange are dead. They have the same damage to their throats, the same unfocused eyes.

"I'm sorry," he says.

"You had to." I squeeze his hand and lean against him. "*I'm* sorry you had to."

"He is a sick, sick . . ." He trails off, snarling as if he can't even find words to finish, and he's shaking, the knife jittering against his leg, and I hug him tight and then take the knife and set it aside, and Jude slides down the wall until he's crouched there, staring at his bloodied hands. I find a napkin in his suit pocket and I wipe his fingers, slowly and carefully, not saying a word until he gives a little jolt, as if waking up, and says, "We have to go. We'll take the dog if we can but we have to leave."

"I know."

Cadence isn't here. It was a trap. The dogs were set free by that laser trip wire.

And the knife?

That knife wasn't lost. Wasn't dropped. It was left, like some kind of bizarre gladiatorial scenario.

And in this next room, you will face a pack of mad feral dogs.
Here's a knife to help you defeat them.

I don't understand that. I'm not sure it can be understood. This man is as mad as he made those beasts, and trying to figure out his motivation is the fast lane to madness itself.

I help Jude stand. He doesn't brush me off. He's still dazed, and when his gaze trips over the dead dogs, he flinches, and I murmur, "Don't."

"I—"

"They tried to kill me."

"But they're dogs . . ."

"Don't think of them that way," I say. "They weren't pets, not anymore, and maybe not ever. Think of them as . . . coyotes or wolves."

"I'd still feel bad if they were."

I give him a fierce hug. "I know. Just . . . let's help Reject. She needs us. It's too late for them. It always was."

I walk to Reject, who's still cowering. "I'll check her as quickly as I . . ."

I trail off as I see his gaze fixed on a spot near the ceiling, his face screwed up. When I notice what he's looking at, I blink, thinking I'm mistaken. Then I rise from Reject's side.

"Is that . . . a camera?" I say.

It is—a tiny wireless lens.

He was watching us? Filming us?

I'm about to say that when I hear a noise that makes us both freeze. It's a muffled sound, but not like the poor dogs. This is a rhythmic banging. One-two-three. Pause. One-two-three.

I glance at Jude.

"I'm going to go take a look," he says, and I shake my head sharply, saying, "No, you can't," but he cuts me off with, "I'll be careful. Stay with the dog." He picks up my bloodied switchblade and then hands me the knife, the large hunting knife. "We have to know."

He starts down the passage, light in one hand, switchblade in the other. I murmur an apology to Reject and follow Jude, just to the corner, so I can keep an eye on him.

That banging continues. It sounds like wood on wood, the same pattern, repeated. One-two-three. Pause. One-two-three.

Jude looks left. He shines the light down the tunnel, and I spot a doorway. There's broken wood at the base, as if that's where the dogs burst through when the trip wire freed them.

Jude peers toward the room and then starts to continue past it. After a few steps, he stops. He backs up to the room. He looks inside. Then he steps through the doorway. A moment later, he's in the tunnel, frantically motioning for me to come, and I do—I run down that passage, even as he's motioning, equally frantically, for me to slow down, to be careful.

Before I reach the room, he disappears inside it. I hear a muffled gasp, then what sounds like a muffled shriek, and Jude saying, "Shhh, shhh. It's okay," and I race through the doorway and . . . there's my sister.

There's Cadence.

At first, that's all I see. It takes a moment to register where exactly she is—she's lying, bound and gagged, on her stomach in a hole near the top of the wall. Her captor stuffed her in there with the dogs right below, leaving them lunging and leaping, desperately trying to get at her.

I'm flying across the room, and she sees me and she yelps behind the gag. Then Jude reaches in to pull her out and that cry of relief and joy turns to fear. "He's with me, Cady," I say quickly. "He's fine. Let him help you."

He pulls her free and gets the gag off as I cut the ropes on her hands, and she says, "I'm so sorry, you look like . . . I thought you were . . ." and then she's free and I'm hugging her and she's collapsing in my arms, and if she says anything else, if Jude replies, I don't hear it.

I have my sister back.

Nothing else matters.

fifty-one

OF COURSE, THAT'S NOT ALL THAT MATTERS. THERE'S THE SMALL detail of escaping and praying we *can* escape what is almost certainly a trap. I'm helping her from the room, wiping away my tears so I can see my path.

I hear something like paper rustling, and I turn sharply. There's a sheet of paper tacked to the wall with a knife. Jude's taking it down. He reads it and his face contorts in disgust and horror. He balls up the page, throws it aside, and takes a deep breath, shuddering.

"Just hold on," I murmur to Cadence, and she leans against the wall as I hurry to pick up the paper.

Dearest Jude,

Congratulations. If you're reading this, you got past the dogs. I knew you would or I would never have set them on

you. If you did fail, you wouldn't be the young man I be-
lieve you to be, so your loss, while regrettable, would not
be overwhelming. But you are the young man I expect, of
course. And here is your reward. A reward and a choice.
I'm sure you've left Winter someplace safe. You may re-
turn her sister to her . . . or you may not. The girl is yours,
either way, to do with as you will. If you make the choice
I hope you will, you do not need to fear repercussions. I'll
take care of everything.

I look at Jude, and he gives another deep shudder of revul-
sion, his look still shock, as if he can't believe what he read, the
interpretation he reached. I pocket the note and give his hand
a squeeze.

"Let's just go," I say.

He motions to Cadence that he'll help her walk, saying,
"May I?" and she nods.

We return to Reject. There's no time to examine the dog
now. No time to do more than stop and tell her that I'll be back,
and I know that's pointless—she can't understand—but I do it
anyway. When we start to leave, she limps after us, and I can't
take that. I just can't.

It isn't just me, either. Neither Cadence nor Jude tells me
to leave Reject. Finally, Jude says, "Can you help your sister,
Winter? I'll carry the dog," and that's what we do—I support
Cadence and Jude hefts Reject into his arms, and maybe that's
not the smart move when you expect a madman to return at
any moment, but it's what we have to do.

We make it to the pit without incident. I go up first.
Cadence follows. She's weak, but insists she's uninjured. Then

Jude ties the rope to Reject, and I hear the dog make that feeble and harsh whimpering sound, and he's talking to her, his voice low, soothing. He comes up next, and she whines and tries to yelp, but he climbs quickly and then hauls her out. When Reject is up top, I expect she'll realize she's free and try hobbling off into the forest. Instead, as Jude unties her, she only licks his face, and then she lets him pick her up again and we head for Reeve's End.

Cadence doesn't say much. Nothing really, no more than, "I'm fine, Win, really," when I keep giving her anxious looks. Partway there, she pulls me into a hug and says, "Thank you, for coming," and I say, "Of course I'd—" and she presses her finger to my lips, motioning at the forest, reminding me to be quiet, just in case.

I still sneak glances at her, and it's not just to be sure she's okay—it's to reassure myself she's actually there. She's cut her hair. It used to stretch down to her waist and now it's barely past her shoulders. It looks good on her. She's put on a little weight. That looks good too—I used to worry about how thin she was, blaming Colton, who'd make snarky comments if she gained a pound.

When we near town, there's only one place I even consider going. I know he was coming back tonight, but I call first to be sure he's home. He is. I warn him we're coming, and I don't say much, just that Cadence is home and something's happened and I need to bring her to him.

We've barely reached the highway when I see the taillights of his old minivan. Those taillights flash, and he pulls a U-turn and veers onto the shoulder in a cloud of dust. The van hasn't even stopped before the passenger door opens and Mrs. Southcott is climbing out and hurrying toward us, seeing us filthy and bloody and saying, "Oh, my God. Oh, my God."

"We're okay," Cadence says.

"The dog's hurt worst," I say. "We need Doc to take a look at the dog."

She looks from one face to the other and gives a choking laugh and then turns to Doc Southcott as he approaches, leaning on his cane.

"They're worried about the dog," she says.

He shakes his head. "Of course they are. Get in the van, and *I'll* decide who needs medical attention first."

We're at Doc Southcott's house. We hold off on our explanation until we arrive, and then I tell the story. The whole story.

Cadence fills in the part I don't know. Somehow her captor knew our father phoned her, likely tracing the call or accessing the message. As she was still trying to figure out how to respond to Bert's plea, she got a call from a man who claimed to be a new guidance counselor at my school. He knew our father had contacted her and he wanted to be sure she understood the severity of the situation, just how distraught I was over Edie, that I wasn't coming to school and I really needed my sister, and he said he'd gladly buy her a bus ticket if she came home right away.

She said no, she'd buy her own ticket, and she *would* come, and he told her that the last bus left in two hours and she promised to be on it. She arrived in Reeve's End and had just started walking home when the "guidance counselor" pulled up and offered her a lift, wanted to talk to her about the "delicate situation" with me. She got in. The next thing she knew, she was waking up in that hole.

Doc Southcott tries to work on Reject as we explain, but he keeps stopping to stare, just stare, and then I take over what he's doing with Reject.

When we finish, he's speechless. Mrs. Southcott is not. She rants about the sheriff and the deputy, and then takes the phone into the next room.

I ask Cadence about the so-called guidance counselor. She tries to describe him, but it was dark and she didn't pay much attention. She remembers dark hair and blue eyes, which is why, when Jude rescued her, with the dim light, she thought she was seeing her captor again.

I'm holding Reject as we talk and Doc Southcott sews one of her larger bite wounds. He's given her a local anesthetic, but he's afraid to fully sedate her, not knowing what else she's been drugged with. My job is to soothe her. She licks my hand and watches me, and I try not to cry, thinking of what she's gone through. Doc Southcott says she'll pull through, and the damage to her vocal cords doesn't seem permanent. Maybe, when she recovers, she'll go back to being that half-wild beast, but this isn't about feeling empathy for a pet dog—it's about feeling empathy for a living creature.

"Not such bad bedside manner after all, huh, Winter?" Doc Southcott murmurs. "It's okay to feel for a creature in pain. And it's okay to recognize that sometimes we can't afford to feel, that it'll hurt too much. You need to protect yourself *and* you need to let people in. It's a matter of finding the right balance." He glances at Jude. "I think you're figuring it out just fine. You two did amazing work on this. Together."

Mrs. Southcott's voice rises in the next room. "You listen here, Ronnie Slate, I'm going to pretend *that* was some kind of joke, a very poor one at that. You are going to get your ass over here and— What? Don't you even—!"

Doc Southcott limps through the door and takes the phone as his wife says, "He's still trying to say Winter and Jude did this. Kidnapped her own sister for attention. I told him about the poor dog and . . . and I don't even want to repeat what he said."

Doc Southcott gets on the phone. "Is that right, Ronnie? It's awful late, and Patsy's distraught over these kids, and I'm hoping she's misunderstanding what you said. Tell me she's misunderstanding."

Silence as he listens.

"Are you drunk, Ronnie?" Doc Southcott's voice turns sharp. "Please tell me you've been drinking or smoking up or *something* to explain the abject stupidity of the words leaving your mouth."

Pause.

"Hell, *no*. Don't you threaten—" Pause. "If you set foot on my property, I swear I'll meet you with my hunting rifle." Pause. "Don't you hang—"

Silence. I can hear Doc Southcott breathing hard and his wife trying to calm him and then asking, "What'd he say?"

"He's coming to arrest Winter and Jude."

Doc Southcott keeps his voice low, as if hoping we won't overhear. Jude and Cadence and I all look at one another as Mrs. Southcott explodes in a fresh tirade.

"Can he . . . can he do that?" Cadence whispers to us.

"He's the local law," Jude says. "It won't stick, but he can do it."

"The doc and Mrs. Southcott won't let him."

"That's what I'm afraid of," I murmur. "I don't want them to get in trouble." I look at Jude. "We need to leave. Get to your father. Sort this out. Once the sheriff throws us in a cell, we're there for a while."

Doc Southcott comes in and says, "Okay, kids. I'm going to ask you to go on upstairs and get some sleep. Whatever you hear—"

"We already heard," I say, and I tell him we're leaving. He argues and Mrs. Southcott argues even harder, but Jude and I make our case quickly, and they finally agree that we aren't children—we've proven ourselves very capable so far and this is the right decision.

We need to leave Cadence with the Southcotts. That's the hardest part. It's also the right decision. No one is threatening her, and she's still weak and shaken from her ordeal.

"Sir?" Jude says to the doctor. "Do you think we'd have time for me to bring the car back before the sheriff arrives? Give Winter a moment with her sister?"

"I can talk to her later," I say. "We should—"

"I'll drive you to your car," Doc Southcott says. "We have time yet. Ronnie lives way over on the county line."

I mouth a thank-you to Jude as they go. Mrs. Southcott says she's going to pack us something to eat and hurries off to the kitchen, leaving Cadence and me alone.

"I made so many mistakes," Cadence says.

"Later," I say. "Right now—"

"No, Win, right now I've got to get this out. I made mistakes. Over and over, I made them. I left you. I left you long before I left Reeve's End. You were my baby sister, and I abandoned you."

"You didn't—"

"I did. I wanted to forget how bad things had gotten. It was easier to stay with friends and pretend you were fine at home. I knew Daddy would smack you when he got into the bourbon, but you were stronger than me. I told myself you could handle him. I told myself if it got bad, you'd come to me. But you would have never come to me. You'd have taken whatever he dished out and kept going, and I am so ashamed. . . ." Her voice catches.

"It's okay, Cady."

"No, Winter, it is not, and please don't say that." Tears stream down her face, tracks through the dirt still on her cheeks. "I was selfish and I was jealous. You were tough and smart and you'd get out and so you could take it, and I couldn't. And then Colton . . ."

"Cady, really, we can talk—"

"Please, please just listen. I said you talked me into going to college and leaving him. That was a lie. I wanted to go. Wanted to go so bad. Not just to go, but to get away from him. I was afraid, though. He said he needed me. Said he'd hurt himself if I left him. Then he'd get drunk and he'd hit me and I'd think it was my fault, that I wasn't giving him what he needed, that I wasn't enough. And deep down, I just wanted to escape. You telling me to go to college gave me permission."

She stops and shakes her head hard. "No, that's a lie. It gave me someone to blame. I could pretend I was doing it for you, to set a good example. And then he . . . he did . . . he did what he threatened, and I couldn't handle it because he'd warned me, which made it my fault. You did nothing wrong, Winter. Absolutely nothing."

She hugs me so tight I can't breathe and she says, "I didn't know how to come home. I didn't know how to say I was sorry. I told myself I was waiting until you left for school so I could visit you at college, but that was just an excuse. I didn't know how to face you after what I did."

I hug her. That's all I can do. That and say, "I love you, Cady," and her grip tightens and then there's a quick honk from the driveway, and she lets me go, saying, "Jude's a great guy, Winter."

"We're not really—"

"I don't know what you two are, but I can tell he cares about you. He *thinks* about you. He treats you the way you deserve to be treated. That's how it should be, whether it's a friend or something more. Such a simple concept. Such an obvious concept. And I don't know why I never saw it before."

"Maybe you didn't think you were worth it before."

Another tight squeeze and a soft laugh. "You're smart, little sister. Anyone ever tell you that?" She steps back and waves toward the door. "Go on. Find Edie. Help Jude find his brother. Just be careful. No more running into abandoned mine shafts. Use his dad's influence and get the police involved. The real police."

"That's—"

"I know. That's what you've been trying to do, 'cause

you're, you know, smart. Both of you. But you've got a witness now, a witness with a story that anyone but that idiot sheriff and his idiot son will believe. Bring them to me. I'll tell them."

Another quick hug, and I'm gone.

fifty-two

WE CATCH ONLY THE BRIEFEST GLIMPSE OF THE SHERIFF'S TRUCK as we leave town. He doesn't see us. As soon as we're on the highway again, Jude agrees that we should go straight to his father, rather than rely on his mother.

"He seems like a decent guy," I say, and then hurry on. "Which isn't to belittle what he did to you and Lennon, how you grew up and all that."

"He didn't have much to do with our growing up. He was gone—first with the law firm, then politics. He was the kind of father who made sure he was there for all the award ceremonies and games and concerts—even if there isn't a news crew on hand—but otherwise?" He shrugs. "He grew up in a world where women looked after the household while men made the money. I'm not absolving him of blame, but he wasn't the one cracking the whip."

"And he may not have been the one saying you were disappointing him. Your mother's the one who told you that."

His fingers drum the steering wheel. "Yeah. I never really thought much about that. I just figured he conveyed it through her. But he was our cheerleader; she was our referee. Which doesn't mean . . ." He shakes his head. "It doesn't matter. I'm calling him now, okay?"

"Okay."

He dials the number on the keypad. The line rings four times and goes to voice mail. He leaves a message telling Mr. Bishop we're on our way and need to speak to him, then explains to me that his dad usually turns his phone off during a party. Then he shuts off the music and says, "That thing I was thinking about earlier. With our father. I've had contact with our maternal grandmother."

"Oh?"

"After I left home, I started worrying that I'd misheard what our mother said on the phone that day. So I tracked down our grandmother, Betty. She eventually admitted she accepted a house to give us up. We . . . worked it out. I've been helping, doing upkeep. Well, *learning* how to do it—that's one thing we didn't get lessons on."

"You're supposed to hire people for that."

"Apparently. Anyway, Betty has told me more about our parents. And . . ." He sucks in air. "I'm beginning to wonder whether Matt Lowe is actually our biological father."

I look over sharply. "What?"

"Betty says Matt was an asshole. Knocked our mother Annie around. Screwed everything in a skirt. Once, when Betty got ranting—and got drinking—she said she was glad there wasn't a drop of Matt Lowe in us boys. When I asked what she meant, she went really quiet and then started blustering that she meant we weren't like him. That we were smart boys. Nice boys."

"Okay. But she's never met Lennon, right?"

"No, and she doesn't know me all that well either. Which now has me thinking she meant something else entirely. You've seen the pictures. Do we look like him?"

I reach into the backseat and take the photos out for a better look. I remember thinking earlier that they took after their mother a lot more. Yet even that resemblance isn't strong. Neither parent has dark hair or blue eyes. The facial structure is different. Which could just be genetics—a throwback to other generations—but there's no proof that Jude is clearly misinterpreting his grandmother's words.

When I admit that, he says, "It's clear we're full brothers, though."

"So you're thinking Annie had a lover, one who fathered you and Lennon?"

"There's more. I asked Betty how the Bishops came to get custody of us. She said our mother—Elysse Bishop—came to her with the offer. When Betty hesitated, Elysse threatened her with a 'secret' about Annie, one that would hurt us if it got out. That's all Betty would say, and she regretted it right away. She has a lot of stuff bottled up and she's lonely and she drinks a little too much, and I think . . ."

He goes quiet, and I let the silence hang until he says, "I think she's trying to connect with me, maybe a little too hard. Annie was her only child. It's important for us to understand that Betty didn't abandon us. I figured she was twisting the truth. She knew I was pissed with my parents and took advantage of that. I figured Elysse said something that Betty exaggerated. I couldn't imagine how Elysse could possibly know a secret about Annie."

"If the secret *was* that you're illegitimate, that'd be an issue, with Matt being a small-town hero and all. I can see Annie taking a lover. But having *two* kids with him?" I pause. "Unless she thought that was the way to make him *more* than a lover." I shake my head. "I'm just speculating. I don't know what else to do with it. You're right, how would Elysse *know* Matt wasn't your father? That makes no sense."

"We need to talk to Betty," he says. "We'll do that tomorrow. Right now, our priority is talking to my father."

fifty-three

Roscoe calls when we're about twenty minutes from the house. Jude has him on speakerphone.

"Hey, bud," Roscoe says. "You find what you were looking for?"

"Yes, everything's fine."

"Good. Then get your butt on home before your momma finds out you took off. She was asking about you and Winter hours ago, and your daddy had to cover for you, saying you two retired early."

"Okay, we'll be there shortly. Can you tell my dad we need to speak to him? He's not answering his phone."

"Probably put it aside for the evening. You know how your momma gets about that—no cell phone checks during social engagements."

"I know. Just tell him we really need to talk."

As soon as we pull up in front of the estate, Roscoe appears, jabbing a finger toward the garage. Jude sighs but doesn't argue. Roscoe meets us in the garage, as Jude looks around, saying, "Where's the Cadillac?"

"Your daddy took it. I never even knew he was gone until I went looking for him. Maria said he took off maybe an hour ago, something about an emergency."

Jude looks at me, his brows furrowing. "But I called around that time and he never picked up."

Roscoe shrugs. "Maybe he was on the line with the other thing."

"Where's Maria? I'll speak to her."

Roscoe checks his watch and arches his brows at Jude, who sighs and says, "Gone home, right?"

"Uh, yeah. Almost an hour ago, along with everyone else. You do know what time it is, right?"

"Fine. Where's Mom?" He sees Roscoe's expression. "Let me guess. Gone to bed."

"Long ago. Last thing she did was ask about you and Winter. It's been a long night for her, and she seemed kind of agitated. Went to her room for a while, which she never does during a party. Bad form, don't you know."

He quirks a smile, but when Jude doesn't return it, Roscoe pauses and then says, "You told her about your brother, didn't you?"

"Yeah."

"Ah, shit." Roscoe shakes his head. "Why do you want to go getting him in trouble like that? Yeah, you're worried. Guess I can't fault you for that. All right, then. You two get off to bed, and we'll pretend that's where you've been all night."

343

"I really should speak to my mother."

"It can wait until morning," Roscoe says firmly. "Let her get some sleep."

There's a guest room made up for me. Jude shuts the door behind us, saying, "I wasn't going to get into it with him, but I'm okay with waking my mother to tell her about Cadence."

I sit on the end of the huge bed. "Will that help? If she's in denial, is it just going to sound like more proof we're hatching some crazy story? Maybe something Cadence and I rigged up to . . . I don't know, blackmail your family? Yes, that sounds nuts, but at this point, I'm feeling paranoid. Other than Doc Southcott, no one's believing us about anything. Should we wait for your father?"

"I don't know." He pulls up a chair and collapses into it. "Why the hell didn't he return my call? I said I need to speak to him and he *knows* we took off on an emergency. Dad and I have never been really close, but he's always been there for me. He was earlier. And then what? Something else comes up, and he can't bother even calling me back? What's that important? Hell, what kind of emergency is he even going to get in the middle of a Sunday night?"

He runs his hands through his hair. "Sorry. I'm tired and frustrated and starting to rant."

"Have you called again?"

"I texted on the way up. I called while you were in the bathroom. It's just going straight to voice mail now, like he's seeing my number and hitting ignore. Which makes *no* sense."

When silence falls, he looks over and then heaves to his

feet. "Yeah, it's late. You don't need my shit. I'm glad we got Cadence back. We'll talk to my parents in the morning."

I catch his hand. "Yes, we got Cadence back, but that doesn't help Lennon and Edie unless we can use it to *make* someone pay attention to us. I wasn't ignoring you. I was just thinking."

I tug him to sit beside me and keep our hands entwined, working up the courage to follow my thoughts where they're leading.

"Back to your grandmother," I say. "It would make sense if Annie had an affair and accidentally got pregnant. But back-to-back pregnancies by a lover? That's intentional and the only reason would be that she hoped her lover would step up and offer to marry her. What's the most likely reason why he wouldn't? Why she'd need to try *twice*?" I look at him. "If he was already married."

He gives a slow nod. "That makes sense. We'll add that to our ammunition for when we talk to Betty."

"Yes, but . . ." I take a deep breath. "You said Elysse went to Betty directly. She wanted you boys specifically. Claimed to know a secret that could hurt you. If that secret is about your real father, how would Elysse know?"

"Like I said, I have no idea . . ." He trails off. "Are you suggesting . . . You think our dad is actually . . ."

"It makes sense, doesn't it? The missing puzzle piece."

"No." He rises, dropping our hands. "Just no. I'm sorry, Winter. Is it possible Peter Bishop is our biological dad? Yes. But you're suggesting he's also the one behind Cadence's kidnapping, which explains why he took off on some emergency. You're saying he's responsible for *all* of this."

"I—"

"Is my dad the man from the conservatory?"

"No, but—"

"My dad was in DC when you were being stalked. That's a provable fact."

"Okay."

"Now you're going to suggest he has a partner, and that's who you saw in the conservatory, the man who stalked you."

"I didn't say a word."

He's pacing now. "You're going to say that's why Cadence freaked when she saw me. Because she thought I was him—my dad. You'll point out that Lennon and I look a lot more like Peter Bishop than Matt Lowe. You'll say Edie's kidnapping came before my dad left for DC, so that *could* have been him. You'll say he could have kidnapped Edie and Cadence, and even Lennon that first time, which is why Lennon didn't want to tell our parents. Because our *parent* is the one who took him. That's why Lennon thought he could fix it."

"I'm not saying any of that, Jude."

"You don't have to."

"Because you're working it through yourself."

His jaw sets. "Peter Bishop is not our father. Any resemblance is superficial. It's dark hair and blue eyes. That's it."

I'm quiet for a minute. Then I say, "Can I show you something?"

"What?"

"Come downstairs. Please. Just . . . trust me."

fifty-four

I TAKE JUDE TO THE SMALL LIBRARY. HE'S STILL VIBRATING WITH anger and confusion, but he let me bring him here. Now he stands in the middle of the room with me, his jaw set, as he says, "What?"

"Look at the portraits."

He casts a cursory glance over them. "Okay. What am I looking for?"

"When I came through the first time, I noticed some of these men really look like you and Lennon. I figured that could be one reason the Bishops adopted you—because you physically resemble them. See this one?" I walk over and point. "He could be Lennon dressed up for Founder's Day."

"Okay."

"You agree he looks like Lennon?"

"Sure, but that *disproves* your theory, doesn't it? This guy looks more like Lennon than Peter Bishop does."

Now I'm the one staring in confusion. Then it clicks.

When Mrs. Bishop was showing me around, she commented on a painting she "brought down" after it was "put upstairs" by her grandmother.

"The portraits . . . Which side of the family are they?"

"Elysse's. It's her house. My dad's family worked the mines—they were definitely *not* sitting for fancy oil paintings a hundred years ago." He looks at me. "You thought this was his family, which supported your theory."

I lower myself to the sofa. "It did. You two do resemble Peter Bishop, but only in coloring. You *really* look like some of these guys. The shape of the face, the mouth, the set of the eyes . . ." I trail off as I work it through. "That can't be coincidental."

"Okay . . ."

"This is Elysse's family. She's the one involved in all this. She adopted you and Lennon. She found you. She made all the arrangements. She made sure you didn't hunt, didn't even want you taking martial arts, freaked when you showed signs of a violent temper. And she's freaking about Lennon, now that she's heard the description of the man in the conservatory. She wanted both of us to stay here, not leave the house, not tell your father, let her investigate."

"Okay, but there's no way Elysse Bishop is my biological mother."

"Who are the male relatives on her side?"

He sits beside me, quieter now, thoughtful. "Her dad's gone. She has a brother, Kendrick, but I've only met him

348

once or twice, when I was little. He's been living in Europe. I wouldn't call them close. But . . ." He's thinking hard, fingertips drumming his leg. "I remember hearing they used to be close, as kids. People ask about him sometimes. I don't know what happened. Between them."

"Do you have any photos of him?"

"There should be some in here." He walks to the bookshelf, takes down one of the newer albums, and then flips through it. "He's a few years younger than her. Okay, here's Elysse graduating from college, and Kendrick's . . ." He stops, his finger on the photo. "He looks . . ." He swallows. "I'm right, aren't I?"

"That he looks like Lennon with longer hair? Yes."

He keeps turning pages. "He's over here, at Elysse's wedding, but it's not a good picture, and then . . ." He turns the page and stops as the color drains from his face. It's a photo of Kendrick; one where he's smiling at the camera, except it's not really a smile. It's a self-satisfied smirk that sends me reeling back into the conservatory.

Do I make you nervous, Winter? Truth is uncomfortable. Ask Jude. He knows all about truth and lies. I only wanted to warn you that the apple does not fall far from the tree. He is his father's son. Remarkable in a way few can appreciate.

"That's . . . ," Jude begins. "I didn't think I got a good look last night, but I . . ." He rubs his face. "Maybe I'm jumping to conclusions. Seeing what I expect."

He's not. Looking at that picture, there's no doubt in my mind. Elysse's brother, Kendrick, was the man in the conservatory.

"Your phone has a camera," I say. "Can you take a picture of this and send it to Doc Southcott? Ask Cadence to take a look? You can include a few other people, so she won't be prejudiced."

He nods, chin bobbing. "Good idea." He swallows again and turns to me. "It's him, isn't it?"

"I think so."

"And if it is, then it fits. It all fits."

"Yes. But send the photo. Cady saw him better."

He's hitting send when the door opens and Roscoe comes in.

"Hey, I thought you guys were going to bed," he says.

"Changed our minds," Jude says. "We're just poking about in here for a bit. Books, you know?"

Roscoe gives a laugh, but it seems a little strained. "Yeah, you and your books." He leans in with a mock whisper. "Might not be the way to impress the girls, though."

"Depends on the girl," I say.

Jude chuckles, but Roscoe doesn't seem to hear me. He's gazing about, as if trying to work something through.

"Were you looking for us?" Jude says.

"Hmm? No. Why?"

Jude looks around at the shelves. "Not exactly the place you hang out on night shift."

Roscoe seems to struggle for a response. "Sometimes. The chairs are comfy."

They actually aren't; they're hard-backed antiques, meant for display, not for curling up with a book.

"We won't be much longer," Jude says.

"Okay, well, I guess I'll go, then. . . ." Roscoe spots the photo album. "Whatcha doing with that, bud?"

There's a moment of silence. It's barely a heartbeat long. Then Jude slowly closes the book.

"I wanted to show Winter an old photo of me and Lennon. I was telling her about the time my mother had this fancy costume made for a Halloween party and Lennon came down wearing a sheet instead."

This is an outright lie. From a guy who does not tell them. Jude has my full attention now, and I'm watching both of them, my brain whirring to figure out what he has.

Jude continues, "But this is the wrong album. I thought I saw a picture of Lennon. Then I realized it was Kendrick."

Roscoe goes still.

"You know who I mean, right?" Jude says.

"Sure, your mother's brother. Your uncle."

"Mmm, he's not actually my uncle."

A pause. "Well, yeah, you're adopted so I guess not, but you'd still call him that, right?"

"Sure. Unless I called him Dad."

Roscoe stiffens. Then he forces a laugh. "Did you guys get into the leftover champagne? Your brother's usually the one for goofy jokes."

"He is. Do you know where I could find him?"

"Huh?"

"Do you know where I could find my brother?"

Roscoe sighs. "This again? I know you're worried, but he's with his buddies. He's been texting your momma."

"How do you know that? No, never mind. Could I ask you another favor? Track that text for me? You're really good at that sort of thing. I was so relieved when you gave us those

GPS coordinates for Winter's sister that I never wondered exactly how you got them. How did you do that?"

"I have a friend, like I said."

"Right, well, you've been very helpful, getting us all the coordinates we need. Even though you're sure Lennon's not actually missing."

Roscoe says nothing. He's thinking hard, and from his expression, he's not a guy accustomed to hard thinking.

"You know Kendrick, don't you?" Jude says. "In fact, I'm thinking he's the one who helped you get a job here, to keep an eye on his sons."

A long pause. Then, "Are you okay, Jude? Your momma's been worried about you, and I'm starting to think she might have a point."

"Tell my mother I'd like to speak to her."

"It's three in the morning. I'm not—"

"Fine." Jude starts for the door. "I'll go—"

Roscoe grabs me. It's so fast I don't have time to react—I'm expecting him to go after Jude. Jude catches the movement and spins, but before he can lunge, Roscoe has a knife at my throat.

"You think you're smart, don't you, Jude? Always have. Too smart and too good for the rest of us. I told your daddy not to bother with you. I've met fire-and-brimstone preachers who weren't as straitlaced as you. No booze, no pot, no pills. You hardly even date. That's unnatural for a boy your age. Your daddy thinks it's a sign—that you've got the itch and you're fighting extra hard to control it."

"Let Winter go. She has nothing to do with—"

"Oh, but she does. She's the bait that keeps you on the

line, boy. You'll do whatever I say, as long as I have her. Your daddy thinks she's the one for you, the key to bringing out *his* side of the family. He's wrong. You don't have that in you. Not the way your brother does. Lennon just needs a little more prodding, and this"—he waggles the blade against my throat—"might be the way to jump-start his engines. The girl he tried to save . . . who ended up falling for his brother. I bet Lennon's going to sing a whole different tune about little Winter now that—"

I stab Roscoe in the stomach. I've palmed the switchblade from my pocket and now I drive it into his gut the moment his knife wavers from my throat. It still hits me, the edge slicing my neck as Roscoe staggers back.

Jude yanks me out of the way. Roscoe charges with a roar. Jude hits him with a hard right and Roscoe goes down. I race over, switchblade ready. Jude leaps in to pin Roscoe, but the older man twists clear and grabs Jude, wrenching him down.

I snatch out my phone and dial 911. Nothing happens. I try again. Then I check my phone. No service.

"You really think we'd make it that easy?" Roscoe sneers. "You're not getting—" Jude hits him in the jaw, which shuts him up.

They're grappling on the floor, evenly matched, and I'm looking for a chance to jump in. Then footsteps sound in the hallway. Jude hears them too and says, "Run."

"I'm not—"

"Winter." He struggles to keep Roscoe down. "Run and get help. That's what I need."

I look at the knife. If I can incapacitate Roscoe long enough for Jude to escape with me—

"No time," Jude says, as if reading my mind yet again. "You need to run. I'll be fine. You will not."

He's right. Kendrick is obsessed with his sons. He won't hurt Jude. I'm not a person here. I'm an object. Like Cadence in that tunnel.

Here's a gift for you, son. Do what you want with her.

I run.

fifty-five

My pursuer is coming down the main corridor. I run for the opposite library door, the one that leads to the side exit.

I hate leaving Jude. Hate it so much. I feel like the helpless girl, running away, leaving her boyfriend to fight. But he *is* the fighter, and I'm helping him in the best way I can. I'll run outside until I pick up cell service and call 911 and *then* come back. I won't sit on the curb and wait for help. I just need to summon it.

When I see the exit door ahead, I slam into it as I twist the knob. The door doesn't budge. It must be locked, but I can't even *see* a lock, as if it's some kind of electronic one.

I wrench and twist the knob to no avail. A shoe squeaks behind me. I spin, my back to the door, knife ready. There's no one there. But I heard that shoe. I know I did. And this door isn't opening.

I race through the nearest door that *does* open and after a couple more, I find myself in the front hall again, the one that returns to the library.

I have to go back. Have to help Jude in any way I can. I can still hear the grunts and thumps of him fighting with Roscoe. And I can hear Kendrick's footsteps. Taking his time. Taunting and teasing as he's done from the start. Rage fills me, and I grip my switchblade and think of running back at him, showing him who he's taunting.

And that's as stupid as my fantasy of leaping from the tree into the feral dog fray.

I must be smart here. For Jude's sake, I must be smart.

Jude . . .

I remember last night, being in this hall, him leading me down it to . . .

To the panic room.

Panic room. Landline. Gun. Steel door that can't be opened even with the code once someone secures it from the inside.

I veer into the outer room. I yank off the painting over the security panel. The code is a pattern; I know that much. And it starts with 25.

2526—

No. I stop, my finger still poised over the 6. *Descending* pattern.

252423.

The steel door clicks open as a shoe squeaks in the hall again. I race into the panic room and slam my fist on the button, and the door slides shut just as a figure steps from the hall. I catch only a glimpse—enough to see a tall, dark-haired man—before the door shuts with a click, sealing me in.

I grab the landline phone. It's an old-fashioned rotary phone, and I lift the receiver to my ear as I dial the 9 and then the 1 and—

The line is dead. I hang up and lift it again.

Silence.

I dial 911, just in case, having not used a rotary phone in years. But I recall enough to know I should hear a tone. I don't and it doesn't magically connect when I dial a number.

I look around, and I spot the corner of *War and Peace* sticking from the sofa cushions.

I need to get help for Jude.

And find Lennon. Find Edie.

What has Kendrick done to them?

Kendrick took Edie for Lennon. Maybe Lennon did know her. Or maybe that whole story was a lie, and Kendrick just kidnapped her like he'd kidnapped Cadence for Jude.

And then . . .

And then . . .

I start shaking. Really shaking.

I need to get a grip. Jude is okay. Whatever—I inhale—whatever else has happened, Jude is okay and he's relying on me to get help. If I can't get help, I must *be* help.

I pick up the gun. I check the clip. It's full, and there's no safety. I lift and aim the gun at the door.

I can do this.

I have to do this.

I don't put my finger on the trigger. I won't be the idiot who

357

accidentally shoots the wrong guy. But my finger is poised. Then I let go with one hand, push the button to reopen the door, and then grip the gun with both hands again, my gaze fixed on that opening door.

Kendrick stands there. He's smirking that same smirk from the photo, from the conservatory. That smirk lets me aim the gun at his chest and pull the trigger without a moment's hesitation.

I feel the trigger move. There's a flash and an explosion and something flies out and hits Kendrick . . . and then falls harmlessly to the ground.

I look down to see wadded paper. A blank. The gun is loaded with blanks.

Kendrick doesn't even flinch, just walks toward me. I dive back into the panic room, to hit the button, to grab the knife. But he's too close. He grabs me and shoves a cloth reeking of chloroform over my mouth and nose, and I kick and punch, and my feet and fists make contact, but he only holds me tight, leans in, and says, "You're a resourceful girl, Winter. I can see why my sons are so taken with you." And then everything goes dark.

fifty-six

I WAKE SMELLING DIRT, AND I REMEMBER THE BUNKER WHERE I found Marty Lawson and for a second, I think I'm back there.

I *am* lying on a dirt floor. I feel it against my fingertips. But the smell is not the same. It's just similar enough that I know I'm underground.

Why am I under . . . ?

The house. The library. The panic room.

Jude.

I try to leap up, but my hands are bound behind me and I don't realize that until I move. My stomach lurches from the chloroform and my gorge rises, and that's when I realize I'm gagged. I'm gagged, and I'm going to throw up, and if I do, I'll choke on my own vomit.

I squeeze my eyes shut and breathe as deeply as I can until the wave of nausea passes. Then I take a moment to assess my situation. Gagged. Hands behind my back. My legs aren't tied, but if I stand, I risk toppling face-first, unable to brace myself.

I blink hard, hoping my eyes will adjust, but there's no light to help. One of my feet brushes a wall behind me. I manage to brace against it and rise onto my knees.

Then I stand. That takes time and effort. I put my back to the wall, my bound hands behind me, fingers outstretched. I feel around, hoping for an edge I can rub the rope against.

I take one sliding step sideways. Then another. My finger-tips move over the concrete wall like blind spiders—searching for a rough edge.

Another step, and my foot hits something soft. At a nudge, it falls against me, and I stumble away, a scream muffled by my gag as I thud down. I rise to my knees, wincing. Then I try to touch whatever fell, but I can't do it like this. I crouch and brush it with my leg. It's soft and yet unyielding. And there's that smell, the one that reminds me of the bunker, and it's more than must and dirt.

I hunker down with my back to the object. Then I reach, fingers behind me, and feel around. I touch something like leather. I rub it between my fingers. Thinner than leather. Fabric? I twist my hand until it hurts and I reach and my fingers close around . . .

A hand. My fingers close around what is unmistakably a hand, and I know what that smell is, what I'm recognizing.

A body. I'm down here with a body.

I scramble away. Something jabs my arm. It's a stick. A sharp stick with a broken end and jagged edges. I close my eyes and try to calm my pounding heart.

Don't think about the body. You can freak after you've gotten this rope off.

I rub my bound hands against the jagged end of the stick. It's not easy—the wood is sticking from something and the base isn't stable, so I have to grip the stick awkwardly as I rub. I can feel strands breaking, though. Slowly, very slowly, one snapping at a time. Sweat beads on my forehead and my wrists scream from holding them at that angle. The wood splinters as I work, and those splinters dig in like needles, drawing blood, which only makes the rope slicker and harder to—

A thump sounds in the distance. Footsteps. I rub frantically, but there's no way I'll get this rope off in time. Then there's a light, just a little, as if a distant one turned on and filtered under a door. I see that I'm in some kind of basement room with dirt floors and concrete walls and . . .

A body. The one I'd bumped into. It's a girl. A long-dead girl, little more than a skeleton in a filthy dress. I instinctively back away from the corpse, and I hit that stick again. I twist and . . .

It's another skeletonized body.

The stick I'd been rubbing against was a broken bone.

My gorge rises, and I squeeze my eyes shut as tight as I can. *Don't lose it, Winter. Don't lose it.*

I turn away and open my eyes, and now I see . . .

She's lying in a crumpled heap, as if tossed there. Her eyes are open. Dark brown eyes. Open and unseeing. Her long blond hair is half gathered in a ponytail. She wears jeans and ankle boots and a cropped leather jacket.

So, what do you think? New boots, new jacket. Am I ready for New York City, Winter?

Edie.

Oh, God, Edie. No. Please no. Tell me this is someone else, and I'm sorry for whoever it is, but it can't be you. It's someone else with your hair and your jacket and your boots.

But it isn't. I see her face and there is no question. No question at all.

This is Edie.

Edie is dead.

I start to sob. Not just cry—I sob against the gag until I can't breathe and don't care. I hear a sound. The muffled groan of someone wearing a gag.

Jude. Lennon.

I scramble toward the sound. When I see a shoe—a heeled pump—I stop. I wriggle up beside Elysse Bishop. She's bound and gagged and blinking hard, as if she's just woken. She's struggling to focus. When she sees me, her eyes go wide. Then they shut. Squeezed shut tight, and she lets out an odd little noise. Her eyes fly open again, wider now, frantic as she tries to speak.

Her mouth is covered in duct tape. A corner of it has come loose. I twist, trying to rub that corner, and she jerks back, as if I'm lunging for the kill. I glare at her and try to motion with my head, and I'm sure she doesn't understand, but she lies still and I twist around, get hold of that corner with my fingers, and pull. There's a gasp, and then, "Jude," she says. "Tell me he doesn't have—"

I shake my head. I don't care if it's probably a lie; I see her panic and I need her calm.

I wave my bound hands and she says, "You've almost broken the rope. Oh, thank God. Yes, let me . . ."

She wriggles until we're back-to-back, and she's pulling at my frayed rope.

"You'll be okay, Winter," she says as she works. "I'll make sure of that. I swear it. These girls—" She inhales sharply and there's genuine pain in her voice, and I turn to see her staring at Edie's body. "I . . . I knew Kendrick had . . . urges. When he was young . . . There was a girl who disappeared, the daughter of a housekeeper, and I thought it was Kendrick, and our father hired an investigator who said it wasn't. I believed him. I wanted to believe him. Told myself my brother had problems, but he'd never do that. Never actually . . ."

There's a noise to my left and we both jump as light floods in. I'm twisting to see the door and Mrs. Bishop gives a half-stifled cry. And then I see Lennon.

fifty-seven

LENNON STUMBLES INTO THE ROOM AS IF SHOVED, AND FALLS face-first to the floor. He's been beaten. A horrible, sustained beating, old bruises mingling with new; fresh cuts intersecting scabbed ones.

He collapses there, and Mrs. Bishop is making these noises, these whimpering noises as she tries to get to him, and I hear that sound and I realize whatever she's done, however distant she's tried to be, she loves them. She cannot help but love them. They are her sons.

Lennon is panting like a dog, and each of those breaths is painful to hear, as if he doesn't have an undamaged rib in his chest. When he gathers enough strength, he lifts his head to look around, and the first thing he sees is me.

"No," he whispers, and he squeezes his eyes shut and tears

glisten at the corners, one falling when he opens them and he mouths, *I'm sorry.*

"Isn't this what you wanted?" Kendrick says as he walks in. "Oh, yes, that one—" He points to Edie. "She was a pretty little trifle that caught your eye. But nothing more. Such a fickle boy."

Kendrick walks to his sister, who's still scrabbling to get to Lennon, making those wounded noises. He kicks her square in the side of the head, and she goes down, losing consciousness. He turns to me and continues, as if he wasn't interrupted.

"Lennon changes his mind so quickly. Tells me about this girl he met at a concert and how she emailed to say she was coming home for the long weekend. He didn't take the hint and offer to meet up with her. So I helped. Got in touch with her and played Cyrano to his Christian. She agreed to come in a few days early. I met her at the bus stop in Lexington, posing as Lennon's driver, to whisk her off for a romantic getaway. Then I presented her to him and what happened? He rejected my gift."

"You . . . you sick . . ." Lennon's face contorts with fury, but even that takes too much effort and he starts heaving breath again.

Kendrick walks over. "You tried to set her free. You betrayed me. And then I had to kill her, and I couldn't even take the time to do it properly because I needed to teach you a lesson. Only it wasn't harsh enough, and you escaped. Then what did you do, you stupid boy? You came back. Tried to pretend you'd changed your mind. Came back to be a proper son. Your only condition?"

He waves at me. "I had to leave darling Winter alone. Sweet, sweet Winter. Who promptly threw you over for your brother."

Lennon pants for breath and then says, "I'll do it," his voice barely above a whisper.

"What?"

He lifts his head, looking at his father. "I said I'll do it. You're right. I tried to protect her. All this?" He plucks at his bloodied shirt. "For her. And she wants him? *Him?*" He glares my way. "Nobody wants Jude if they can have me."

"Well, well," Kendrick says. "I knew you had it in you." He walks over, crouches, and hands Lennon a switchblade. *My* switchblade. "You don't have the strength to do a proper job, but let's see you make a good start."

Lennon takes a moment, just holding the knife. He hits the switch. The blade pops out. He backs up onto his haunches. Another moment, breathing deeply, gathering his strength. Then he lunges at Kendrick, who slams him in the chest hard enough that there's a crack, and I wince as Lennon crumples, making a muffled noise, as if trying to contain a scream.

Kendrick retrieves the fallen knife. "Yes, I saw that one coming a mile away. I had to give you a chance, just in case. But I knew better."

He crouches in front of Lennon, who's curled up on the floor, trying to stifle his whimpers. Every time Kendrick turns away, I pick madly at the frayed rope. I'm taking it one strand at a time, and I don't seem to be making any progress. My heart is thumping. I know Lennon is in trouble—serious trouble—and I have no idea where Jude is, how badly hurt *he* might be.

"You're weak," Kendrick says to Lennon. "Soft. You had

me fooled for a while. I thought I saw something in you. But when I actually gave you a gift, you couldn't even consider it."

Kendrick raises his voice to a mocking falsetto. "Y-you want me to do wh-what?" He lowers it again. "So shocked. So horrified. As if you haven't fantasized about it. Of course you have. You just don't have the guts to go through with it. You're all surface. Your brother is the one with depth. He won't disappoint me."

Lennon laughs. It's a ragged laugh, painful to even hear, but he can't seem to help it. Anyone who knows Jude can see he doesn't have a scrap of real darkness in him. But their father is desperate. Lennon has failed him; Jude cannot.

"Ellie? You joining us?" He walks to Mrs. Bishop and grabs her by the hair, shaking her until she regains consciousness. "I was just saying that I made a mistake. You made the same one, Ellie. You're not exactly maternal, but there's a little spark of it in you, and you aimed it at the wrong boy. You're very fond of Lennon here. He reminds you of your Peter, and so you are charmed, in spite of yourself. Jude, though?" Kendrick scrunches his nose. "Jude is too complicated. Too cold. Too much like you. But he's the one with talent and brains and depth. The one who reminds you of me, too."

Mrs. Bishop chokes on a laugh, not unlike Lennon's earlier. "You? No, Kendrick. Jude is difficult. He tries my patience. He can be overly dramatic, and he has a temper. But whatever taint is in your blood, it thankfully passed him by."

"You're wrong, Ellie, but the point is that you like Lennon. You might even love him. So that is how I'll pay you back for keeping my sons from me."

Kendrick walks to Lennon. I'm frantically trying to get

this damned rope off. I'm twisting and turning and blood is streaming down my wrist and I don't care—I just need to get it off. I know what's coming, and Mrs. Bishop doesn't. She's just lying there, glowering up at her brother, her eyes blazing with hate.

Kendrick smoothes Lennon's hair, and Mrs. Bishop relaxes. I try to yell a warning against my gag as I madly struggle with the rope.

Kendrick runs his fingers through Lennon's hair. Then he yanks it, pulling Lennon's head up, and the blade flashes and I leap to my feet and dive at them, hitting Kendrick with my shoulder as Mrs. Bishop screams, and then I hear a voice shout, "No!" and Jude races through the doorway, blood on his shirt, a cut on his cheek.

Jude grabs the knife from Kendrick and hits him with an uppercut, sending him flying. Then he turns to me and the rope finally snaps. I rip off my gag. Jude hands me the knife and launches himself at Kendrick, who's struggling to his feet. I kneel beside Mrs. Bishop.

"We're going to get you help." I cut her bonds and say, "You need to call 911."

She blinks at me, as if in a fog. Then she reaches for her pocket as if she'll find her phone there.

"You need to *get* a phone," I say. "Quickly. Please."

She sees Jude, still battling Kendrick, and she takes a step in that direction.

"Go," I say. "Please. He's fine." I lift the knife, letting her know that if Jude can't subdue Kendrick, I'll hardly cower here, whimpering.

She takes a step toward the door. Then another. I move to

help Lennon, my gaze still fixed on the combatants. Jude grabs his father by the hair and slams his head into the concrete. Kendrick slumps. Jude hurries to me, and we're crouching by Lennon's side when Jude looks toward his mother, heading into the hall, and says, "I've already—" and then "Mom!"

He shoots to his feet, and I hear a rasping breath from the hall and then Jude is racing toward that hall. I get to my feet, taking a running step toward the door as I see what Jude sees. It's Roscoe, bloodied and beaten, limping toward Mrs. Bishop. There's a gun in his hand.

I hear the gun fire. I hear Jude shout. I see his mother sail backward. I see blood. I'm running toward them, shouting for Jude to get down, just get down. He dives as Roscoe fires again. The bullet whizzes past me. Jude hits Roscoe's legs and knocks him flying, the gun clattering to the cement floor.

I'm running for the gun when I see a movement behind me. It's Kendrick. Blood streams from his forehead, but he's rising, his gaze fixed on Lennon. I run at him and kick as he lunges at Lennon. Kendrick snags my foot and yanks. I manage to hold on to the knife as I go down. I resist the urge to slash at Kendrick—that risks letting him get hold of my knife. Instead, as he comes at me, I punch with my free hand, and that surprises him.

When Kendrick grabs for me, I jab him in the eye. As he falls back, I go for his other eye, jabbing with my thumb. He snarls, but he's blinded, and with a few adrenaline-fueled and well-aimed blows, he goes down.

I flick open the knife then. It's poised at his throat. He blinks, clearing the blood enough to see it. And then he chuckles.

"You going to kill me, little Winter? Maybe I picked the wrong pupil. You seem to have that certain something my sons lack. Be sure to look into my eyes as you kill me. Be sure to enjoy it."

I pull back the blade, my fingers wrapping around it. Then I stab it, as hard as I can, into his shoulder, picking exactly the right spot so it buries itself in the muscle. Kendrick screams and clutches his shoulder as blood streams from it.

I climb off him and grab Lennon by the shirt. He's passed out. I haul him to the doorway, where I can keep an eye on him. Down the hall, Jude and Roscoe are still fighting. I run to them. I have to step over Mrs. Bishop. She's lying on her back, her sightless eyes staring up, and I feel a pang of grief at that. Whatever she did, she tried, in the end. She cared, in the end. It was just too late.

I run over and grab the gun. When Jude sees I have it, he throws Roscoe aside and staggers to his feet. I give him the gun and keep my knife ready.

"Lie on your stomach," Jude says to Roscoe. "Hands on your head."

Roscoe starts to lie down. Then there's a crack down the hall. The sound of footsteps, multiple footsteps, moving fast.

"Jude!" I say. "Get—"

"We're in here!" he shouts. And police storm through the doorway.

epilogue

"I WANTED TO BE A HERO," LENNON SAYS. HE'S PROPPED UP IN his hospital bed. It's been over a week, but he still has to strain to speak; so many broken ribs makes even breathing difficult. He's refusing the morphine drip, a fact he and Jude have been arguing over. Lennon says the pain's not so bad, but the truth is that he wants to suffer, to do penance. Helping him out of that dark place is going to take more than a week. Part of it is letting him explain, however many times he needs to do that.

"I couldn't save Edie," he says. "So I thought if I could gather evidence for the cops, no one would remember that I was the screwed-up kid who started following his psycho father. They'd only remember the hero who caught him."

I squeeze Lennon's hand. "You *were* a hero. You made sure he didn't come after me."

Lennon manages a pained snort. "No, that was my *stupidest*

mistake. Telling Kendrick to lay off you let him know you were important to me. That's when he targeted you."

Jude shakes his head. "He targeted Winter the minute he saw you two together. By asking him not to hurt her, you piqued his curiosity. That's what kept her alive. Kendrick knew you wouldn't hurt her, which meant she didn't work as a possible victim for you. He had to observe and figure out how she *could* be used. That's what saved her." He glances over. "And then she saved you and saved herself."

"I'm not the one who called the police," I say.

Jude makes a face. "Only because you couldn't. Stop ducking compliments."

"I will if you do."

"Not happening, for either of you," Lennon says with a half smile. "I'll admit, when I tried to play hero, I hoped it might win me the girl. But you know what? I like this ending better."

We talk a little more after that, about other things, like Jude going back to finish his senior year, moving into the family house again. Things that help us forget the horror of what happened. No, not forget. Just temporarily distract me from memories of Edie's body, of the bodies of those two other girls, now identified as ones who'd been on my list, both disappearing a few years ago.

I knew those girls. Not as well as I knew Edie, but I knew them. They are not nameless victims, not to me.

The police found two more bodies, also from Reeve's End. That's not coincidence. As Lennon mentioned, Elysse and Kendrick's family used to have a summer house in the area. After suspicions arose when that housekeeper's daughter went missing, Kendrick decided to target a place where kids *do* go missing and picked Reeve's End. Finding out Lennon knew a girl from there must have seemed like a sign, proof that it was time to take his son to the next stage.

When Lennon is too tired to talk, we head into the hall, and Mr. Bishop rises from where he's been waiting.

"Is he still awake?" he asks.

"Just ready to doze off," I say.

Mr. Bishop heads into the room, and I see him gripping Lennon's hand, leaning over to talk to him, brushing hair back from his forehead. Then one last squeeze and he joins us.

"There are a couple of reporters in front," Mr. Bishop says. "We'll duck out the back. I already brought the car around." As we start for the stairwell, he glances at Jude. "Everything okay?" There's an edge of anxiety in his voice. There always seems to be these days, along with the constant checks.

"Everything's fine, Dad."

Mr. Bishop relaxes most at that last word, confirmation that he is still the boys' dad, no matter how badly he might feel he's failed them. He never suspected that Jude and Lennon were his wife's biological nephews. Mrs. Bishop didn't want children, so when she had a change of heart upon hearing about two orphaned brothers, he was too pleased to question it.

Jude holds the passenger door for me, and I'm still climbing in when my cell rings. It's Cadence.

"I'm roasting the chicken," she says.

I sigh. "Didn't we already discuss this? Fried chicken is your specialty. Fried chicken is fine."

"That's home cooking. This needs to be special."

"Your fried chicken *is* special, Cady."

"How about both? I could do both."

"We don't need—"

"It's seven people. I should do both."

"Seven? You, me, the Southcotts, Jude, his father . . ." I squeeze my eyes shut. "You invited Dad, didn't you?"

"He wants to come," she says quickly. "He hasn't had a drink since I came home, and he went to his first AA meeting last night. He'd like to meet the congressman and apologize to Jude. You need to let him do that, Win."

I fight against the urge to argue. My sister wants to make peace. I will let her try, even if I know it's not that easy.

I agree we'll be at the Southcotts' at six for dinner, and then I talk to Jude and Mr. Bishop for the rest of the ride back. I've been staying at the estate to avoid the media, but it's time for me to go home. Get back to school. Try to live with my father until I can escape to college.

When we arrive at the house, Mr. Bishop drops us off and drives into the garage. Before we even reach the front door, mad scratching erupts from the other side, followed by the shout of an alarmed maid. Jude opens the door and Reject leaps on him as the maid runs to save the door from further scratches.

"I've got her," Jude says, and he bends to rub Reject behind the ears as she bathes his face in kisses. We both try to keep her from jumping. She's not quite recovered enough for that. She can bark, but it's soft, and we aren't sure if that will get better, but she seems happy, and that's the main thing.

"How about Squeaky?" Jude says as she prances around us, squeaking excited yelps as we walk through the house.

I give him a look. "That's almost as mean as Reject."

"Hey, I'm not the one who picked it. You come up with a name or I will, and yours will be better. Remember, I'm still the guy who called you babe."

"We can call her Hardy," I say. "If you're done with it."

He looks over and nods, his lips curving in a faint smile. "I'm done with it. Let's go with that, then."

We head up the stairs and he pats his legs, saying, "Come on, Hardy."

She bounds along after us as he entwines his hand with mine. When we reach the second floor, though, I pass our bedrooms and continue to the back steps, leading him up to the turret room and then over to the piano. Then I sit, and he takes the spot beside me on the bench. I put my fingers over the keys, take a deep breath, and play the first few chords of "Hey Jude" as best I can remember them, and it's terrible—hesitation over each key, even my tin ear able to tell that I get about a third of them wrong. But when I look over he's smiling, and he reaches, hands cupping my face, and he kisses me, the sweetest kiss.

When I pull back, I look at the piano and say, "That's the only part I know." He smiles again and says, "I think I know the rest," and when I say, "Will you show me?" he takes my hands and positions them over the keys, and we play it together.

acknowledgments

TO MY EDITORS AMY BLACK AT DOUBLEDAY CANADA AND Antonia Hodgson at Little, Brown UK, thanks for sticking with me as I shift gears into YA thrillers. And thanks to new editor Phoebe Yeh at Crown, who took a chance on me and my new direction.

To my agent, Sarah Heller, thanks for being such a good sport when you were expecting a new YA fantasy . . . and got a book proposal without a hint of the fantastical.

And finally, thanks to my daughter, Julia, for your last-minute continuity catches. I meant for Winter to have *both* a gas lantern and a battery-powered one. Really. You can never have too many lanterns.

about the author

KELLEY ARMSTRONG IS THE #1 *NEW YORK TIMES* BESTSELLING author of the Darkest Powers (*The Summoning, The Awakening,* and *The Reckoning*), Darkness Rising (*The Gathering, The Calling,* and *The Rising*), and Age of Legends (*Sea of Shadows, Empire of Night,* and *Forest of Ruin*) trilogies for teens, and most recently the YA thriller *The Masked Truth.*

Kelley lives in southwestern Ontario with her family. You can visit her online at kelleyarmstrong.com.